Ella —

Thank you for
Supporting me!

:)

ENNIS ĆEHIĆ

SADVERTISING

VINTAGE BOOKS

Australia

VINTAGE

UK | USA | Canada | Ireland | Australia
India | New Zealand | South Africa | China

Vintage is part of the Penguin Random House group of companies
whose addresses can be found at global.penguinrandomhouse.com

First published by Vintage in 2022

Early untitled versions of 'Poeticules', 'Collaborationist', 'Meetings', 'Click here', 'Dido'
and 'UI vs UX' were published in *Going Down Swinging*, edition #38, 2018

Cover design by Sam Maguinness
Typeset in 12/18 pt Adobe Caslon Pro by Midland Typesetters, Australia
Printed and bound in Australia by Griffin Press, part of Ovato, an accredited
ISO AS/NZS 14001 Environmental Management Systems printer

A catalogue record for this
book is available from the
National Library of Australia

ISBN 978 1 76104 243 0

penguin.com.au

This project has been assisted by the Wheeler Centre's Next Chapter scheme.

Penguin Random House Australia wishes to acknowledge that Aboriginal and Torres Strait Islander people
are the first storytellers and Traditional Custodians of the land on which we live and work. We honour their
continuous connection to country, waters and communities. We celebrate their stories, traditions and
living cultures. We pay our respects to Elders past and present.

CONTENTS

POETICULES

On Wednesday, they announced they were all poets.

They'd had enough of being called copywriters. At lunch-time, they got together to discuss a plan. They decided a formal announcement was necessary and invited the entire agency to join them in the common area at five o'clock.

Jamie, the most poetic of them all, took centre stage. He adjusted his thick-rimmed glasses and stepped up on a carton of beer, a book of John Berryman's poems in his hand. When the office murmur died down, he began to speak.

He called for briefs to be named distillations. Team lunches to be poetry readings. Meeting rooms to be named after famous wordsmiths. Desks to be adorned with fresh flowers in ceramic vases. Brainstorms to be held in parks and Friday afternoons to be declared wine-drinking soirées. Then he announced that the copywriters would stop writing advertisements with calls to action. Advertising needed to be taken seriously; it was the poetry of consumer goods.

When he stopped talking, the other copywriters gathered around him. Together, they bowed before their colleagues like actors in a play. Loud cheers and applause followed. Excitement crackled through the air.

WE MUST TRAVEL IN THE DIRECTION OF OUR FEAR, they yelled proudly.

The cheers intensified. Their colleagues clapped harder, whistled and urged them on. The reception felt rhapsodic, almost revolutionary. But then they saw – at the back of the roaring crowd – the expression on their CEO's face. They knew what it meant: he'd offer them a separate bookshelf for the new poetry books they brought in to read. Then he'd tell them to get back to work.

THOUGHT CHATTER

As soon as she got on the train, Elvira heard it: the voice of someone stressing about an Instagram post.

She thought it was part of the song she was listening to on Apple Music, but when she paused the app, the voice got clearer. *Oh God, why did she post that?* she heard the voice say. Elvira looked at the commuters around her; most, if not all, were men staring at their smartphones. *What's with my eyes in this shot? I look so awful.* Baffled, Elvira turned off her phone's wi-fi and Bluetooth connections. Still, the voice was present, prattling on about the post.

She refreshed her apps, then turned off her iPhone completely. The voice was still audible.

Can you hear that? she asked a schoolkid next to her, but the kid shrugged.

She took out her earphones and stuffed them into her pocket. With a deep inhale, she shut her eyes. It definitely wasn't her own voice. She was sure of it. She didn't have Instagram, so it couldn't even be some wishful version of herself emerging out of the subconscious.

She held on to the railing as the train sped along and listened. The voice was soft but anguished. She tried to match it to a face on the carriage, scanning over features of the other women around her; but they too were staring at their smartphones.

She looked to the other end of the carriage but it was teeming with people. When the doors opened at the next station, more flooded into the train, pushing Elvira to the side of the door between three boisterous businessmen who were in the midst of a conversation. The voice was steadily becoming more distressed but Elvira struggled to hear it over the droning businessmen.

Quiet! she yelled in desperation.

The three businessmen stared at her.

Elvira stumbled away from them until she was right up against the door. She pressed her head on the window, shut her eyes again and finally gave in. She listened with complete and utter concentration.

By the time the train arrived at the central station, she knew everything about this woman.

Tears welled up in her eyes. *The pressure we put ourselves under.*

Elvira desperately wanted to find her and tell her she *was* beautiful. That her jealousy was needless because she was only jealous of illusions – we all were, envious of relationships and lifestyles that do not exist in reality. Elvira wanted to hug her, tell her she didn't need to worry so much about not getting enough likes. Or feel so sad about the message she sent to a friend last night that had been seen without a reply.

She learnt more: the young woman's high heels were killing her feet. She wished she wasn't wearing the red lipstick she had carefully applied this morning. Last night, she masturbated, imagining broad shoulders pressing against her chest, suffocating her loneliness. She preferred the company of her bookish father over the presence of her domineering mother. Sometimes she felt so paralysed by her resentfulness that she wished the shows she watched on Netflix never ended, that they continued for years. Unlike the people she followed on Instagram, who unceasingly posted inspiring quotes, photographs and videos, she felt like she lived with an unbroken chain of questions, not a rigid system that inspired happiness.

In the future, Elvira learnt, the woman wanted to get a tattoo on her face just to spite her mother. Today she was thinking of eating sushi rolls with too much wasabi. She was not looking forward to going out after work on Friday and feeling like the ugliest one among her colleagues. And it shocked Elvira how afraid she was of simply cutting her hair.

The train slowed down again, and Elvira began to move frantically through the airless carriage. *You're not alone*, she yelled, pushing herself through the crowd. She approached every single woman. She stared at their dumbstruck faces, examined their lips and shoes. Each time, she apologised with increasingly desperate eyes.

You're not alone, she yelled again and again.

When the doors opened at the central station and the commuters began to disperse, Elvira heard one final thought; that today she would buy that backless dress from Net-A-Porter, no matter what.

HORROR VACUI

How did they miss it? wondered David as he slammed
a book on the corner of his desk.

The cleaners were always thorough, but this corner, for the past
month or so, hadn't been wiped down. He could see the dry,
circular marks from the cloth they used. The rest of the desk had
been wiped, but they had bypassed the far-left corner entirely. To
David, the corner seemed the most logical part to start cleaning
from, so, why didn't they? Did they want to annoy him as well?

He stared it down, the smattering of dust that had turned
into a heap. He wondered what it was made of. Lint from people's
clothes? Their hair? Debris from the ceiling? Dry skin? He swallowed what felt to him like dryness. The thought of dry skin flakes
falling from people's heads and arms and landing on his desk made
him tingle. He opened a drawer and began to frantically search

for anything to remove this thought from his head. He hoped for a small bottle of hand sanitiser but found only a scrunched-up tube of moisturiser. He applied it onto his arms, neck and face. He sat back to feel the relief traverse through him.

But it was short lived, this moment of repose.

He noticed, as he glanced about, that streaks of leftover dust were still visible. Behind his 27-inch monitor. Around his paper weights. His loose pamphlets, brochures, reports and piles of books. The dirt, grime and dust hadn't been wiped away at all; it had merely been brushed over.

He slammed down some more books and walked off to make himself a coffee.

As usual, he was one of the first people in the office. His desk occupied a corner at the end of a row of four desks. Ahead of him, three more rows extended to the other end of the wall. To his right was the kitchen and a long dining table where employees usually ate lunch together.

All along the left side were floor-to-ceiling windows from where he could see the far edges of the city. He loved arriving early to watch the last bit of the sunrise in silence. Amber light would stream across the floor, lighting up various objects. The plants on Janine's table. The Superman toy on Mike's. The open novel on Vinni's desk, the one he read secretly when he thought no one was watching. But as the day progressed, the windows would also begin to reflect people's personal belongings: the gym bags, extra pairs of shoes, umbrellas, old printers, cameras and clothes they had piled beside their desks instead of under them, next to their feet. From his corner, these ugly piles would always annoyingly double in his view from the reflection in the window.

With a coffee in hand, David returned to his seat and observed the desks in front of his as though they were rows of unwilling soldiers.

He sat back down and began his day in the same manner he did every morning, by opening up Microsoft Outlook, Excel and Project and looking over emails, timelines and budgets, pondering where his small digital team was at with their latest deadlines. As an executive producer, his job was to shepherd a project through its timeline, ensuring that each member of his team was completing their daily tasks efficiently. Hours passed and David didn't notice that the morning of the office had begun, that the rows around him and ahead of him had filled with chattering heads bobbing back and forth in front of screens and laptops.

David's colleagues had long ago stopped asking him why he was so quiet. He wasn't a man for small talk, so their tendency to pop by his desk to say *What's going on?* dwindled fairly quickly after his arrival. It wasn't that David didn't get along with them – he was simply an introvert who preferred to mind his own business – but this open-plan office tended to treat natural homebodies with incredulous disdain. *Why so quiet? Hey, are you okay? Is something the matter? You don't seem yourself, is everything okay?* These questions used to bother David. *I'm fine*, he'd always reply but instead of letting it go, they would disparage him behind his back. To them, a rock-solid prerequisite for working in their office was to be like them – extroverted and vociferous loudmouths who never turned down a chitchat or a one-to-one. *Standoffish*, someone called David once. But someone else thought that was too polite. *He's an arrogant prick*, they said.

Fortunately, management didn't care.

Of the five executive producers at the agency David was the only one to have never missed a deadline or blown a budget. He always – irrespective of what people thought of him – delivered a project successfully. And his digital team, which consisted of an assistant producer, two digital designers and a mid-level copywriter, loved working with him. They shared an unspoken approval of his behaviour because it meant they were the only team in the agency that never had to stay back late, or come in on the weekend. To them, the absence of group lunches, after-hours drinks, office gossip or personal reflections on life didn't matter. They, unlike many others, had a life outside of work because of how David managed their workload. For this they were devotionally grateful and always stepped in to defend David if anyone talked behind his back.

After lunch, David could see, from the corner of his eye, Mike, a copywriter from another team who loved an office chit-chat, walking towards his desk. Immediately his gaze was drawn to the loose hairs on the shoulder of Mike's jacket.

David, I'm bored, said Mike.

You're always bored, said David.

It's a stress state, you know? said Mike, picking up a book from the top of the pile. *Have you read this one?* Mike began flicking through the pages of *Sapiens: A Brief History of Humankind* by Yuval Noah Harari.

Of course I have, replied David.

Been meaning to read it. Is it good? asked Mike.

Don't you have copy to write? asked David.

I should read more non-fiction, shouldn't I? I'm such a fiction snob, said Mike.

Good for you, mate. Good for you, said David.

You know, said Mike, still leafing through the book, *the story behind boredom supposedly lies in the body. Bored body language is a whole thing. Weird, huh?*

It's not weird at all . . . look at you, said David, with his eyes fixed on Mike's chest.

Mike looked down at the slight paunch protruding through his T-shirt. He loosened it, placed the book back on top of the pile and wandered off.

This, thought David as he watched Mike and his unkempt appearance move away, was the kind of behaviour that made him fume. This idleness, this constant need to converse only to say nothing with clear purpose.

He felt a need to breathe deeply, to open a window or inhale the air of a lush green forest. Instead, he opened his bottom drawer. Inside were old manila folders and odd books he'd forgotten about. He placed them on top of the stack he'd started. The pile was just above eye-level now, and he had to lift himself up to see past it. He felt surprisingly relieved – it blocked the view he hated: people's crap and shit that he'd see reflected in the windows.

By the end of the week, he had constructed two towers on the left side of his desk made up of books, folders and loose papers. Together with his monitor, they blocked from view a fair chunk of the office. Now, even when he pushed his chair back, he couldn't see the rest of the desks before him. He also noticed a change: his happiness. He was applying himself with newfound gusto. Being crowded in gave him psychological space.

Quite a pile you got going there, said Janine in the kitchen one afternoon.

She was standing in line behind David at the coffee machine but he was too focused on frothing his milk to answer.

Yes, I do, Janine, it's quite the pile, she continued, with obvious sarcasm.

Sorry, said David. *Almond milk's a bit hard to foam up.*

Janine peeked into the fridge while David continued to froth his milk.

Excited about the clean-up? she said, her eyes scanning the contents of the fridge. *The shit people leave in here. Look at this!* she said, pulling out half a plum. *Why would anybody leave half a fuckin' plum?*

David poured the milk into his coffee cup.

What clean-up? he asked.

I don't know, mate. Either that or you hate us all, she said, laughing right in his face.

David couldn't help but stare at the metal fillings in her mouth; her bottom row of teeth was full of them.

As he walked towards his desk, he became conscious of ogling eyes and whispers. Seeing his colleagues so scandalised by his simple desire to be left alone made him want to retreat further.

He rearranged his monitor immediately, shifting it further to the side, which left a bit of space in the centre of his desk from where he could still see everyone. Janine waved at him through the gap.

He's alive! she yelled, making everyone else laugh too. David walked away.

A short while later, he returned. The others watched in disbelief as he strolled towards his desk carrying another monitor.

He placed the monitor right next to his other one. Now they couldn't see him at all. He put his headphones over his ears and got back to work.

It didn't take long for David's colleagues to come up with a name for his towers. *The fort*, they called it.

It's just a joke, his team repeatedly told him during their scheduled catch-ups and meetings. *They're just having a gag.* While it appeared that David didn't care, each day the fort got bigger. The others began to talk about David's constant walking back and forth from the office library. And when he got tired of books, he started to bring in obscure objects from home. They were surprised that he had now begun to stockpile ceramic cups too. They were tilting in mid-air like the Leaning Tower of Pisa and everyone was waiting for the sound of porcelain smashing on the floor beside him. Mostly, they wondered about the electric typewriter. *Where did he get it from?* When he wasn't at his desk, the others would crowd around it, take photos to post on Instagram and Twitter. David enjoyed that these piles and towers were being called a fort. After all, they were beginning to look like one.

In the mornings, when he was alone, he'd reflect upon the fort from the kitchen. From there, it looked more like a bunker. A total of six book towers crowded around his two monitors now. Three old printers were stacked behind his chair, with the electric typewriter levelled on top of them.

It fascinated David that an act to minimise conversation, to guarantee fewer personal workplace relationships, seemed to be doing the opposite. By this time, the fort was all anyone could talk about. Not a single person walked past David without asking about it, laughing about it or giving him ideas to add to his collection. Some even brought stuff (old hardcover books and lamps) from home and left it there for him, with unsigned notes of support and encouragement. A handwritten letter with a heartfelt note about *doing your own thing* and *protecting your personality* took him by surprise – he wasn't a martyr for introverts.

A few weeks later, most of the office were rushing to a monthly talk by a guest speaker.

Are you coming? asked Mike as he passed David near the kitchen.

You know I don't come to these things, said David.

Mike knew this well, but he always asked David anyhow, because secretly, he was on a personal mission to get him to participate in something communal and collective. But David found these speakers as cringeworthy as a LinkedIn influencer.

As he passed the bathroom on his way back to his desk, the promotional poster for the talk caught his attention: Working with Different Personalities: A Talk by Tim Sheer.

What the . . . said David.

Guest speakers were usually experts in trend forecasting or industry insights. They had never had a speaker come in to talk about intra-office relations.

Entering the common area from the back, David leant against a column far from the others who sat up closer, near the speaker. Tim Sheer was standing before them, dressed in a casual suit. He was tall with greyish sideburns. With enthusiasm and charm, he was addressing the many different personalities that exist inside an office. From debaters to entertainers, he clicked through slides that outlined tactics and strategies for healthy interactions, with a variety of relatable examples.

David watched in horror how his colleagues reacted to the slides. They laughed and giggled at Tim Sheer's obvious jokes. They asked questions and made silly suggestions. He couldn't believe how gullible they were, inflating Tim's ego like that.

David began to feel increasingly sickened by this talk. Just as he felt that he'd had enough, Tim Sheer clicked through to a slide that read: Dealing with Introverts. The audience quietened down.

This one always makes the crowd go quiet, said Tim Sheer, grinning.

David paused. His heart began to pound.

Introverts are very good collaborators, said Tim, pointing to an illustrated slide of a lonesome stick figure. *They bring a sense of calm, reason and thoughtfulness to the collaborative process,* he said.

David couldn't believe it. He felt a quiet concentration of eyes grow around him.

Generally speaking, continued Tim Sheer, *introverts get along with others pretty well as they are excellent listeners. But when it comes to interaction with others, it needs to be on their terms and in their time. They don't appreciate having their thought processes and workflows interrupted by someone else's agenda. And in an open-plan office such as this, you need to respect people's individualities to ensure a healthy culture.*

Bullshit, blurted David.

He stormed off towards the CEO's desk. *Think this is funny?* he yelled, to the surprise of a few people nearby who didn't attend the talk.

Calm down, mate, said the CEO.

Exasperated with David's outburst, he took him by the arm and ushered him into an empty meeting room.

Just calm down, he said.

Did you organise this talk because of me? David asked without hesitation.

Look, said the CEO, *it's the best I could do without talking to people directly and making you feel more isolated.*

David couldn't stand still; he paced around in circles aimlessly.

I can't believe it, he said. *I thought—*

Mate, you're building a fucking fort! In AN OFFICE! What the hell am I supposed to do?

Too angry to think straight, David was at a loss for words. He kept shaking his head and pacing.

You need some time off. A holiday. Positano, I tell ya, wow. I just spent a week there a month ago. The CEO placed his hand on David's sweaty shoulder. *You'd love it there. It will liven you up, and there's so many peaceful hidden beaches nearby for you.*

I don't need a vacation, I was just annoyed with the dust! yelled David.

What dust? asked the CEO.

Never mind, said David.

He stormed out of the meeting room, slamming the door behind him, then made his way through reception and down the stairs, his steps resounding loudly through the concrete stairwell. He wanted free, outdoor air, some kind of country expanse, anything other than the suffocating air of judgement he felt in the office. When he got to the ground floor, he found that his legs were shaking, so he sat down on the armchair in the foyer to calm down.

Just then, the elevator doors opened and Tim Sheer walked out, rearranging the contents inside his messenger bag and talking at the same time through his AirPods.

It was good, he was saying. *The usual – typical office crowd. I know how to work them!*

Of course you do, murmured David as he watched Tim Sheer stroll out of the building, passing him without even so much as a glance. It was as if David wasn't even present in the foyer.

Through the glass front door, he watched Tim Sheer leisurely hail a cab, jump into the back seat and disappear up the road like nothing was the matter at all.

He slouched into the seat. He felt tired, his body heavy. Anger controlled him still, but now he felt more betrayed than angry. Stabbed in the back, like Julius. How could he face them again? As he got up, he made his mind up. He would hand in his notice and be done with this place.

Upstairs, the common area had cleared out. But a commotion somewhere in the office could be heard; people laughing and joking. As he neared his work station, he saw them.

Mike and Vinnie were standing on his desk, adding books on top of the towers. Even Janine was helping, passing items and books to them.

What the hell are you doing? asked David.

Building you a proper fort, said Mike.

Vinnie turned around and gave David the thumbs-up. His own team were on the ground, creating an archway that led to the desk. They waved to David.

Come in! someone yelled.

Janine strolled over and took David by the arm.

Go on, she urged.

He didn't know what to think, but he let Janine guide him through the archway. He sat down behind his desk. Above the monitors, Mike's face appeared.

You guys are mad, said David, still in shock.

This is going to be a window, said Mike.

We're thinking of stacking the books on top of a plank.

Oh, added Vinnie, *maybe you could have a little curtain, so when you close it, we know not to disturb you.*

David shook his head. As hard as he tried to dissuade them, they didn't stop.

For the rest of the evening, they kept up their collective pursuit and built a proper fort out of books in an office of a top tier advertising agency. To Mike's pride, David ended up participating himself – wholeheartedly. Mike watched him pile books with a sense of accomplishment, as if he were solely responsible for David's participation.

When they finished, they retreated to the kitchen to admire their handiwork. The fort looked disastrously out of place among the orderly rows of desks and computers. David's desk was now completely hidden by duct-taped towers of books, glued-on monitors, stacked-up old printers, vases and frames. Every bit of space was covered, with only a side entrance left open and a hole to see out of.

It's contemporary art, someone said. Everyone laughed.

Mike reached into the fridge and took out a cold six-pack of beers. *It's like a hermit's wet dream,* he said.

David poured wine into cups. Vinnie set out chips and other snacks. Someone else ordered pizzas. Then Janine, after staring quite intently at the fort, said, *Guys, wouldn't this be a great idea for a mental health campaign?*

PATIENT ZERO

The following year – not this one, but the one after – a young man wearing a Gucci sweatshirt over a Kappa tracksuit, with AirPods still playing Dua Lipa in his ears, will be found unconscious on a bench inside the Fotografiska Museum in Stockholm.

It won't be snowing, but there will be a light drizzle visible through the windows.

He will be found by a man in a cream-coloured Burberry overcoat who, by fortuity, will happen to be a doctor on vacation from London. This doctor will examine the man wearing the Gucci sweatshirt over a Kappa tracksuit, with AirPods still playing Dua Lipa in his ears.

To the shock of onlookers, he'll pronounce the man dead.

Live tweets and stories from the scene will amplify the incident online. For a period of forty-eight hours the story will trend. Many local and international readers will offer condolences to the dead man's loved ones in the comments section of the reported articles. One reader will ask whether he passed away in front of a Cartier-Bresson photograph.

No one will entertain this insensitive question.

When the doctor in the cream-coloured Burberry overcoat returns to his home in London, he will feel overwhelmed by the young man's passing. The official cause of death will be recorded as a spontaneous coronary artery dissection, but that won't sit quite right with the doctor.

A particular image will haunt him: the young man's left hand solidly fixed to his smartphone, his thumb twitching over the screen. This image will preoccupy the doctor's mind obsessively. For days, he'll remain quiet and aloof, hardly leaving his study. He will ask his wife not to be concerned, but she will be concerned anyway.

I am investigating something, he will tell her.

Over the following weeks, the doctor's unforthcoming behaviour will continue. Despite his wife's protests, he will remain in his study, pursuing his investigation. There, he will meticulously retrace the dead man's life. He will discover that his name was Andy Cole. That he was a twenty-three-year-old fine arts student at New York University and his trip to Sweden was part of his first trip to Europe. He lived in on-campus housing in Manhattan but was originally from Providence, where his parents still lived. All this he will piece together from Andy's digital footprint.

A close review of Andy's social media presence will reveal more. From what the doctor will gather, Andy followed an unusually high number of accounts. However, he never posted anything himself. His Twitter feed was empty. His Instagram grid had zero posts, just a bio that read, *I only live in Stories.* To the doctor, Andy appeared to live online as an obsessive observer. A close-watching, digital prowler who seemed to carefully loiter behind people's profiles like a stalker. With no likes, comments, shares or retweets left behind to analyse, the doctor will be compelled to make further enquiries about this curious human behaviour.

The first will be a phone call to his 20-year-old niece, Brittany. While being initially wary at receiving a phone call from her bookish uncle, Brittany will brighten when she grasps that he has called her to talk about something she knows quite a bit about: social media. In this one-sided conversation, the doctor will gain insight into the conduct of online lurkers, contributing only one reply: *I see, I see.*

From Andy's parents, whom he'll go out of his way – all the way to Providence – to meet, the doctor will find out that, other than being an anxious couple, Mr and Mrs Cole were openly dissident, prone to believing in alternate theories of reality, especially in the political realm. The doctor will regard this to have influenced Andy's upbringing, making him a suspicious kid. His childhood friends will confirm this: *He just kept to himself.* The doctor will hear similar accounts from Andy's college classmates: *Nice guy, but kind of a lonely NYU hipster,* some will say without hesitation. Others will reveal that he didn't really have friends, just acquaintances. That he'd hang out with people, but he was *never really there, you know?*

22

It is after the doctor speaks to Andy's ex-girlfriend, Jane, that he will become convinced his research will be of great consequence, but only after being told repeatedly that she wasn't Andy's girlfriend, that they only hooked up once.

He was a bit creepy, she will tell the doctor, *always on his phone, following everyone. It was so fucking obvious what he was doing, it's not like I didn't know. You can't imagine how surprised I was when I woke up to find he liked one of my photos. I took a screengrab of it – look!*

It is exactly this detail that will cement the suspicion he had been forming since the museum: that Andy hadn't died of a spontaneous heart attack.

Over the following months, the doctor will continue his research. He will write copious notes about Andy – how Andy preferred the internet to reality, but fear of being judged had turned him into a lurker. Though the beauty of this allowed him to keep to himself while immersing himself in the lives of others, it became a profound online compulsion, an extreme craving that came with all the behavioural signals usually associated with chemical addictions: smoking, drugs and alcoholism. But Andy's addiction, he will argue, was entirely unique. It displayed a manifestation he'd never seen before: a kind of chaste voyeurism.

The doctor will note this down with the elation only the onset of a fresh idea emerging in the mind can elicit.

Here, he will put forward the argument that no, Andy Cole didn't die of a spontaneous heart attack as previously concluded, but from Lurker's Syndrome; a death caused by acute stress-induced cardiomyopathy that happens only when a lurker, such as Andy, accidently takes action, such as liking a photograph. Lurker's Syndrome, he will argue, will be easily identified by a hand solidly fixed to a smartphone, with a thumb twitching over the screen.

This will be the first recorded death of such a case.

NMBA

What the fuck was I thinking? said Kendall Jenner.

Her publicist was quiet on the other end of the line.

Seriously, continued Kendall. *I'm about to become the face of the worst commercial of all time.*

It'll blow over before you know it, said her publicist.

But Kendall wasn't so sure.

I should've listened to my gut, she said, *I questioned the goddamn script, remember?*

It's just an ad, give it another twenty-four hours and it'll be done, trust me, repeated her publicist.

No one will respect me now. Fucking Pepsi, said Kendall and slumped onto her bed.

The agency, the director, the art director, the stylist – everyone, in fact – assured her that advertising worked best when it tapped into popular opinion, especially if that opinion was of a sensitive nature, like social justice movements. Well, here they were. Twenty-four hours had passed and they were in a shitstorm of a worldwide backlash.

I'm trending faster than Trump's tweets, she said.

She could hear the coarse breathing of her publicist. Then she heard a sneeze.

Did you read this article? asked Kendall. *It claims it's the greatest failure in advertising history. Who the fuck do they think they are, writing this?*

It's not! You were . . . hang on, replied her publicist.

Kendall scanned her nails as her publicist blew her nose. *It felt like such an honour at the time,* said Kendall.

It still is, said her publicist.

Cindy Crawford's successor, that's how they pitched it too, remember? Now I'm the internet's favourite joke.

Just be patient, pressed her publicist.

Still, Kendall couldn't shake off her embarrassment. She hung up and stared wide-eyed at her bedroom ceiling. After brushing away a single tear that fell down her cheek, she turned off the light and went to sleep.

The next day, she stayed in bed. The day after too. But on the third day, Kendall Jenner woke up with a thought that riled up her nervous system. A commanding voice was telling her to channel her disgust, sadness and rage into something actionable. An idea.

For days, Kendall let the thought graze around in her mind. *There's something to it,* she reminded herself each time she saw a commercial, drove past a billboard or checked out stories on

Instagram. Every single post suddenly revealed itself to be what it really was: predatory corporatism and legalised lying full of manufactured fears. Advertising – from brands and individuals – wasn't enlightening people. It was failing culture.

Kendall took a good, hard look at herself. She had to acknowledge that she – like the rest of them – was part of the problem. She consciously perpetuated this grotesque cycle of legalised lying without remorse. But unlike the rest of them, Kendall figured that she had the privilege and the power to do something about it.

On the seventh day after the release of Live for Now, her now infamous Pepsi commercial, Kendall was sunbaking alone beside her pool. Without opening her eyes, or moving her body, she told Siri to dial her assistant.

Register NMBA, Kendall said when the assistant picked up.

Sorry, what? the assistant asked.

NO MORE BAD ADVERTISING! screamed Kendall. *Just register it!*

And just like that, NMBA was born: a not-for-profit mission devoted to banning every terrible commercial in the world, starting with the Pepsi commercial that ruined Kendall's year.

When it launches, her sister Kim will make videos about it on Instagram. Lil Nas X will sing about it on TikTok. Dua Lipa will passionately rave about it in interviews. Justin Bieber, Harry Styles and the Hadid sisters will walk around wearing #nmba T-shirts. Even Pepsi will get behind the movement, creating a limited edition can.

Kendall's vengeful mission will remove a whopping forty-six per cent of bad advertising from Western media. The leftover space – on billboards, bus stops, airport displays, print magazines, mobile ads in taxis and Ubers, banner ads on Twitter, Instagram, Facebook, YouTube and Snapchat, even those ads above urinals in public bathrooms – will be replaced with J. M. W. Turner's paintings and Jenny Holzer's poetry.

This accomplishment, while it will only last a week, will become a period of remembrance in western society. Not because a modern celebrity did something altruistic, but because people will remember it as the week they felt free from the shackles of consumerism. And Kendall? She will become the most respected celebrity of the internet age.

CROSSOVER

Like Steve Jobs, Maurício did his best thinking while walking.

Whenever he had to mull over a complicated idea with his team or think deeply about a business problem the agency was facing, he would take a long walk by himself. It would take him, as he would say, to the breadth and depth of creativity.

It typically happened in meetings. Maurício would quieten down in the middle of a brief or presentation. His eyes would glaze over and to the people present it would appear as if their Chief Creative Officer had already departed. *I'll leave you guys to it*, he'd say, and leave the room. He'd proceed to his desk, place his belongings neatly on the table: his smartphone, watch and the two golden rings he wore on his fingers. Then he'd take the elevator to the ground floor and from there, head out onto the street and disappear for a while.

Often a very long while.

When the elevator doors reopened and his co-workers made out his signature look – fitted blue jeans, a pair of Converse, white or black cotton T-shirt, a tailored blazer and, of course, his silver head of hair – whispers would spread through the floor. By the time Maurício had reached his desk, every single person in the office would know that he had returned.

He would slip the watch around his wrist, slide the two rings back onto his fingers, and check the messages on his smartphone. After a quiet fifteen minutes of note-taking and replying to emails and text messages, Maurício would ask his senior creative team to join him in the boardroom. There, he would outline new concepts and routes to tackle the problems they were trying to solve for their clients. After each of these meetings, his team would walk away with newfound resolve.

One afternoon, Maurício set off on a walk and didn't return.

It was around six o'clock when his absence was first noted, but his team assumed he had gone home for the day after his walk. It followed, after all, a difficult briefing they had had with a new client. The next morning, they didn't question his absence either, knowing he had an external meeting visible in his diary. It was only after his wife called, concerned that Maurício hadn't been home – or in touch – that the office became alarmed.

The police were immediately notified. Interviews were conducted and CCTV footage was analysed. But after a week of strenuous investigations, Maurício hadn't been found.

News reports circulated, intensifying the mystery of the man who walked out to think but never returned. Over the next twelve months, the advertising industry began to commemorate

Maurício's achievements. Industry experts and colleagues wrote articles, talking up his personality, his leadership style and his singular creative approach. When two years passed and Maurício still hadn't been found, an honorary award was created in his name. A memorial service soon followed, where during speeches, guests clapped ardently while his wife held back tears.

But his agency, despite how bleak it sounded in the ether of media, never lost faith that Maurício was alive. They kept his small corner office unoccupied. And once the police released the smartphone, watch and the two golden rings that he left on the table, his wife agreed to keep them sitting where he had left them – just in case he returned.

As the third anniversary of Maurício's disappearance approached, the agency started to grow exponentially. They had won multiple new pitches and a different organisational structure was established to herald this inspiring chapter. With that, the office's departments had to be rearranged to fit a new floorplan.

It was a sunny Friday afternoon when the big move started.

Everyone was tools down. Boxes were stacked up beside desks. Cleaning products and cloths were in hands, ready to wipe away grime and filth. Employees were turning off their laptops and screens, packing up their personal belongings and moving to their newly designated spots.

It was a lively commotion, the air filled with the anticipation of eagerly awaited change. Maurício's office, although it had become a quiet shrine of remembrance, was set to finally be disassembled. No one knew who would end up cleaning it out, but most believed it would be someone from senior management, or perhaps one of his mentees from the senior creative team.

Everyone was so busy with their own storing and restoring, that no one paid attention to the tall figure that emerged from the elevator hallway.

He walked purposefully, his eyes focused straight ahead. His clothes looked dirty and tattered from age; the jeans had many holes and the T-shirt he had on was frayed at the collar. Through this surprising appearance, they could still recognise his silver head of hair.

Maurício, they whispered under their breath.

A quiet frenzy of astonished faces followed him.

The loud chatter and sounds of packing and unpacking dwindled then stopped, as if time had frozen. Maurício, not noticing the shock on people's faces, walked on until he reached his small office. As if by habit, he slipped his watch around his wrist, slid the rings back onto his fingers, then picked up his smartphone to read his messages.

He fiddled with the switched-off phone, then he glanced up. A swarm of bodies was standing, huddled around the door to his office, gawking in disbelief. He looked at them absent-mindedly, then turned back to his phone. No one said a word. They kept staring, until, through the bodies, the CEO emerged.

Maurício? She gasped. *Oh my God . . . where have you been?*

She pulled him into a tight hug, but Maurício was unforthcoming.

Within an hour, his wife and children, along with the police, arrived. People stayed close, curious to find out what had happened. Like trained sentries, they kept watch over Maurício's office, eagerly awaiting answers. At eight o'clock, the doors opened, but only for the police officers to tell them all to go home.

They went to a bar instead. Over drinks and bar snacks, they discussed the possible theories behind Maurício's disappearance. Some suggested that, like Forrest Gump, maybe he had spent the past three years walking to clear his head. Others wondered if perhaps he had been hiding in a shack on some remote coastline, writing a bestseller about creativity and walking. A few were convinced, given his appearance, that he'd been stranded on an island like Robinson Crusoe, while others held off speculating, convinced that the truth would be even stranger.

The following week, details filtered through.

Maurício's wife relayed his story to his closest colleagues, who in turn, summarised and recapped the story further to others in the agency. Then it began to circulate through the nexus of text messages, phone calls, DMs and group chats. No one could believe what they had heard: Maurício, while walking and thinking, had activated a gleaming incision in the air ahead of him. When he passed through it, he entered another dimension, proving that a multiverse of realities exists.

A multiverse? Everyone immediately thought something was at play. None of it made any sense. They chewed over other hunches; was it a nervous breakdown Maurício was hiding? Or a wild international affair? History was full of stories of men who hid second families. Tax evasion? A conspiracy theory about him being a government spy was another contender, but no one believed this either. The abounding theories did not explain the reality of the puzzle; how no single trace of him had been found for three whole years.

True or not, the agency attempted to stop the spread of Maurício's story. They feared that if the preposterous story got out, it could damage their renewed reputation. Luckily for them, he was hospitalised and placed under psychiatric supervision, leading people to naturally refrain from further gossip out of respect for his family's privacy.

But people could not help themselves. What if it was true? They asked in hushed voices and secret group chats. Did anyone know where he was admitted? Which hospital? Maybe the government was involved? Or the military?

They didn't have to wait long for an answer.

Maurício walked into the agency just after lunchtime one day. He stormed into the common area, where most of the employees were chit-chatting and holding casual meetings. He looked frazzled and out of breath. It was also the first time anyone had seen him wearing a collared shirt, which was oversized and worn over a pair of wide-legged slacks.

Join me in the boardroom, he said with surprising clarity.

Without hesitation, everyone dropped what they were doing and followed him like they did after all his walks.

He stood in the far back of the boardroom as it began to fill up. He rubbed his hands as if he were cold and kept looking out of the window, down at the street below. People squeezed in from all corners of the agency. When his own team saw him, they smiled with reverence and rushed to sit right before him.

I don't have long, Maurício said without waiting for everyone to sit down, *but I can tell you, it is as physicists have predicted: pocket universes, quantum tunnelling and eternal chaotic inflations are the true models of measuring cosmology.*

No one knew what he was talking about. So no one said a word.

You can speculate all you want, he continued. *But trust me, state of mind is the access key to the universe.*

Maurício looked out the window again. Everyone was still quiet, but he could sense them retreating, huddling closer together.

This is what I've come to tell you, he continued. *It wasn't until that day that I understood the power of this stupidly simple, human act. With each step I took I could feel this remarkable clarity coming. I don't know why but I began to walk faster, speedier, and somehow, after an hour, maybe longer, I ended up all the way at the park. Inside me, I started to sense this equilibrium rising, this complete joining of my body with the rhythm of my feet and the life around me: sound, air, materiality, the skies . . . I really felt a change. Then I saw it: this incision. It's as if someone sliced through the pathway in front of me with a sword. I could see a light emitting from it, and without hesitation, I walked in. I had to. Anyone would've.*

Maurício stared across at the entrance of the boardroom, where six security guards waited. He smiled and faced the crowd again. Some of the co-workers got up to block the guards from entering.

Sir, would you please come—

He's not going anywhere! the group said, confronting the guards.

What is existence? asked Maurício. *That's not the question. What's the extent of existence — that's the question.*

Sir, we need you to please come with us, repeated the security guard, but Maurício ignored his request.

I saw another reality, he continued. *I stood and faced an ocean of waves, but the water wasn't transparent like here. No, over there it was black. Yes, black water! Think of the varied law of physics! The moon in the sky was the shape of an egg and the trees that rustled beside me slithered in the air like snakes. Minutes there became years over here, but I knew immediately that the state of mind I reached was the activation – the key.*

They know. He pointed at the security guards. *That's why they are here.*

Maurício paused to take a breath. He suddenly appeared frail, skinnier and paler than before, as if the abrupt speech had depleted his energy. The security guards pushed through the crowd.

Sir, please come with us now, they repeated.

Walking, people, just keep on walking, said Maurício.

And here, just as he put his hands up in surrender, Maurício, legally known as Maurício Cristiano Mendez, who was 43 years of age, 1.85 centimetres in height, weighing 83 kilograms, voluntarily let himself be escorted out of the building by the six security guards.

We believe you, yelled some people from the back of the crowd who had followed him to the SUV parked outside.

Maurício never said another word. And as you'd expect from a story with such an ending, he was also never seen again.

INTERRUPTER

Today, Lydia learns more than just the story of her favourite tea.

Did you know Lady Grey was created by Twinings? says her colleague Giselle, who is sitting across from her.

The backs of their monitors are facing each other, and Lydia has to lean to the side to look at Giselle.

They made it for the Nordic market in the early nineties.

This fact doesn't interest Lydia, but she lets Giselle continue because she can tell Giselle is excited.

Can you believe the Vikings found Earl Grey too strong for their taste? The Brits had to make Lady Grey to get into the Scandinavian market.

Geoff, who is sitting next to Giselle, interrupts.

I heard a different story, he says.

He doesn't have to move his head to the side, because he can see Lydia clearly between the monitors.

Supposedly, he goes on, *back in the day, Earl Grey caused strange impulses in women because of its citrus aroma and taste.*

This piques Lydia's interest and she stops writing her article and looks over at Geoff.

Giselle thinks this is ludicrous. *That's bullshit,* she says.

Geoff moves closer. *No, seriously,* he says. *Excessive drinking would lead women to feel compulsive desires. It was said that it increased their heart rate and made them feel irritated for no particular reason. Horny, too. And that's why Lady Grey was created – to ease women's minds and . . . you know.*

Geoff laughs while Giselle shakes her head in disgust. Lydia keeps quiet.

Tale or not, Lydia walks off to the bathroom believing what Geoff just said. Maybe having had to grow up motherless, raised by a single father who only ever bought Earl Grey tea had caused the angst and low self-esteem she experienced during her childhood. As she sits on the toilet bowl, she looks up Lady Grey on Google and finds some additional information.

Lady Grey was the better half of Earl Grey, the namesake of the tea, also known as Charles Grey, a British Prime Minister in the 1830s and author of the Reform Bill of 1832. Now there are three stories about her favourite tea and Lydia can't make up her mind which to believe. Having always been anxious and pedantic, she resolves that Lady Grey was definitely created to ease women's minds, because that's what it does for her. The additional lemon and orange peel produces a gentler flavour, much more palatable than any of the other black teas she's tasted.

Lydia walks back to her desk. To her relief, Giselle and Geoff have their headphones on. She doesn't like being interrupted by small talk. Earlier this morning, Giselle had been bored and kept talking about everything, from Miley Cyrus's teeth to Nikola Tesla's asexuality, and the stream of useless information had completely derailed Lydia.

What's it going to be today? Giselle suddenly asks.

She doesn't move to look at Lydia, she just says it behind her monitor, but Lydia knows she is addressing her.

I don't know yet, replies Lydia, and places her own headphones over her ears.

It annoys Lydia that Giselle takes so much interest in her ritual. So what if she only drinks Lady Grey tea? And so what if she has two mugs on her desk? And does it really matter to Giselle that one reads *I've Done Nothing* and the other, *I've Done Everything*? And so fucking what if Lydia drinks from each depending on how she feels at the end of the day? To Lydia, her feelings are a valid reason for the habit.

I think you did great today, adds Geoff, with a laugh.

Lydia pretends she hasn't heard him through her headphones.

This daily ritual she practises allows her to calmly reflect on her achievements. Or failures. With each sip of tea, Lydia analyses the tasks she did that day.

Have you ever tried it with camomile tea? Or Japanese green tea? asks Giselle with a smirk.

Lydia knows Giselle is the office jester but now she's pissing her off. Didn't Giselle think her silly ritual was a good thing? It meant Lydia was able to leave the office at the office – something most people here, including Giselle and Geoff, were incapable of doing. To Lydia, there was nothing more troublesome than going home with work on her mind. It made her anxious and it meant (as much as she hated the phrase) that she didn't work to live but lived to work.

Just shut up! screams Lydia.

Giselle and Geoff look at each other in shock.

Lydia is slightly shocked herself. She didn't mean to say that, it just announced itself out of her mouth. She can usually take a joke.

Hey, says Giselle, standing up and looking at Lydia over their monitors. *I'm sorry, you know I love to joke around.*

Lydia doesn't respond right away. She drums her keyboard harder, the hits resounding through the air, until she stops and looks up at Giselle.

It's okay, she says. *Just trying to finish off this report.*

Giselle sits back down, unconvinced.

Geoff crouches behind his monitor and mouths, *Is everything okay with her?*

Giselle just nods and tells him with a shrug to let it be. They both know that, as with most things when it comes to Lydia, deeper meanings can be extracted from her actions and objects. Every choice somehow informs her self-perception. The black clothes she wears signify sophistication. Eliminating sugars and maintaining a diet rich in wholefoods prevents her – allegedly – from ever becoming obese, and while they tease her about all these little things, they don't mean anything by it. It's just innocent kidding around. Except that one time Lydia told them that she only dates men who know about the honorary side of the street – to Giselle, that definitely meant she was asking to be teased.

To Giselle, Lydia was just too interesting to be left alone. And the two mugs on her desk? She couldn't let them be. They were designed specifically to measure Lydia's productivity and self-worth at the end of each day. Giselle respected this practice, because she knew about Lydia's anxiety. At times when Lydia had too much on her plate, her worries would spike. Her left leg would constantly bounce, she would pee a lot, and bite the inside of her lower lip, sometimes until it bled.

Don't you have that meeting soon? says Giselle a little later.

Fuck, says Lydia.

She did forget, whispers Giselle to Geoff.

Lydia gets up frantically, unplugs her laptop and grabs her notepad and pen.

You still have fifteen minutes, says Giselle.

But I gotta finish the rest! yells Lydia and walks off towards the kitchen.

Fifteen minutes later, they see her in the glassed-in meeting room that's visible from their desks. The creative team is listening to her deliver her latest report on consumer habits of online skincare purchasers. It is a pleasure watching her, thinks Giselle, because she's dominant in meetings and it's a rare sight for an office that is governed by too much dick.

Giselle checks the time.

I've got about five minutes, she says to Geoff.

He turns to her. *Five minutes for what?* he asks.

She takes out a mug from her drawer. *This*, she says.

Fuck off! yells Geoff. *You can't fucking do that!*

Giselle looks towards the meeting room. Lydia is still presenting. She gets up, and leans over her monitor.

Trust me, she'll have a laugh for sure, says Giselle but Geoff is sceptical.

I don't want a bar of this, he says.

She places the mug in between the two on Lydia's desk.

Don't say a fucking thing, she says to Geoff, who is trying not to pay attention.

A part of Giselle does feel bad, and as she goes back to writing her article, she wonders if she should hold off, keep it in the drawer for another day. But she doesn't. Believing whole-heartedly that this is exactly the kind of prank Lydia needs to loosen her up a bit, she reaches over and pushes the mug even more into line with the others.

Here she comes, says Geoff just as Giselle retreats.

Giselle looks up and sees Lydia walking towards her desk. She's not smiling but she also doesn't have that look of intensity on her face, the one that tells you right away it'll be the *I've-Done-Nothing*-Lady-Grey-tea-infused-self-reflection day.

Lydia places her laptop on the desk and stretches. She's quiet, a little too quiet.

How was it? Giselle asks.

Lydia continues to stretch her arms out. *They don't get it*, she says and sits down.

Here we go, thinks Giselle.

She reclines further into her seat, a little out of fear and a little out of anticipation. Geoff keeps a close eye on Lydia from his desk and Giselle watches his face to catch his reaction to Lydia's reaction. He moves his seat forward so he can see Lydia more clearly and watches her take off her jacket and sling it around her chair. When she reaches over for her mug, she stops. Geoff clenches his teeth and Giselle bites her lower lip when he does this. Lydia sees the third mug. She turns it around. Like the others, it bears an inscription in the exact same handwritten font, but this one reads, *I've done enough.*

She continues to look at it, deeply, as if she's seen something that she hasn't seen in years, something suddenly remembered, like an old picture from her past or an object she adored as a child.

Giselle can't hold it any longer. She gets up and hovers over Lydia.

Is something the matter?

Lydia doesn't answer. She continues to stare at the third mug, trying earnestly to extract the meaning behind its sudden appearance. She doesn't ask where it came from, who placed it there, or why. She kind of understands that this is a prank, a prank courtesy of Giselle, but this doesn't seem to bother her.

Geoff gets up. *Lydia, are you okay?* he asks. He sounds genuinely concerned.

Still, Lydia stares at the mug without saying a word. She can hear Giselle – *It was just a joke, I'm so sorry* – but her voice is now fading into the background, like a song nearing its end. This thing in front of her is so very suddenly eye-opening that Lydia feels she's looking at her life from another perspective – a different camera angle, a celestial viewpoint that is showing her just how ridiculous she is. How structured and planned, controlled and organised every single aspect of her life has been.

And here is this object with an inscription meant as some kind of senseless trick to make her laugh, or cry, or loosen up, but instead it is both causing her to feel the texture of her own worthlessness and telling her something she genuinely needed to hear: that, much like the origin story of Lady Grey, everything is pointless.

COLLABORATIONIST

Jules always felt confined by her job description: copywriter.

She knew she could do more. In addition to being a copywriter she was also an experienced planner. A nifty strategist. A critical-thinking UXer. Quietly speaking, she was also a pretty good art director.

For years she resigned herself to the copywriter title, but after her thirtieth birthday she began to give serious thought as to how to expand her skillset.

One Thursday morning, as she smoked a cigarette on the office balcony, an idea came to her. She asked for a hot desk in every department so she could collaborate with everyone.

Soon she was everywhere. Everyone knew her; everyone asked for her.

It was an idea that slowly changed the makeup of the agency. Jules became a new kind of creative. The first of her kind. The *collaborationist*, they called her.

But the idea didn't change Jules alone. It inspired a significant change in the agency. After finally grasping that the active exchange of ideas is the truest way to innovate, they made collaboration their most important capability.

Now they're killing it.

EXHIBITION 1

Her friend was upset he missed the exhibition.
What was it like? **he asked.**

But the friend to whom the question was posed didn't really know how to answer because she hadn't yet fully comprehended what had just taken place at the exhibition.

I need a cigarette, she said.

He passed her one. *Tell me, how was it?* he asked.

It was weird, she replied after a few frantic puffs.

I knew I should've gone! said her friend.

My boyfriend had to wait outside.

You serious?

It was for art directors only.

What the fuck? said her friend.

I had to fucking prove I was an art director. It was so awkward.

46

I didn't have a business card so I had to show them my LinkedIn profile.

Her friend lit a cigarette too. *God, that's wanky,* he said.

So many people got pissed off they couldn't get in.

Her friend laughed. *Of course an ex adman that becomes an artist has to become a dick. What was his name again?*

Konrad J. Krusemann, she replied.

Wanky name too, remarked her friend.

I dunno, this exhibition, it was something else, though, she went on. *There were just these desks where designers were sitting. They'd only let ten people go in at a time, and they called us Hoverers. Like, there'd be these whispers coming out of speakers just saying that from time to time, like ridiculing us. We'd be guided to stand behind each designer and were told to just watch. We couldn't comment on anything, and it was really frustrating because so many of the designers were doing a shit job, and they genuinely needed feedback, but we weren't allowed to art direct.*

The audacity of this fucking guy! said her friend, shaking his head.

It's not even funny anymore; the exhibition has been picked up by every major institution. It's gonna be touring, worldwide.

Fuck me, exclaimed her friend.

Just wait, it gets worse, she continued. *At the third desk, this one creative director couldn't take it anymore. He pointed to a CTA button on a screen that the designer had placed in the wrong spot. It was just bad UX, but he nudged the designer, and told him to move it lower. He was laughing the whole time, and we thought it was funny too, but then out of the blue, a security guard came and dragged this guy out of the exhibition.*

Her friend had his hands on his face. *Are you fucking kidding me?* he asked.

Yeah, it got fucking scary and in the last room especially. It was this small space with a designer sitting behind a desk. There was this huge ticking clock timer above his desk. We didn't know what was going on, but suddenly the guards came out again. They said they were going to tie our hands behind our backs and gaffer-tape our mouths!

Her friend stared her down. *You're lying*, he said.

I'm serious! That's why I had to sign the fucking waiver before I got in. Some people got out right away. And the worst part, after they did all that, we had to stand behind this designer who was actually DESIGNING A WEBSITE IN PHOTOSHOP for like ten minutes. Like, we had to stand there for that long man, watching this shit. This one girl eventually tried to get out, but the security guards wouldn't let her till the timer finished up. She was screaming and crying and saying she'll sue the shit out of the gallery. Then there was this song, like choir music coming out of the speakers that slowly ascended with more and more insults. It just kept repeating, Hoverers, hoverers, hoverers. *Like, endlessly. They forced us to stay there till the clock timed out.*

Her friend took his phone out of his bumbag and checked a message. *I can't believe that fucker*, he said. He typed out a reply, then lit another cigarette.

Some crazy performance art, I tell ya.

Fuck that, said her friend. *He's just taken the whole hovering art director joke and turned it into an art show.*

Yeah, but he single-handedly got like three hundred thousand followers overnight.

Her friend shook his head again, then offered her another cigarette.

She took it.

That's not art, added her friend.

I don't know what it was. I just had to take a Zoloft afterwards.

SPAM

According to the internet, the first SPAM email was sent to six hundred people over the ARPANET on 1 May 1978. This is the story of one of the recipients.

On the morning of this historic day, Jake S., from the University of Utah, arrived at his office thinking about the ruggedness of the Marlboro Man. On the highway earlier, he had passed a newly installed 'Come to Marlboro Country' billboard and the image of the cowboy lighting up a cigarette next to a black horse impressed him. It represented freedom, red-blooded strength and rustic adventures. By merely lighting up a Marlboro, Jake thought, one could be transformed into a ruggedly handsome rancher. So, as he strolled through the grounds of the university, pondering this thought, Jake lit up. He took subtle drags, and consciously blew the smoke out of his mouth with pursed lips.

At his office, he placed his packet of smokes neatly on the table and booted up his computer. As he did this, he caught his reflection in the small screen. He stopped and examined it. There was no doubt that Jake enjoyed being a computer science lecturer, although it clearly wasn't as sexy as being the Marlboro Man. But, as he stared at his raised eyebrows, his rough stubble and his cool new gaze, he thought – just maybe – it was possible to transform yourself, one Marlboro at a time.

Relishing this renewed self-confidence, he started to hum a tune. A hit of the times, 'Go Your Own Way' by Fleetwood Mac. If anyone had passed his office in that moment they would've seen a happy, joyous man starting his day. With a little hip movement, Jake hung his jacket on the coat rack beside the door, and took another look at his computer. The machine was making a sluggish sound. It felt slothful to Jake, like it was being dragged. It must be something to do with the disk space, he thought. Just as he began to investigate the issue, his desktop loaded up normally. He smiled, lit another cigarette, took a drag, then placed it carefully in one of the indentations on his ashtray.

When he opened up his electronic mail service, he finally saw the problem.

What is this? Jake wondered in confusion.

There, as fresh, and pioneering as the Marlboro Man, sat the first ever unsolicited email.

Nobody should be allowed to send a message with a header that long, he muttered.

The emailing system Jake used had limited capacity for addresses and messages. The idiot that had sent the email had typed the addresses into the TO header, which then overflowed into the CC header, the subject field and the message field as well. At the bottom was a marketing message, typed out in capital letters inviting Jake and 599 other recipients to a new computer product presentation in California. Jake looked at the mess in disbelief. But before he could delete the email, his computer shut down.

Fucking thing used up all my disk space! yelled Jake.

He gave it a minute, then tried again. The computer still wouldn't start. The euphoria he had felt earlier, of being a ruggedly handsome rancher, vanished. He reached for the cigarette on his ashtray. It was out. Rage rose within him, spurred on by a combination of anxiety and frustration. It immediately tightened his chest. Jake sighed, then rubbed his upper body with his palm. *What the fuck was that?* he yelled.

And here is when it happened.

As Jake sat in his office chair, with his head tilted backwards and his palm on his heart, his mind was strenuously working on a new defence mechanism. You see, this first ever unsolicited email didn't just use up Jake's computer's disk space; it infiltrated his mind in such a way that it immediately fortified his entire psychological system in order for this to never happen again. When he saw the so-called invite in his inbox, Jake developed an antagonism towards unsolicited communication. He found the intrusion of this marketing act highly unethical and corrupt. It bothered him so much, that from that moment on, he devoted his life to fighting SPAM. Inside that little office, while chain-smoking cigarettes and channelling Marlboro Man energy, he started the work that would be the work of his career: computer software that blocked SPAM messages. He became so vehemently devoted to this singular pursuit that SPAM itself became afraid of him and the iron curtain of software he ended up building against it.

Jake fiercely (and successfully) avoided SPAM emails in his inbox for the rest of his life. That is, until an unremarkable day in May 2025.

While living at an aged care facility in Salt Lake City, Jake will receive the second SPAM email of his life, and with it, a memory he hadn't thought about in fifty years.

By this stage, Jake will be battling dementia. Things will feel recognisable, but they won't make sense to him. His level of focus and concentration will gradually decay, as will his memories. But on this day, a distantly familiar feeling will take hold of him.

He will wake up before dawn, not knowing what time it is. He'll reach for his iPad on his bedside table. When the screen brightens, instead of focusing on the time, Jake will notice a red circle on the blue icon of his email service. This will puzzle Jake, but he will click it nevertheless.

As the mail service loads, an unfamiliar email on top of the rows of messages from friends and family will load up. And immediately that raw fury he experienced fifty years ago will come surging back. The sight of this intrusive message will awaken that historic day in 1978 with more clarity than he'd had in years. He'll remember the Marlboro Man. He'll remember how the billboard made him feel. He'll recall the damp smell of his office and his indented ashtray. But most of all, he'll remember how that invasive invite knocked out his whole computer.

Jake's hands will shake, but he will manage to reach for his phone. Instead of a nurse, he'll dial 911 and tell the operator to send the police right away. His shaky voice, the fear in his mumbled speech, will frighten the operator and they will immediately dispatch emergency vehicles.

Within five minutes, two officers will arrive. The nurses and night staff will be shocked to see them ringing the doorbell of the aged care facility. Together, they will rush to Jake's room. They will find him scrunched up like a baby against the wall with the iPad pushed to the foot of his bed, below his feet.

What happened? the frightened nurse will ask.

Jake will point at the iPad. *It's come for me,* he will say. *It's finally come for me.*

What's come for you, Jake? What has come for you? the nurse will ask.

As she attempts to calm Jake down, the police officer will carefully pick up the iPad. He will turn it on and see an opened email on display: an image of a ruggedly handsome rancher with a satisfied woman on his arm. Below the image, a tagline: *You know what you're made of. Buy Viagra today.*

What's there? the nurse will ask, while holding a very frightened Jake by his shoulders.

The police officer will wonder if this is all a practical joke. He will re-read the email, look at Jake, and laugh. Then in a somewhat ironic tone, the police officer will reply, *Ah, it's just SPAM.*

GFC

The decline of a Greek advertising agency experienced through Christmas parties during the Global Financial Crisis.

2006

A two-day cruise through the Aegean Sea with a stopover in Mykonos. In the words of Galen, a web developer who attended the cruise, *It was the greatest Christmas party ever.*

2007

A five-course dinner at a celebrity chef's restaurant in Athens followed by a warehouse after-party featuring a renowned DJ. Sponsored by Mythos Beer (their client).

2008

Private room in a shabby restaurant with catering (limited to finger food, beer and wine) which was fun, until the photobooth promised by management didn't arrive.

2009

Casual drinks at the office.

APHANTASIA

Here is a story about an art director who lost his imagination.

Just after a late afternoon tea break, Ben was gazing at a bowl of M&M's on his desk. His colleague, Usman, who was sitting beside him, was disturbing this quiet moment with loud and obnoxious humming. Instead of telling him to quieten down, Ben tried to imagine a red M&M jumping out of the bowl and spitting in Usman's face.

But, try as he might, he couldn't. Creating this mental image suddenly felt like pushing a boulder uphill.

Unnerved, he tried to imagine other things. He stared at the pencil on his desk. In his mind, it wouldn't form wings and cruise through the office. His headphones wouldn't change into the hot pink colour he was trying to picture. Not even the sky outside would glaze over with the furious lightning he was describing to himself. Strangely, he could easily think of the individual elements of each thought – the wings, the lightning – but he could not see the complete images in his mind's eye.

Usman, said Ben.

Yeah, man? replied Usman.

If I asked you to imagine an M&M jumping out of this bowl and spitting at you, tell me what happens in your mind.

What . . . Usman frowned. *What are you talking about?*

Like, what do you think about in your head, said Ben.

By the concerned look on Ben's face, Usman saw this was a serious question indeed.

I think of those M&Ms from the commercials, he said. *I think of them chatting, jumping out, forming a mouth and spitting. Why?*

But you just think of the idea of it, right? asked Ben.

No, it's like a picture. You know?

Ben leant over and gripped Usman's shoulders. *You see a picture? A visual component?*

What the fuck, dude?

Oh my god, mumbled Ben. Sweat formed around his temples. His hands began to shake, his heart beat accelerated.

You see, without imagination, Ben was left with only what he could see: his world as it really was. And the world as it really was, was the art department of a small creative agency on a late afternoon at the beginning of the week. Where, behind rows of messy desks, bored bodies attempted to stay busy until the hour finally arrived when they could go home. This world was familiar to Ben, yet its familiarity suddenly became disturbing. It was as if someone had plucked out its essence, leaving it lifeless before him.

He got up and marched around. He slid his fingers over desks and monitors. Picked up pens, papers, stained coffee cups and water bottles. He examined them closely as if they were prehistoric objects. He pressed his hands and face against windows. *Why does everything feel so dispassionate?* he kept asking himself. He stomped his feet on the grey office carpet, trying to discern what the hell was the matter with him. While at the same time, his colleagues – who observed him quietly and fearfully – wondered the same thing. He went back to his desk and tried to imagine more concepts; but like before, nothing could be conceived in his mind.

He screamed.

Usman, who had returned to his humming after their brief, awkward chat, froze in shock. He turned around just as Ben slapped the bowl of M&Ms from his desk. The little multi-coloured chocolates scattered through the office, hitting heads, computer monitors, chairs and walls.

Jesus, man, what the fuck? yelled Usman.

But Ben wasn't listening. He began to cry and scream and slowly went down on his knees. Then he fainted.

His colleagues thought this was it, Ben was having one of those millennial burnouts they'd read about on newsfeeds. They called an ambulance.

Ben woke up in a hospital hours later. He was strapped to a bed, dazed and high on Valium. Usman, who had come along with him, watched the scene in bewilderment, but he no longer thought Ben was going through a millennial burnout. Something very serious was happening to him.

After extensive tests and psychological exams, doctors determined that Ben had permanently lost the ability to create mental images in his mind's eye. If you asked him to describe a green square, he wouldn't be able to understand the question. He would think of the idea of a green square, but all else would be blank. Behind his eyes. Next to his ears. Blankness in every nook and cranny of his brain.

This strange occurrence, the doctors observed, gave Ben the ability to see what was truly in front of him, with no personal point of view or bias. He was – unlike any of us – truly free. Ben, however, wasn't curious enough to see this change as a gift. No, all Ben worried about was how the hell he was going to be an art director if he couldn't imagine anything anymore.

META ENNIS
PART I

In the city of Sarajevo, a slow-growing decision is being settled by the brain areas of a young woman called Ina Ahmetović.

This decision isn't about choosing burek over a vegetarian stew for lunch. It is of much more serious consequence. Ina's mind is weighing up the option of either (a) continuing to pursue a career in advertising or (b) risking everything for her art.

There's no option c.

As we'll soon comprehend, Ina believes that major endeavours in life – especially art – deserve full, undivided attention. While you or I may think it's perfectly fine to work full-time and pursue art on the side, Ina is of the opinion that a person who chooses to become an artist chooses divine responsibility. *You cannot undertake anything else,* she would say. Dabbling, to her, is not conducive to great accomplishment. *You must devote yourself religiously to one quest: that of mastering great work, and great work alone.*

Every decision, in its simplest sense, is an act of choosing between two or more courses of action. With more weighty decisions (such as Ina's), intuition, reasoning, personal value and cognitive biases come into play. Ideally, a final choice is based on an analysis of these influences, but sometimes . . . it's not.

Humans, especially creative ones (like Ina), often wait for signs from which to draw meaning. They seek out sublime interventions. Experiences they would consider meaningful coincidences. In this instance, we're lucky. Meaningful coincidences are perfectly rational beliefs, and given what we're about to do, it will no doubt influence Ina's mind to lean more towards our preference. But before we get to this moment in our story, let's first get to know Ina.

Born during the opening ceremony of the 1984 Winter Olympics in Sarajevo, Ina came into the world more curious than afraid. She hardly cried as her mother held her in her arms. When her father, a professor of comparative literature, caressed her face for the first time, he immediately knew that Ina possessed that sixth sense that allows us to experience time with more cognition. As her little body stretched its arms into the air, he recognised that she would have the ability to perceive life more intensely. He was proud.

Consequently, from an early age, Ina was encouraged to pursue her playful wonderments. Her father loved observing her as she coloured in bountiful spirals with crayons or smudged paint over sheets of baking paper with both hands, dragging her fingertips through the colours to make squiggles. At the age of six, she developed a love of edges. She started playing around with drawing them, then painting them. Sometimes she would become obsessed with painting hard edges onto copious sheets of paper, other times they'd be soft and smooth and cover the walls of their Austro-Hungarian apartment in central Sarajevo. The concentration on her face, her joyful expression, was what her father loved the most. He regarded it as evidence of her intelligent personality. But before he was able to hearten her mind and soul into further pursuits of artistic expression, the war began.

Well-armed Bosnian Serb forces, backed by neighbouring Serbia, laid siege to the city of Sarajevo in early April 1992. Ina's father, who always donned suits and ties, was suddenly clothed in an army uniform. No longer a studious professor, but a principled soldier, he had to postpone his daughter's education in order to protect their homeland.

Now, war is certainly sweet to those who haven't experienced it, but for the purpose of our story, it isn't relevant. So, we'll skip the horror of the forty-four-month-long Siege of Sarajevo and draw our attention to a few moments during the short-lived exile Ina and her mother experienced in Paris, where they stayed as refugees until the war ended.

In 1995, a year after arriving in Paris, eleven-year-old Ina was admiring her pair of hand-me-down Nikes with a pink swoosh when the telephone rang in their small apartment. Her mother ran to pick it up, anxious to hear of her husband and news from Sarajevo. It only took seconds for her silent listening to turn into a chaotic cry. Her body loosened and she fell to the ground. This is a moment Ina has never forgotten: her mother's slackened body, the terror on her face, as she listened to how her husband had died.

Even at Ina's young age, she knew that her mother would never again get up from this fall. It would be a permanent plunge into mourning.

Ina's mother was bedbound with grief for several days before Ina decided steadfastly that a trip outside was necessary for both of them.

In honour of Father, she said to her mother, who couldn't understand where her daughter suddenly found this burst of energy.

On the seventh day of their conjoined grief, Ina led her mother through the streets of Barbès, their neighbourhood in Paris. They ventured to a little café for tea and cakes. A local market for fresh strawberries. Through the Marais for window shopping. And so, the morning hours dwindled and soon they found themselves before the doors of the Pompidou Centre.

We must go inside, begged Ina.

There was something urgent in Ina's tone that made her mother immediately agree. At the counter, while she paid for two tickets, Ina asked an attendant where she could find the works of Sonia Delaunay. Initially, her mother didn't understand. But after they had spent several minutes standing like silent monks before the giant works of Delaunay's art, she remembered.

How did you know? she asked her daughter.

Ina observed her mother's grieving figure next to the strong colours and geometric shapes of Delaunay's work. Her mother looked lonely to her, her dark sorrow entirely exposed.

He used to make me imitate her, explained Ina. *Sonia was his favourite artist.*

With the death of her father, Ina's mother assumed sole responsibility for her daughter's artistic development. Soon, they spent less time at home and more time in galleries around Paris. It was an education Ina will forever cherish. Those lonely days, together with her mother, strolling from the Pompidou Centre to the Louvre, staring at and trying to understand the works of Van Gogh, Monet, Degas, Picasso, Gauguin, Rousseau, Matisse or Derain. Ina was aware that her mother did not know how to respond to art as well as her father, but it didn't matter – she was grateful for her mother's renewed zeal.

In 1999, they returned to Sarajevo.

After being devastated by the siege, physically and emotionally, the city had begun to find its feet again, albeit slowly. As Sarajevo gradually healed, Ina entered high school, where she abstained from taking part in sports or active debating. Instead, she fastened herself to poetry and literature, art classes and critical thinking. Many nights, her mother would find Ina in her dead father's study, underlining passages from Goethe, Sappho, Rilke, Mak Dizdar, Rumi and Mikhail Bulgakov. The spitting image of her father, thought her mother.

Ina never refrained from asking existential questions, or sharing her own poems.

Why am I? she once asked her mother.

You mean who? replied her mother.

Why is a more important question, Ina said sternly, then let her be.

Her mother watched her pass through their living room, her eyes voraciously examining the many paintings on their walls. She was impressed with the fluency of Ina's curiousness. Ina didn't seem to be affected by the turmoil left behind by the war. It seemed to her mother that Ina lived in her own world, where she couldn't get her ideas down fast enough. One idea simply led into another. Stacks of filled-in notepads soon piled up in her bedroom.

Privately, Ina deeply missed her life in Paris. She found it hard to adapt to Sarajevo again. But time, as we'd know if we were ever conscious of it, heals all wounds and yearnings. Soon, she reconnected with lost childhood friends – those who had survived or returned to the city like she had – and she began to listen intently. To stories of horrific exiles. Violent deaths. Rape. Ethnic cleansing. Genocide. These devastating stories of what happened to her people hardened her, made her more politically aware and proud to be back where she was from.

She began to fall in love with the rebirth of Sarajevo. She felt like a pioneer, a witness to the city's second coming. She entered the Academy of Fine Arts and quickly established herself as an excellent student. She had a strong work ethic; studied, painted and drew with admirable gusto. But throughout her time at the Academy, Ina never publicly exhibited her art. No doubt she was urged to – by her mother, friends, tutors and professors – but she always refused, as if she wasn't bothered by time or mortality.

At the age of twenty-six, an unexpected opportunity arose while she was studying. Now, she often thinks back on this moment, as it is the one encounter that led her to the crossroads she currently finds herself at. A classmate approached her and, having always loved her eye for detail, wanted her to join him as an art director at the design studio where he worked.

There's so much work coming in, he said, *brands are throwing money at us. Seriously, you'll get the freedom to design ideas how you like.*

Immediately, she refused. Commerciality did not interest her. As we know, she despises the idea of dabbling. But over the following months, her classmate pushed and prodded, convincing her to give it a shot at least. What did she have to lose by trying?

It was a question that startled her.

I'll quit if I don't like it, she demanded.

Of course, said her classmate.

This marked a new moment in Ina's life. The first time that she began to apply all her learnings about art, philosophy and theory into something other than her own practice. At first, she began to view communication design with contempt. It was a burden she approached cautiously, but the work soon turned into a joy. At times, she felt like an investigator who was digging into metaphysical problems for brands. Other times she compared herself to a pastry chef who was trying to blend different ingredients into a uniform mixture. She combined the useful with the interesting to create all manner of work: stand-alone logos, full brand identities, posters, billboards, print advertisements and online content for a variety of new companies trying to take advantage of a post-war economy. Unlike her own work, which never seemed to have an end in sight, there was always a finale in this field: the work would appear on TV screens, billboards, magazines, and eventually, on social channels. The more time passed, the more she injected her individual personality and style into the work. She committed herself to this new creative journey and enjoyed the unknowable outcomes that she was producing. But what she had initially thought would be a short period, turned into a role that continues to consume her till now.

Today, aged thirty-six, after nearly a decade in this field, Ina has come to a standstill. The work has finally gotten to her, this dipping in and out of art and work, that she never wanted to commit herself to.

What have I done? she asks herself, almost daily.

This may sound demoralising, this period of an artist's life. But look at it this way: she still gets lost looking at rays of light filtering through grass like she did as a child. When she walks through the mahalas of Sarajevo with her friends, she's the one who always points up at lit-up windows, telling her friends how there's a story behind every one of them. When her mother (who is still alive) speaks of boredom or restlessness, Ina tells her to pay attention to boredom because it can be unbelievably interesting. When her friends recall the siege and the war, Ina doesn't get angry like they do. She stays still, let's them vent their frustrations, then she recites the poetry of Mak Dizdar. Each and every time, this reminds them that every great suffering turns into an equally great strength. No, Ina might be at a crossroads, but she has not lost her artistic sensibility whatsoever.

She spends every Saturday at the Ministry of Ćejf, a café in an area of Sarajevo called Kovači. She arrives just after they open and sits at the corner table beside the window that overlooks the sloping cobblestoned street that leads into the old town, Baščaršija. Every time she sits here, her heart pounds. She loves how the smooth cobblestones reflect the light of the sun. She loves the remnants of Ottoman architecture that can be found in the burgundy-coloured wooden panels around the shopfronts.

She always stares into these quaint little stores, where local crafts-men make coffee pots and decorations out of brass and copper. She can hear the pounding of their hammers even when they're not working. To Ina, this pounding is the heartbeat of Sarajevo. Usually, as she listens and looks around, she re-enters her own world again. She forgets her work. Her life. The need to create art arises and she begins to draw onto her notepads, sketch ideas and write, sometimes for hours on end.

And just here, on this particular Saturday, while she sips on her coffee, ponders the great intersectional questions of life and art, and deliberates over her decision, we will introduce her to the author of our book, i.e. *me*.

I won't preach and lecture Ina on the reasons why she shouldn't pursue advertising. I love advertising, that's obvious – but I also know what happens to the artist in advertising. What I must become is the sublime intervention she seeks; the mean-ingful coincidence.

There's good reason for this.

Within a year, Ina's work will catch the eye of a director of a London design studio. He will throw everything at Ina to convince her to join his team – which she will. After all, it's not every day that Bosnian people find themselves presented with opportunities like this.

London, with its double-decker buses and milky teas, its red phone boxes and carpeted pubs, will charm Ina immensely. Her life will ease into an enjoyable existence. She will visit Sarajevo off and on, but after she falls in love with an Englishman named Edward, life will hold her in London. She will marry Edward and bear his children. Regret, however, that comes along with letting

71

go of dreams will follow. A hollowness, like that of a rusty metal tube, will live inside her. She'll be able to suppress this cavity-like feeling, but privately, it will haunt her. It shouldn't surprise us then that the question, *What if?* will be the last thing she'll utter on her deathbed.

Of course, Ina isn't aware of this destiny. To some extent, we're not either. We know what will happen to her scenarios, but we cannot control her will – we can only influence it. England, London, Edward and children sound great, but we don't want this to happen. We want Ina to remain in Sarajevo.

Here, something entirely different will shape her life.

After her mother passes away, Ina will be consumed by grief. She will start to examine the timeline of her life: every moment will be probed for answers. Alone, in her parents' apartment, her father's study unchanged since she was a child, she will plummet into work. The existential pain she'll experience won't let up, it will only push her further into seclusion. She'll free herself from the burden of work and commit wholly to her art. The pain (and all its glory) will for years drive Ina until she arrives at a completely new body of work: the first and only work she will ever exhibit. *Art washes away from the soul the dust of everyday life*, said Pablo Picasso. This is what Ina's work will do: it will wash away the pain the people of Bosnia and Herzegovina still feel from the war they experienced in the 1990s.

Her work, a set of large-scale paintings and marble sculptures, will raise again the question of her people's suffering. A collective, public interest in her art will emerge, which will spread to the far corners of this heart-shaped land. They will ask themselves, *How much longer do we need to live like the war only ended yesterday?* From this moment onwards, an uprising will begin that will inspire the people of Bosnia and Herzegovina to protest and demand a better future. A future they will attain.

Sure, you can sit here, she says when I ask to join her table.

Perhaps, at the beginning, when I ask Ina if she is an artist, she isn't all that interested in having a conversation with me. But then we chat: about Nikolai Gogol and Aleksandar Hemon. The advertising of United Colors of Benetton. Balenciaga. Yeezy. We speak about Swiss design and Bauhaus. My tenacity, and likely my honesty, intrigues her.

I'd like to tell you a story, I say when we finish a slice of carrot cake together.

I like stories, she says with a smile, and I begin.

Years ago, I met a woman in a bar. It was in Melbourne in 2007, when I was twenty-four years old. The woman was alone, sitting next to me on a barstool in a darkly lit cocktail bar off a laneway. Playing with the large ice cube in her whisky, she asked me, very much out of the blue, if I was a writer. I laughed, and said I was an aspiring writer, who also had just started working as a copywriter in advertising. Really? *she asked. She said she didn't expect my answer and was blown away by the serendipity. If I cared to listen, she said, she needed to tell me a story.*

I did, even though this was a time in my life when I listened more to reply than to understand. But on this occasion, the sombre tone of her voice made me keep my mouth shut for the duration of her story.

Fifteen years ago, said the woman, she was bright and ambitious, fresh out of university. She had studied philosophy and literature and was inspired to pursue these studies for the rest of her life. She lived and breathed novels. Poetry and metaphysics were to her what getting

73

laid and partying were to others. Shortly after graduation, she got a job in a university as a research assistant. She moved out with a girl from campus who had just started working in advertising. After only a year, her research job fell through. With mounting debts, she needed to find something quickly. And that's how she found herself at an interview for a copywriting role at her housemate's advertising agency. She thought, Why not? It's a job with long hours, but she could still manage to work on her stories and poems afterwards.

The moment she entered the office, she felt an energy that excited her with astonishing immediacy. There were people playing ping pong without a care in the world. A team drawing on a wall, while others meditated nearby. On the balcony, there was a crowd drinking beer and barbequing. It was nothing like she had ever seen at a workplace. In the interview, she expressed her jubilant desire to join the industry. The agency was impressed with her writing samples and offered her a junior copywriting role.

Within a month she found herself writing ads for Skittles. A month later, she was on a photoshoot. Two months later, she was writing a script for Nike. Every Friday night, she was out at different parties with different people who all displayed versions of cool she had never encountered before. With time, she began to lose interest in her devotional pursuits. I can always write later, *she'd tell herself.*

But years went by. She became a senior creative, working on projects all around the world. When she was promoted to creative director, she became a pitilessly ambitious leader. Fifteen years after she took that junior role at her housemate's agency, she had become one of the most awarded female copywriters in the world.

The evening I met her, she had just flown in from New York after accepting yet another prestigious advertising award. On the

74

flight over, she was sitting next a young man who was reading Letters to a Young Poet *by Rainer Maria Rilke. She hadn't seen that book since university, and the young man's attention to it reminded her of her younger self.*

She wondered how many stories, poems and novels she could have written by now. It surprised her then, when she realised she had become an advertising stereotype: someone who lacked the will to pursue their dream of being an artist, and so had ended up in advertising, working on other people's dreams.

When her fellow passenger with the Rilke book noticed her staring at him, he closed the book and adjusted his arse in the seat. Nothing to see here – Yet, *she felt like saying to the young man, but there was no point. She would never write a book like the one he was reading. She had already become that person who talks for forty years about the novel they are writing, but never, ever finishes it.*

She didn't go home that night. She came to the bar directly, lamenting her success, trying to justify to herself that there was still time for art. It wasn't that she couldn't undertake it; she had the means, she said, but time had drifted her away from the raw energy art needs to mature into something great. What is the point otherwise? *she asked.*

After telling me this story, she stopped and looked at me gravely. Does your heart burn for literature? *she asked.*

I was shaking – for I didn't know how to answer.

She got up, paid for our whiskies and said, Never choose security over art, especially if your art comes from need.

Ina Ahmetović listens intently to every word I say about the woman I met in a bar when I was twenty-four years old. And, much like the woman I had met, I leave soon after telling Ina the story.

She watches me walk off down the cobblestoned street. She admires, I think, my clothing, and liked how I mixed athletic wear with a formal, woollen coat. But I could also be dead wrong. She could hate it. As she sips on her pressed apple tea, and watches me disappear in the crowd near Sebilj, she thinks how, in the end, all hearts break and all lives end. As it plaits implicit meanings through her mind, Ina wonders if she would rather have her heart broken and her life ended through the pursuit of her innermost dream, or, like the woman in my story, only realise when it was too late.

Can I please get another pot of tea? Ina asks the waitress, who is taking away empty cups from a nearby table. She takes a sharpener from her backpack and sharpens her pencil, then opens her sketchbook to a fresh sheet of white paper and stares at it. She doesn't feel threatened by the stark whiteness, or by not knowing what to draw or write. She unexpectedly discerns how the fine, uncoated texture of the paper looks a lot like the sun-cracked skin of her father's hands.

Inshallah.

SIDE HUSTLE

His girlfriend recommended laughing yoga classes.

They would do you good, she said. And she meant it. Since she had started giggling out her bodily tensions, she felt great.

Sam said nothing in return but kept staring at the vase with the single purple tulip on their coffee table.

Looking at him moping like that, with his shoulders slouched and his head dangling, his low spirits seemed so unexplainable to her. After a prolonged pause, he looked up at her.

I don't feel like a grown-ass adult anymore, he said.

Don't be silly, she replied. She reached over and touched his knees.

He pulled them closer to his chest. This rut he was in, he thought, she didn't get it.

You always say a person needs to fail harder, said Anne.

Not this time, he replied.

He was sick of saying shit didn't work out. Not just to his girlfriend, but to everyone else.

What happened to that alarm clock app that yells at you?

Oh, the developer pulled out.

What about the accounting software for freelancers?

Someone got there before me.

What about Syrious?

Well, the Syrian war ended.

That had been the hardest one to swallow. Inspired by the devastating Syrian civil war, Sam created a monthly event that centred itself around honest discussion of critical debates. It had the best fucking tagline: Dangerous ideas in civil discussion. But after the conflict faded away from daily news, people had stopped coming.

It was a bit PC, they'd said.

And now? What was he going to say about his latest side hustle, the perfumed matchsticks? *The investors pulled out, even though the idea had serious legs. Imagine if your house smelt like Tom Ford's Tuscan Leather from one single strike of a match?*

Nah, he was over it. Today was the day; he knew it. His entrepreneurial hat would be hanging right next to that stupid DHL x Vetements long-sleeve jacket he'd bought but never wore.

I just feel like I'm going through an endless cycle of failed ideas, he said to her. *Like, seriously, could one just work out?*

She caressed his arm this time. *It's okay, babe, just keep going. I'm here for you. Let me get us some Uber Eats.* She opened the app on her smartphone. *Feel like Thai?*

Sam nodded and pulled himself up to the centre of the couch. The challenges I'm facing aren't fleeting, he wanted to tell her. They were systemic and he was annoyed she didn't see that.

That week, he stayed back at work every night, more to avoid his girlfriend's grating positivity than to work. He didn't know exactly when, but he was sure that at some point over the last year she had become one of those people who were too optimistic about failures. They listened intently, and always had encouraging advice, but never really got the gist of a circumstance because they never tried anything risky themselves. He hated it.

He glanced over at Tom, a digital art director who specialised in web design and development. A long-time collaborator, they sat next to each other in a co-working space they freelanced out of, a converted inner-city warehouse full of energetic creatives who dabbled in myriad artistic fields: interior styling, urban architecture, 3D printing, editorial design, product development and screen printing. Sam was the space's only content strategist, and he was good at helping businesses take that much-needed leap into the world of content marketing, but his heart was elsewhere.

He listened inattentively to Tom as he designed a website for an art gallery in Sketch.

Thinking of switching to Figma, said Tom. *It's such a cool program. We can work together in it, in real time, you can add copy while I design the sites.*

But Sam wasn't listening at all; he was rearranging the apps on his smartphone.

Hey! said Tom.

What? replied Sam, looking up.

I'm talking to you.

Sam repositioned his arse in the swivel chair and placed his elbows on Tom's desk.

I'm so over everything, he said.

Tom turned to face him directly. *Dude, you worry too much*, he said. *You're making good money, got a great girlfriend.*

She doesn't get it! said Sam angrily, staring at the ground.

That's not fair, replied Tom. *Anne's always there for you, don't forget that. She never discourages you from trying out new shit.*

Sam looked up; his eyes watery. *I know, but still*, he said. *She downplays it all.*

Tom put his hand on Sam's shoulder. *Give her a break*, he said.

I just wanna make it as an entrepreneur, man, added Sam.

That weekend, Anne tried to cheer him up with a surprise. She got up early and drove out to the farmers' market while he was still asleep and brought home a box full of fresh farm vegetables, free-range eggs, smoked salmon, Persian feta and honey. He woke to an aroma wafting from the kitchen.

Anne? he called but she didn't reply.

He found her stirring scrambled eggs at the stove in a black Calvin Klein leotard.

Wow, he muttered.

Her hair was tied up into a bun and when she turned towards him, he saw that her eyes were gently rimmed with eyeliner. He stood there speechless, thinking she looked more silly than sexy. The boner she was hoping for never rose to the occasion. Sam merely kissed her shoulders, thanked her and went back to bed after he ate.

His sulky state of mind continued for the next week.

He re-engaged with the investors to see if they would reconsider their offer for his perfumed matchsticks, but none did. This made him angrier, so he kept staying back at work.

Do that again, he said one night.

What? asked Tom.

That thing you did with the blur, he said.

This? said Tom, who punched a button on his keyboard and made a row of text blur into a coloured background.

Wow, Sam said, *that's beautiful. Like really beautiful.*

You're a fucking idiot, said Tom.

I've always loved this, he said.

Tom pushed an empty glass towards him. *Pour me one,* he said.

Sam looked around for the bottle of Laphroaig.

It's under your chair, said Tom. *It's kinda therapeutic . . . here.*

Sam placed the glass, now filled with Laphroaig, next to Tom's keyboard and went back to his smartphone.

The following week, instead of mucking around on Instagram and drinking, Sam began to pay closer attention to Tom's work. There was something mesmerising about it.

I love that, he said. Tom was adjusting the colours of a chessboard-like layer in Sketch. Every time he pressed a button on his keyboard, the squares changed colour.

Yeah, it's cool, said Tom. *It's called shared styles. You can't do this in Photoshop.*

He kept watching Tom's screen. The way some of the greyscale wireframes filled up with colour. The way Tom zoomed in and out of different sections. Added images and animation effects.

This is really ... I don't know, it feels good watching this, he said.

Tom laughed. *I'm glad you're into it,* he said.

The idea didn't come to him immediately.

In the way ideas tend to, its arrival took Sam by surprise. He was outside on his balcony enjoying the morning sun. With a fresh coffee in hand, he was watching a neighbour across the street hang their laundry on a clothesline. The neighbour seemed to have a system. The underwear and socks were carefully hung up on the string closest to the wall. The longer items – T-shirts and shirts, jumpers and pants – were placed further out. On the last strings, closest to the balcony railing, the neighbour hung his coloured linen sheets and pillowcases. Then he sat down and admired his handiwork. That did it. Sam ran back into the living room. He grabbed his notepad and began to scribble something down.

What's wrong? asked Anne who was stretching on a yoga mat in between the kitchen and the dining table.

Nothing, said Sam. *Nothing at all, babe.*

He was conscious of its strangeness, but that was what attracted him to the idea.

For weeks he continued to sit around Tom. Using multiple health apps he downloaded to his smartwatch, he monitored everything from his pulse to his heartbeat variability, blood pressure, cholesterol and sugar intake. He kept on top of his mindfulness practice and noted down every change in his emotional state.

After analysing the data with a therapist friend, he knew there was something to this idea. The simple but peculiar act of watching designers design was having a positive effect on him.

It was remedial. Soon he found himself laughing without the laughing yoga classes his girlfriend had recommended.

Much later, when he proposed the idea to Anne, she didn't understand.

It's called Therapy by Design, he said. *Do you like the name?*

Wait, what happens again? she asked.

I told you already! he said.

I don't get it, love.

There's nothing there not to get, he responded. *It's simple! People come and sit behind designers and watch them design websites, products, services – whatever. Then they feel better.*

She was slicing cucumbers in the kitchen and he waited for her to look at him.

But how? she asked without lifting her head. *I don't get how you make money.*

Like any therapy session, said Sam annoyingly. *It's charged by the hour and the design studios that participate get a cut. I'm trialling it with Tom, and later down the track, it could also be video-based therapy. I don't understand what you don't understand – I outlined it in the deck I sent you. It even has the analysis I conducted with Dr Simmon, the therapist.*

She stopped slicing the cucumbers and reached back around into the fridge. *Sam, that deck is a hundred pages,* he heard her say. She pulled open the bottom drawer of the fridge. *Didn't we get zucchinis?* she asked.

Instead of an answer she heard the door slam.

These days, Sam doesn't like to speak about Anne all that much. It's when Sam and Tom recount to others the early stages of their business that Sam thinks back on his old relationship. This tends to happen at start-up festivals where people ask all manner of questions, especially about the beginning of their business.

How did you know there would be a global therapy market with watching designers design websites?

During these moments, as he lets Tom sometimes answer this question, his mind drifts back to thoughts of Anne. His stomach churns at the thought of her years of unwavering support.

This would never have happened without her, he'd confess to Tom after a few heavy drinks at the end of the day. *I mean, she paid rent for a year when I started freelancing on my own,* he'd add. *In those six months when I was developing TBD, I just kept thinking she wanted me to fail again. I thought she didn't believe in the idea. I treated her like shit – then I just fucking left. Who does that?*

These soliloquies usually end with extended sighs and exhalations. But right after, Sam makes a wise remark – the same wise remark he makes whenever Anne becomes the centre of their conversation.

You win some, you lose some, hey, Tom?

VERSUCHS-KANINCHEN

Sitting there, alone, with a pint of weissbier in his hand, Rainer couldn't stop thinking about the fragility of happy occasions.

He had seen the phrase earlier, on a wall plaque in front of an artwork at the Pinakothek der Moderne. Since then, it hadn't stopped coursing through his mind. He was on the verge of coming to a conclusion about its meaning when his mind registered that the pressure in his lower abdomen had reached its limit. He needed to take a piss – badly.

He stepped off the barstool and ran up the narrow spiral staircase that was just behind him. Upstairs, a few patrons were sitting around talking on low stools in dimly lit corners. He noticed a bright blue jumper and heard a loud, irritating cackle. It made the pressure in his bladder more intense. He pushed open the door of the bathroom. The urinal, on his right, was occupied by a broad-shouldered man in a hoodie who was talking loudly to himself. Rainer headed straight for the cubicle, unbuckled quickly and positioned his dick towards the piss-stained toilet bowl. When the last jet of urine had streamed out, and the remaining trickles had dripped into the yellow water, he finally felt relief.

The man at the urinal had abruptly stopped talking. Rainer could hear him slurring and bumping into things like a drunk. He flushed and began to drift back into the thought he'd paused on earlier – the fragility of happy occasions. It occurred to him that the meaning of this bittersweet sentiment related to his current situation: Friday, early evening. The beginning of his personal loosening of the week's built-up angst. This loosening, to him, felt heightened, even blissful, upon the first taste of beer. But this joy was transient, momentary; Monday was always around the corner. He lived, thought Rainer, with the fragility of happy occasions weekly, like everyone else. It was nothing more than a poetic expression of a universal malaise.

He walked back down the spiral staircase, mildly dejected about his interpretation. The seats at the street-facing window had by this time become occupied by a large, chatty group. More patrons crowded the counter, where two bartenders tended to orders. Still, he was able to jump back onto the same stool where he had left his jacket. The bartender, not a friend yet, placed another weissbier before him. *Danke*, said Rainer. The bartender responded with what looked like a suggestive wink. Rainer didn't wink back but excitement flitted through him. He wondered whether he was being subtly courted. He didn't mind.

His friends were still at Café Jasmin down the road on Steinheilstraße. He liked waiting alone in bars in winter, watching Friday night crowds roar with laughter. Tonight, their interactions and conversations looked as if they were praying for the quick return of summer.

Earlier, a fresh sweep of Siberian winds had blown ferociously through Munich. The icy cold it unleashed was unbearable. Much like Rainer, many of the city's denizens were finding comfort inside warm restaurants, late-night cafés and bars like this one, Café Kosmos – a two-storey bar with hip retro décor. It was the Google description of Café Kosmos, but Rainer enjoyed using it when people asked him what it was like.

It had become his favourite haunt since he moved to Munich a year ago. He came to the Alte Pinakothek to finalise his thesis research on the urinating figure in art; the little winged chubster who peed into fountains, vases and basins and onto adults, cupids and angels in paintings from as early as the twelfth century. Rainer was looking for lost historical uses of the figures and was initially enticed by Peter Paul Rubens's painting of *The Drunken Silenus* but he continued his stay in Munich to also study the archives, convinced more could be found. After all, the Alte Pinakothek was one of the oldest galleries in the world.

Entschuldigung, is this stool taken?

Rainer turned to the left. A pretty face, he thought. *Nein, nein, bitte,* he said and motioned his hands to sit down.

Mein Deutsch is schlecht, sorry, said a woman with long, curly brown hair.

That's okay, said Rainer. *The seat is free, you can sit.*

She sat down. Her nose was red from the cold. She unwrapped a scarf from her neck and placed it on top of her quilted handbag on her lap.

Thank you, she said. *It's freezing outside.*

It's bad, Rainer agreed.

This whole week. I've been trying to see the city, but it's so hard, she said. *I was heading to my hotel, but I couldn't get a taxi quick enough. Then I saw this cute bar and I thought I'd at least have a drink. It's so nice here!*

She picked up the menu and leant forward onto the counter to signal the bartender. The same guy who'd placed the second weissbier in front of Rainer and supposedly courted him with a wink, appeared immediately. By the way he eyed the woman, Rainer wasn't so sure any more about his racy wooing.

Can I please have this one? She pointed at the menu. *The Hot Buttered Bourbon?*

Of course, the bartender replied with a prolonged stare. And there, just as he moved away from her, Rainer saw him give her the same wink.

It's a nice place, she said.

Better than outside, said Rainer.

I'm Louise, she said. *I hope I'm not bothering you.*

I'm Rainer, he said. *Pleased to meet you.*

He stretched out his hand and Louise shook it.

*Sorry, my hands are so cold. I don't have any glov*es, she said. She clasped them together against her chest and laughed.

They'll warm up, said Rainer. *You're not from here?*

No, she said, *but I always wanted to visit Munich. It's maybe not the best time to visit, but I still love it. I've been to Berlin a few times, but I think Munich's cultural scene is so underrated. The museums are definitely better. I spent all day at the . . . Pi-na-ko-thek. Hehe. Sorry, I can't pronounce that well.*

It's Pina-ko-teck – that's how you say it, said Rainer.

Ah, thank you! replied Louise, shyly.

Did you go to the old or the modern one? asked Rainer.

Both! replied Louise enthusiastically.

Wunderbar, said Rainer proudly. *That's kind of why I'm here.*

What do you mean? asked Louise.

I'm doing a PhD in art history but it's just disguised medical research, really.

Wow! said Louise. *That's so admirable!*

Thank you, said Rainer.

I'm so impressed with people who pursue academia, continued Louise. *I hated university, and couldn't wait to get out. It was always so stuffy to me. And I never liked theory much. Oh, that was so long ago now, but I could never go back. Is it hard? Do you like it? What are you working on? German art?*

No, no, laughed Rainer. *It's a very niche field. I'm looking for lost historical uses of the urinating figure in art. You know, those sculptures and paintings of little children that piss into fountains?*

That's so interesting! said Louise just as her drink arrived before her.

Thank you, she said, handing the bartender a scrunched-up twenty-euro bill.

Noch ein Bier, bitte, said Rainer.

The bartender nodded.

Just then, Rainer felt a familiar constriction in his abdomen.

Not again, he thought.

Scheisse, he blurted.

Huh? said Louise.

He moved up and down in his seat, just to check if he could hold off a little longer but it was too uncomfortable.

Sorry, just gonna run up to the bathroom, he said. *You don't mind holding my seat?*

No, not at all, said Louise, and placed her scarf on top of his jacket.

He opened the bathroom door. The urinal was free this time. Rainer spread his legs, unzipped and began to piss. He looked around, read the scribbles on the walls: German slang and dicks; tits and arses. Toilet art was always the same, no matter what city you were in. He looked down, and on top of the urinal, a screen lit up. A black frame faded away to reveal a broad-shouldered man dressed in a Spartan military uniform looking at him, a beer in his hand.

Whaaaat? thought Rainer. Video advertising on urinals?

The man knocked on the screen. He said something, but there were no speakers on the urinal. Then he began to wave as if he could see Rainer.

What the hell is this thing selling? thought Rainer as he zipped up and headed back downstairs.

Sorry, he apologised to Louise.

No worries, she said, moving her scarf from his seat.

He noticed the crowd behind them: Café Kosmos was even more jam-packed. The floor-to-ceiling window that faced the street was now completely condensed. He could see steam floating off people's jackets, faces and mouths as they murmured how cold it was outside.

Interesting, said Louise.

Rainer rearranged his arse on the stool. *What's interesting?* he asked.

Your PhD slash medical research, she said and laughed.

Ah, that, he said. *Yeah, it's quite a subject.*

Louise moved her seat a little closer to avoid the jostling crowd beside her. *How did you come to study that?* she asked.

That's a long story. But, basically, I'm relating the pissing figure to today's scientific research about urine being nutrient-rich. You know it's a great tooth-whitener?

Louise stared at him. *What?* she asked. *That's crazy.*

No, seriously, said Rainer, *there's quite a lot you can do with urine. There's also this theory that came from an ancient Germanic text, that urine from certain people, if collected under extreme duress, can be of great value. Supposedly, excessive stress activates some kind of supernatural quality. And that's why I've been spending my days in the archives, studying sculptural phalluses for clues. You'd be surprised at just how far back the motif of the pissing figure goes — it's in so many works of art! St Augustine had this interesting saying that we were born between urine and filth. I kind of like that. Anyway, that's me!*

Louise exhaled with admiration. *You are incredible! I don't know anything about that and I work in skincare! I want to buy you a cocktail. Can I please?*

Rainer looked at his watch. They should be here by now, he thought.

That's so sweet of you, I'd love one, he said.

It's nice to meet you, though! she said excitedly. *Thanks for hanging out with me. I don't know anyone here and I haven't spoken to anyone all day. As you can see, I talk too much!*

Rainer smiled politely and they continued to chat for the next hour, by which point they were feeling like old friends.

As Louise was telling Rainer a story about the first time she went to Greece, he checked his phone.

Shit, sorry, he said.

Is everything all right? Louise asked.

Rainer looked at the messaging apps on his smartphone with concern. *Weird*, he said, *my friends were supposed to be here by now but they haven't even messaged me yet.*

Am I holding you up? Louise asked.

No, no, said Rainer. *This is just unusual for them. Where were we? Actually, hold that thought*, he added, getting up. *Just going up to the bathroom again.*

Upstairs, there was a line. He stood behind a guy who took off his jumper, revealing a tank top and a tattooed back.

Fuckin' 'ot 'ere, he said in a harsh English accent.

Rainer stared at the floor, hoping the line would move quickly. He entered the bathroom at the same time as the English guy, who headed straight for the cubicle. Rainer took to the urinal fast.

As soon as he began to piss, the screen above the urinal turned on and text appeared. Du bist ein match, Rainer.

Rainer didn't notice the message at first, and kept on pissing. Then the text started to flash alarmingly. It faded in and out, displaying his full name now, before a new page appeared:

Colour: Yellow

Appearance: Clear

Specific Gravity: 1.023

PH: 6.0

Glucose: Positive

Bacteria: Few

Crystals: DNR

What is this? Rainer laughed, waiting for the punchline.

Behind him, the English guy finished up and strolled out of the cubicle, only to be replaced by a groaning man, who made an urgent dash for it. Rainer wasn't even pissing anymore, he was just holding his dick in his hand as if safeguarding it from harm. New text faded in:

NAME: RAINER MÜLLER

AGE: 35

GENDER: MALE

HEIGHT: 1.85CM

RACE: CAUCASIAN / EUROPID

BLOOD TYPE: AB-

MARITAL STATUS: SINGLE

SEXUAL ORIENTATION: BISEXUAL

NUMBER OF CHILDREN: ZERO

OCCUPATION: STUDENT

SALARY: €2033/MO

Is anyone else seeing this? asked Rainer.

He turned around; there was no one behind him. The personal information faded.

SEE YOU SOON, the screen read.

Rainer kicked the urinal. *How did you . . . ?*

He stood, stunned, dick still in hand, until he was shaken out of his stupor by the sound of the toilet in the cubicle flushing. He zipped up quickly, moved over to the basin and frantically washed his hands. In the smudged, dirty mirror, he could see his startled face. He put his hands under the dryer but no air blasted out.

Fuck, he exclaimed, and wiped his hands on his jeans quickly. He was eager to get back downstairs and complain about this. It felt illegal and totally over the line. He reached for the bathroom door, but a pain in his left temple halted him. Before his hand went up to touch it, he collapsed.

Downstairs, Louise was sipping on her third Hot Buttered Bourbon. Occasionally she checked her watch, but otherwise sat idly by. After some time passed, she dug into her handbag and took out her smartphone.

Would you like another drink? asked the bartender.

I drank that quickly, didn't I? She laughed, fingering her empty glass. *Sure, I guess I'll have another one, you do make them really good.*

Thank you, said the bartender. *And your friend? Will he have another one too?*

Louise looked down at Rainer's jacket hanging over the barstool. She picked it up and handed it to the bartender.

Please dispose of this, she said sternly.

The bartender looked around, then took the jacket and disappeared into the backroom.

Louise untangled her earphones. She placed them into her ears and opened an app on her smartphone. It loaded up a dashboard with live views from several different surveillance cameras. She clicked on one of them.

Rainer opened his eyes.

Above him, a white ceiling fan spun slowly. He realised immediately that he was on his back. He clenched his muscles, as if to test whether he was still alive, then quickly clambered to stand.

What the hell? he said when he saw his bare arms and legs.

He was dressed, head to toe, in a Spartan military uniform. He looked around: nothing but stark white walls. Fixed to one of them was a porcelain urinal, and behind him, on a white table, a glass of cold beer. It frothed like it had been poured moments ago. Above him, fitted to a corner of the ceiling, he saw a small monitor with a camera attached to it. His head hurt. He pressed his temple, where the pain was the fiercest, and felt a small bump.

What the hell is going on here?

He pounded the walls, searched for an exit, a door, but there was nothing. He began to yell for help and waved at the camera. Still, nothing happened. He pulled the table towards him and jumped on top of it. He was now face-to-face with the screen watching someone look at him stupidly from the same urinal he was in earlier.

Hey! he yelled, knocking on it. *What the fuck is this shit? Is this some kind of joke?*

A red light started to blink inside the lens. *Hello?* he said.

He heard a sound, much like the sound of a microphone being touched.

Welcome, Rainer, a familiar female voice said. *This won't take long.*

MEETINGS

There was nothing more meaningless to Jo than being stuck in meetings.

She was a doer. And meetings, she felt, were the enemy of doers. She hated the idea of sitting in a room with her colleagues, discussing how to solve this and that. Planning ahead. Going over things, again and again, until the very idea of their idea had boiled into something so generic it had no value whatsoever.

One day, Jo calculated that out of the fifty hours she spent at the agency each week, she spent about fifteen of them in meaningless meetings. This realisation outraged her. There must be something she could do about it. A side project, perhaps? Anything, really.

Then it came to her: over the next twelve months she would write a book called *The Meaninglessness of Meetings*. And the

96

challenge she gave herself was to write it while she was in meaningless meetings.

Three years later, Penguin Random House published the book
to critical acclaim. *The Meaninglessness of Meetings* became the
bible of new-age work ethics, and the advertising industry took
note: they cut forty per cent of meetings and devoted the time
saved to creativity.

WAR ROOM

They called it the war room.

Like in the movies. But unlike in the movies, theirs didn't contain maps of front lines and plans for imminent battles. Still, it felt authentic. For, much like the real deal, this ad agency war room dealt with critical real-world problems, from reducing global warming to tackling income discrimination, rebuilding food and water security, raising education levels and lowering unemployment.

To enter the war room, one had to be chosen.

The select group would receive the long-anticipated email, specifying the date on which their presence would be required for twenty-four hours. Only five participants – aptly called ideators – made the cut every year. The elation of being selected has been described as *inimitable*. There were tales of people missing their mother's funeral, postponing weddings and even serious health appointments. Nothing would stop them from taking their place in the spotlight of the war room.

Still, admittance was not guaranteed. Strict conditions had to be met. Ideators had to discipline their bodies with a month of intermittent fasting. This was encouraged to reset their appetite's thermostat, which the creators of the war room believed perfected brainstorming for the critical real-world problems they aimed to solve. Working knowledge of Oulipo literature and pastoral poetry was a prerequisite to put the mind in an unconventional state prior to the tasks ahead. Lastly (but most importantly), ideators were forbidden from consuming news or social media for the month leading up to occupation.

One's state of mind must be clear of superficial turmoil, said the creators of the war room, who, by design, were the founders of the ad agency.

Before the doorway, the ideators were confronted with one more rule.

They had to surrender their smartphones to a hired guard, dressed entirely in black leather. They would watch him place their smartphones on a sturdy tree trunk and smash it with a sizeable hammer. Then they would be asked to take off their socks and shoes, and offered one single cigarette to take in with them.

Our lack of context is wilfully deliberate, said the creators of the war room, who propagated the notion that confusion concentrates the mind better than clarity. To the ideators, this did not matter. They were trained problem solvers.

The moment they stepped inside the war room they felt something akin to unhinged ecstasy. *We had to ready ourselves,* they said. *After all, this is a specially constructed room in our agency. Not everyone is privy.* Inside, they confessed, the walls were intimidatingly blank. It was furnished starkly with a three-seater leather sofa, a dead clock on the wall, a table with five chairs and a box filled with unopened Sharpies and Post-it notes.

At 9 am, it all began.

A piece of paper slipped in from under the door. The dead clock on the wall would start ticking, but in reverse. On the paper, they would find a detailed brief about one of the critical real-world problems the war room attempted to solve.

They would get to work right away. They'd read and re-read the brief. They'd scribble thoughts onto the Post-it notes and pin them up on the walls so they could ruminate on them visually. For an extended period of time, the ideators would lie around, productively procrastinating. Some would sit on the sofa, others on the chairs. Some would press the soft cushions of the sofa against their chests because they feared the pressure of the war room was making them creatively constipated. Others would flip the single cigarette between their fingers, not knowing what to do with it. When they thought an idea popped into their minds they would jump out of their seats and say, *Fuck, okay, imagine this.*

The participant groups remarked that, despite the exhaustive preparations, a recurring problem persisted in the war room: they couldn't focus their creative energy on real-world problems in a pressure-cooker environment like this.

We often tried to bring overlaps into the equation, which is what you do in advertising, they said. *We considered issues from the perspective of unrelated subjects, like a donkey and weather patterns,*

a UFC fighter and bushfires, artificial intelligence and the holy books.
But nothing linked.

At the end of the sessions, the ideators admitted that they were appallingly unfit for service. Real-world problem solving wasn't their cup of tea. They were much better suited to capitalist interests – figuring out how to raise awareness of oat milk, or trying to change the perception of Jägerbombs, that sort of thing.

Perhaps, this is why, in the five years of the war room's existence, not a single original idea emerged. Statistically speaking, it was daunting, yet the creators of the war room have expressed no regrets. They have, however, expressed interest in flipping the idea on its head. They feel that a room called the 'peace room' with a highly appealing reward system could spawn greater (and faster) results.

WAR ROOM

CLICK HERE

It's all about action: that's what Zak was told when he started out as a junior copywriter.

The writing had to make people do something. That's what advertising was: persuasion. The more immediate, the better. After spending a year writing banner ads, Zak was disillusioned – no one was clicking on them. His copywriting wasn't making people do anything. He felt he wasn't cut out for advertising but all his colleagues told him not to worry. *No one ever clicks on banner ads,* they said. It was just about awareness. They gave him stats to make him feel better.

Zak wasn't convinced. He thought there must be a way to get people to click on banner ads. To test this theory, he created a campaign for his uncle's lawn mowing company. Instead of showing sunny front lawns, blades silently slashing through grass like butter with huge red call-to-action stickers, he did the opposite.

He created banner ads that depicted the demise of suburban aesthetics: sparse blends of grass, clover and weeds interspersed with sad, bald patches in backyards. Instead of inspirational, product-specific one-liners, he wrote about the anxiety men experience while trying to maintain an impeccable bed of grass.

It was touchingly miserable, and in complete contrast to anything Zak had ever been taught.

When the banner ads went live, they made people brood and contemplate their own existences. He didn't expect the internet to listen, but it did. Suddenly everyone was clicking on the banner ads for his uncle's lawn mowing company.

Within a year, they became the most effective banner ads of all time. They dumbfounded the industry and disrupted statistics. So much so that his uncle's lawn mowing company grew from being a small suburban business to a national conglomerate.

Zak was eventually awarded the Best Banner Ad Writer of All Time by the British advertising and design association D&AD. Till this day – much like Bob Dylan – he doesn't like to talk about the accolade all that much.

If at all.

CLICK HERE

DIGITAL NOMAD

Other people's lives. They're fascinating, aren't they? How do people other than ourselves survive this perpetual ongoingness? Maybe this is the reason why we like to stare into windows. After all, behind every window is a story.

And speaking of windows (and stories), there's a large window on the third floor of a building on Carrer d'Avinyó, in the El Gotic quarter of Barcelona, not too far from Plaça George Orwell, that is worth talking about. It is revealed daily, right around eight o'clock in the morning, when its exterior brown wooden shutters are opened and the white silk curtains drawn aside. If you look through the curtains, you'll see a large and airy apartment.

Every morning, a young man named Cooper steps onto the balcony that is attached to this window. Wearing nothing but white Calvin Klein briefs, he closes his eyes and moves his athletic body meditatively, stretching his limbs. In the background, coming from a good-quality speaker, you can hear music. It sounds, if you listen closely, like slowed-down Enya. After his stretches, he performs a number of physical exercises: crunches, squats, push-ups and lunges. This routine lasts about thirty minutes.

And, just like us, the lives of others intrigue him. He also peers through his neighbours' windows. In Barcelona, during summer, when clothes stick to bodies and sweat pours from every orifice, he loves to watch how they cool themselves down. If they use the ceiling fan or air-conditioning units, or if, as he some-times witnesses, they just rest ice on their faces and bodies.

Today, Cooper is gazing at a woman who is cleaning the bi-fold doors of her own balcony, right across from his. They're level with one another. He lights a cigarette, leans against the railing and stands there, watching her. The woman doesn't mind his ogling. Actually, we should state here that no one really does in Barcelona. Buildings are very close to one another in El Gotic. The architecture is intimate. The spaces between buildings are so narrow that you could easily jump over onto neighbouring balconies. This is what Cooper, our digital nomad, often thinks about, the possibility of jumping into another home. Another life.

If you're used to living in houses divided by fences, this close-ness to others can be confronting. But in Barcelona, being close together is true living.

Our digital nomad is fascinated by his neighbour's domestic dexterity, how absorbed she has become by her menial task. The windows and panes are sparkling clean, yet she keeps wiping them. After she reaches the far corners – by standing dangerously on the railing – she climbs back down, sits on a bucket, wipes the excess sweat from her gleaming brown legs with a tea towel and lights a cigarette herself. Then she proceeds to watch the action on the street below, an activity our digital nomad Cooper also loves.

Below them, Carrer d'Avinyó usually fills up by midday. A thousand voices, both foreign and familiar, can be heard. It is the sound of languages alien and known colliding into each other, becoming an indistinguishable murmur. Together, without interacting, the two of them watch and listen to this ascending commotion from their balconies.

Barcelona is often called the City of Lifestyles, and the hum and energy on its streets is one of the reasons why Cooper is here – he feels like he's living inside the very concept of freedom. Often, he stands on his balcony, reflecting upon the two great myths of Barcelona's origin. The first is that the city was founded sometime around 230 BC by Hamilcar Barca, the great Carthaginian general, known more popularly as the father of Hannibal. The second is that the city was founded by Hercules. When Hercules joined Jason and the Argonauts in search of the Golden Fleece, one of the nine ships they sailed with got lost in a storm off the Catalan coast. Hercules found it wrecked near a hill. It's said that he was so moved by the beauty of the site that he and the crew stayed, founding the city Barca Nona: the Ninth Ship.

To our digital nomad, the second myth has always held more appeal. Not just because it's more interesting, but because he believes Barcelona has retained something of Hercules within its confines: energy. Each time he watches the streets below his apartment, he feels surer that it was Hercules who had founded the city, not Hamilcar Barca.

But why? You're asking, right? Why are we bringing up Cooper when there are a thousand other windows we can peer into?

Well, from his spacious apartment, our digital nomad makes a living being a motivational influencer. That is, he uses self-help rhetoric to boost the morale of people who need it, especially those in the corporate world. At the moment, he is in communication with 89,235 followers on Twitter, 135,002 on Instagram and believe it not, 195,763 on LinkedIn. He hasn't written a book yet, but he's doing well. His engagement is high and he markets himself like all great influencers: with a carefully calibrated version of brutal honesty. He tells it how it is regardless of insult or transgression. In other words, he makes it clear that he lives free from concern, which is what his followers want: to be shown how to live free from concern.

But while he portrays himself to have achieved this life he preaches all on his own, he, in fact, hasn't. In a previous life, prior to his success as a motivational influencer, he worked in the property industry. It was there he learnt his true forte: *legalised lying*, a term H. G. Wells used to describe advertising. This is how he falls within the 'yeah, but' category of people. *Yeah*, he's done well for himself, *but* only because his dad is a successful property developer in Australia.

You're right, this still doesn't answer our question. Does it?

Well, we're about to get to it. Cooper (or Coops, as his dad calls him) has finished smoking and ogling his neighbour, which means he's now ready to get to work. His work appears on all fronts to be inspiring and creative, but the truth is, as successful as Cooper has become, the only original idea he's had is TrapContent™ – a software algorithm he created that gathers (i.e. steals) content from the internet, much like a prawn trawler nets prawns from the ocean. It tracks, finds and downloads anything interesting that pops up online that deals with his own agenda.

Right now, with a cold tetra pack of coconut water in hand, Coops is sitting down behind his clean white desk, logging into the back-end of TrapContent™ and carefully looking through the stolen content his secret invention has gathered for him.

For the rest of the morning, amid eating, drinking, shitting and generally piss-farting around, Cooper will select up to twenty images, videos, quotes, messages, articles (both short and long form), tweets, Reddit threads and comments, and various blog posts, which he will strip of any metadata, and then repurpose as his own. He will refashion them with his own fonts and backgrounds, rewrite a couple of lines, edit the videos, then blast them far and wide across all his channels to followers who will unknowingly accept them as his own, original thinking.

See, revealing this nasty business is a worthwhile reason to take interest in our digital nomad. But, it isn't the only one.

Just like there's a story behind every window, there's also a story behind every browser window.

In Cooper Coop's case, over the past year since he's been living in Barcelona showing people his *free from concern* life, someone other than us has been observing him with fierce attention. They aren't curious, distant observers like us; they are hell-bent on justice. And justice, as we all know, is a dish best served cold-heartedly.

In a short while, after Cooper has his midday shower and his favourite low-carb lunch (garlic-butter steak bites with zucchini noodles), he will recline on the sofa with his tablet and begin to respond to every comment he's received from his followers (this is how he maintains his high engagement rate). Before he begins, he'll say, *Okay Google, play my Hot Hits playlist.*

But he won't hear the playlist come on through his good-quality speaker this time around. Instead, he'll hear a distorted static sound. A crackling.

You okay there, Google? he'll ask.

His Google Assistant won't answer.

Cooper Coops will be puzzled. He'll reach over for his laptop to press play on the playlist himself but he'll find his eyes staring in horror. His cursor will be moving all on its own, taking control of his machine and permanently deleting TrapContent™, right in front of his eyes.

That won't be all. The objects on his table, his side boards and kitchen cupboards will begin to wobble. The windows we are peering through will crack, the wooden shutters splintering. Before him, the vibrations of the sound from his Google Assistant will start to coagulate, and begin to jell into a transparent human-like shape; a being with a face that won't smile. A body with a voice that won't be polite. Yes, he's pissed someone off. But who?

Well, not even I, the author of this story, is fully aware of whom Cooper Coops has offended. I could speculate and predict it to be Kyberia, the faithful new goddess of technology, venting her anger at his theft through the fibreoptic cables under the sea. Or maybe it is Hamilcar Barca coming in hot and angry, determined to forever squish this myth playing against the foundation of his city.

No, I doubt it is him. He doesn't have much to do with this story. But Hercules? He could be here for his lost and often-debated thirteenth labour, to punish poor Cooper Coops and be enthroned as the saviour of millennials' precious content.

No, no. This is a vengeful deity that doesn't like to be pissed off. It seems to me that this pissed off deity is worse than a pissed off mother-in-law and our digital nomad Cooper Coops will soon come to understand why you shouldn't – ever – fuck with the Internet.

FEMME FATALE

Kim doesn't know that today will be the day of her greatest rebellion.

How could she? The results of our actions are only known to us after the fact. It will take another ten years for Kim to realise the significance of today. Right now, she's just enjoying her stroll to work in the city.

It's Wednesday. The sun is shining. Kim is listening to Elton John and wearing a new skirt she bought on Farfetch. Every now and again, she checks her phone to see if her daughter has read her message. It annoys her that she hasn't.

She looks up from her phone just as the pedestrian traffic light ahead of her turns to flashing red. She initially speeds up, but then decides to wait instead of dashing across the busy intersection. She places her phone back into her handbag, and as she looks up again, she notices something strange about the little figurine displayed on the pedestrian traffic light.

Goodness, she says, when she realises that it no longer depicts a man. *It has a skirt*, she almost yells.

This amuses a younger woman who is standing next to her. Kim feels goosebumps ripple all over her arms and shoulders. When did this happen? How did I not notice it before? she wonders.

At the office, she nods and mumbles *hello*s to her colleagues as she makes her way to her glassed-in cubicle. It's right at the end of the open-plan office she works in, where, for the last sixteen years, she has controlled the finances of the agency. As she sits in her chair behind her desk, she admits, she feels tired. A little too tired for good old hump day.

She turns on her computer and, as the machine starts up, Kim thinks of the pedestrian crossing light she saw earlier. It amused her as much as it delighted her. For some reason, it's now tinkering with her memories, taking her back to her naive girlhood in the country town where she grew up. Her shy university days in Sydney. Her first love, her most recent heartbreak. This peculiar sense of nostalgia keeps rising within her, but she's unsure what she's pining for, exactly – or why.

Impatiently, she gets up and strolls over to the communal kitchen to make herself a cup of coffee. A few people are standing around the coffee machine.

Good morning, Kim, someone says as she approaches.

It's Cory, one of the new interns. There's too much enthusiasm in his voice. Too much youth, thinks Kim.

Hello, hello, she says.

Let me make you a flat white, says Cory. *I've finally mastered them!*

He looks at Rachel and Asmira as he says this. They are standing in line behind him.

Sorry, you guys mind? he asks.

All good, says Rachel then she turns back to face Asmira.

I was told I needed to man up, Asmira says.

She's a new account director whom Kim has not met properly yet. Her eyes look gentle and kind, thinks Kim. She leans against the marble kitchen bench and busies herself rearranging the bowl of fruit on the counter.

Seriously? says Rachel in shock.

Rachel is a senior planner whom Kim considers too ferocious.

Fuck that little slimy bastard! yells Rachel. She turns to look at Kim, but Kim stares fixedly down at the mandarins in the fruit bowl.

He has no fucking right to say something like that, continues Rachel. *Did you speak to HR?*

Asmira glances around. More people are coming into the kitchen and she seems reluctant to pursue the conversation.

It's okay, says Asmira. *Not a big deal. I'm sure he didn't mean anything by it.*

Kim immediately knows who she's speaking about. It's the thin-haired man with whom she never got along either. She always thought him to be a bit slimy herself.

How have you put up with all this shit for so long? asks Rachel.

It takes a moment before Kim realises Rachel is speaking to her.

You've been in this dick-filled industry for so long, adds Rachel, clearly angry.

Kim feels confronted and would prefer to not have this conversation.

Here you are, says Cory.

A saviour, thinks Kim as she takes the flat white from him.

Thank you, she says.

She can sense Rachel is still waiting for an answer. She turns towards her.

Well, it's the price we pay for admission, replies Kim.

She doesn't know why she said this. She can hear Rachel laugh with reproach. With the coffee in her hand – *the perfect flat white,* as Cory had proclaimed – Kim turns around and heads for the balcony. She has never liked confrontation, especially with women. And Rachel's attitude is not the kind she knows how to deal with. No, Kim doesn't want any of that. She prefers to let matters slide away, instead of deepening and escalating them. What's a little bit of sexism in the office anyway?

On the balcony, she stares out at the cityscape. It's a view she's always enjoyed, especially in late summer. Again, the traffic light figurine flashes through her mind, as if on a mission not to be forgotten.

How long has it been now? she wonders suddenly. Maybe forty or forty-two years. That's how long she's spent in this wild world of advertising. This dick-filled industry as Rachel called it. Oh, I've definitely seen it all, she reminds herself. The long-gone era of the 80s, replete with its three-martini lunches, glamorous clothing, and, of course, the too-normalised sexism. The pre-internet days of the 90s with their cheesy radio infomercials and fuzzy television commercials. To her, that had been the golden era of advertising, when the right slogan, catchphrase or jingle could become part of Australian lore. She remembers when they starred Natalie Imbruglia in a Twisties commercial. A young Cate Blanchett in a Tim Tam spot. She laughs when she recalls the Cadbury Roses jingle, and how much she had hated it.

Yes, Kim has seen it all, ploughed through every triumph and hardship of the industry – even the rise of social media, which has upended traditional advertising as they knew it. It all makes sense to her. Except for one thing. It dawns on her with a rapid surge of humiliation.

What was it all for? Kim asks herself.

She stands up abruptly. The question keeps echoing through her head. She feels mounting shame. A personal, self-inflicted disappointment fills the inside of her stomach. Kim looks down into the remaining froth in her mug. It wasn't a perfect flat white, she thinks. It was a latte.

She walks back to her office.

There's lots to do. Today, she is supposed to get on with her analysis of department budgets and the agency's cash flow. Plus, it's pay day. Processing payments for 165 employees always makes her nervous.

The day carries on. With purposeful self-restraint, Kim quietens the strange thoughts and feelings that are brewing within, and she is able to accomplish everything she needs to. She attends meetings, some with enthusiasm, others with disguised boredom. Mechanically, she tills through the rest of the afternoon.

By four o'clock, she's ready to head home. Instead, she decides to ease into the last hour and make herself a cup of tea. On her way to the kitchen, she ducks into the bathroom to wash her hands. Inside she hears the sound of quiet sobbing, but it stops as soon as the bathroom door closes behind her. She thinks she must have imagined it and turns on the faucet. Then she hears loud sniffling coming out of the last cubicle.

Hello? asks Kim.

No reply.

Are you okay in there? she asks.

I'm okay, I'm okay, a shaky voice replies.

Kim steps up to the cubicle.

Asmira? she asks.

The stall door opens and Asmira walks out, trying to hide her red, swollen eyes.

Oh my god, what happened? Kim says, thinking of him. *What has he done?* she asks.

Asmira looks up at her in surprise. *It's fine, really,* she says.

No, it's not, says Kim. Her own audacity surprises her.

I don't know why he keeps picking on me, says Asmira. She wipes her nose with her sleeve. *When I was presenting the work earlier, he kept smiling at me. And then when everyone left, he said:* I can't take you seriously with what you're wearing.

Kim passes her a tissue. *It's appalling,* she says.

Asmira looks up at her: she seems frightened, fragile. Like a lamb, thinks Kim.

She clasps her arms around her. *It's okay,* she says.

Asmira continues to sob into Kim's arms. Kim holds on to her and observes their embrace in the mirror, outraged at the world. The angrier she gets, the clearer her head becomes and suddenly an idea speeds through her mind. At first, it's unclear, fuzzy, but as Kim listens to Asmira crying, the idea becomes purer and forms into a specific, justified action. It's so resolute that she knows she will have to do it.

Years later, she will ask herself, *What came over me that day?* Possession, maybe. *The devil got into you,* her husband will say. It will be criminal, and she'll think herself lucky to have avoided being charged. But this is the instant she stopped giving in. The instant she didn't let a matter trickle away and be forgotten like she used to, but instead, fought against it.

Take the rest of the day off, please, says Kim. *I'll take it from here.*

Asmira wipes the tears from her face. She reaches out and presses her shaky body against Kim one more time.

Thank you so much, she says.

Kim walks her over to the elevator. *You need me to get anything from your desk?* she asks.

No, says Asmira, pressing her handbag. *Thank you.*

Kim waits for the elevator doors to close, then rushes back to her office.

If anyone looked up from their screens, they'd see Kim dashing across the floor as if she's on a life-saving mission. Her expression is one of sheer determination. Her body tense and upright. She slams her office door, seats herself behind her computer and, without hesitation, gets to work.

First, she creates two Excel spreadsheets and sorts everyone in the agency into one or the other according to their gender. She types in their monthly salaries next to their names, starting from the lowest paid employee to the highest. When she finishes entering all 165 employees' names and salaries in the spreadsheets, Kim cross-references each role to see the difference between male and female salaries. She isn't shocked to discover the gaps.

Some are minor, others hugely disproportional, but it no longer matters. Angrily, she swaps Asmira's monthly pay with the thin-haired man's.

She takes a deep breath. She feels victorious, righteous. But she knows it's not nearly enough. She leans back into her chair, stretches, and then switches over every other monthly salary in the spreadsheet. Now that she has a clear picture of everyone's new earnings, she opens up the online payroll system. She schedules in the new wages and processes the payments. It takes a gruelling hour. With shaky hands, she logs out of the website, closes all other applications, neatens her desk, then shuts down her computer.

She sighs. She can't quite believe what she has done, but courage is pushing her through this with great calmness. She doesn't care about the consequences. The aftermath.

All she cares about today is long-overdue justice.

She swings her jacket over her shoulders, picks up her handbag and heads for the elevator. In the foyer, she sees him coming towards her. His hair has thinned even more. Soon he'll have to shave it off and commit to baldness.

Hope you had a good day, Kim, he says dispassionately, as he passes her.

Kim stops and faces him directly. *Oh, a most wonderful day indeed.*

BRAND MANIFESTO

It wouldn't be unrealistic to say that in any given city right now there is a poor copywriter sitting behind their laptop, sweating over a brand manifesto.

And given the oft-repeated statistic that ninety-nine per cent of advertising comes from other advertising, we can confidently presume that our poor copywriter is watching commercials of some of the greatest brand manifestos ever written. This list would include Write the Future by Nike, Go Forth by Levi's, Litany by the *Independent*, Your Verse by Apple, 100 by Leica, The Getaway Car by Volvo and Style is Why by Specsavers.

It's a good list. No wonder it is making our poor copywriter scratch their head and mutter praise and admiration. Their sweat glands are feeling it, too, because watching this collection is more intimidating than you might think. Every word is heard crystal clear. Every visual cue is memorised. The music deeply considered. Each video is watched multiple times, because our poor copywriter is trying to achieve two things from this task: (i) understand the nuances, simplicity and power of each video's narrative and (ii) convince themselves that they will, regardless of budget, write a better one.

Conviction about the second point is crucial.

This is why we'll find them so focused right now – their facial expressions stern, their eyebrows straining inwards. In their eyes, their colleagues see pure concentration. Their bodies are slouched to protect themselves from the loud, irritating reality around them – particularly against those eager chatterboxes that exist in every advertising agency.

Most of our copywriters are wearing noise-cancelling head-phones (top of the range), but no music is playing through them. It's a front, another layer of protection that tells everyone, *Fuck off, don't talk to me, I'm writing the greatest manifesto ever!*

If they're lucky, they have found the quietest spot in their agency to make damn sure they're left alone for this vital under-taking. Some – the more courageous – are using the opportunity to nurture their inner poet. They feel the winds calling them, and may even be sitting outside in parks near their offices where they believe every blade of grass is singing to them in secret.

Now, before we venture further, we should clarify here that a brand manifesto is not your typical piece of marketing.

It is something that isn't admired, but respected. And not just by advertising agencies, but, more importantly, by clients. A brand manifesto is the call to arms that makes the most profound of statements. It explicitly doesn't sell a product or service. Instead, it sells the feeling. The story of their glorious why. Best of all, when it's brought to life cinematically, in a thirty-second video composition with a god-like voiceover (like the ones our poor copywriter is watching again and again), it becomes so inspiring, so emotionally contagious, that it makes the audience think and feel and cry and love.

Now, imagine yourself in the sneakers of our poor copywriter.

No doubt you'll immediately feel the pressure of this creative expedition. You'll see how daunting it is to write a brand manifesto that impresses both the agency and the client. But give it a few hours, and when you're comfortably settled in, and have attempted a few drafts of writing yourself, you'll feel a new, subterranean fear emerge. A fear that is entirely singular.

You'll notice that no one in advertising, not a single person other than the poor copywriter, understands what it requires to pen a brand manifesto. Only the poor copywriter understands that to write something that great, to make the audience think and feel and cry and love, a copywriter must become a *writer*.

Think about that for a minute.

It's the ultimate test. The one that undeniably determines whether they are just another word slinger who punches out sharp, quirky lines about household goods and lifestyle services or whether they are what they believe themselves to be: a frustrated writer with high literary ambition, currently just honing their skills in advertising. Only our poor copywriter knows that the best brand manifestos tap into the inner struggle of our existence, the struggle only a real writer knows how to rip out and use. Indeed, many fail in this endeavour. But some, don't.

There is a deified group of individuals that our poor copywriter thinks about before they finally submit themselves to the grand task. They remind themselves, how just like them, these people walked in the same shoes, trying to demonstrate the narrow limits between advertising and literature. From Salman Rushdie to Peter Carey, James Patterson to Bryce Courtenay, Don DeLillo to Martin Amis, Joseph Heller to Mary Higgins Clarke, J. G. Ballard to William S. Burroughs. They think of them all, even recalling the great poet, Mayakovsky and how he insisted, very vehemently, that the poet should work in advertising in full force of their talent.

So with that, it is not hard to believe, that right now, in a country not so far away, in a city not too old or not too new, on a street with no great or notable architecture, in an unassuming office on the fifth floor of a tired-looking building, in a corner beside a fake palm tree, there is a poor copywriter named Ivo sitting on a couch with his legs crossed and a smile on his face that tells everyone around him that he's no longer sweating over a brand manifesto.

Well done, Ivo. Well done.

FINAL
FRONTIER

**For a brief moment Cameron thought he had it:
an original idea.**

He stared at the headline in his notepad as if he'd just discovered why there are exceptions to every rule. He was transfixed. His hands were shaking mildly from elation and in this brief, excitable moment, Cameron's mind went straight to accolades: promotions, awards, interviews and fame.

He looked up from his desk for the closest face. He desperately wanted to tell someone, to share this ingenious thought but he composed himself: there was time. He quickly went back through his research. He re-read his notes. Looked over the sketches he'd made yesterday on Post-it notes. He rewatched every single commercial and YouTube video he had saved in his reference folder. He sifted through his browser history, carefully reviewing every artwork, painting, collage and poem he'd clicked on to make sure he hadn't accidently copied the headline from somewhere else. Nothing came up.

Cameron sighed. Then he remembered.

He first went outside to have a cigarette to prepare. Then he got back to his desk, swallowed hard and opened up Google. With his shaky hands, he typed the headline into the search engine.

Nothing on the first page.

Nothing on the second page.

Nothing on the third page.

Cameron's excitement grew and grew. By the time he got to the sixth page, his elation had turned into hysteria. He pounded the table. He swore freely. He jumped around like a headbanger at a heavy metal concert.

FUCK YEAH, he said.

Again, he thought about accolades. How he'd accept awards for the best idea in a dark double-breasted suit with the white Repettos he always wanted to wear. He waved over the entire creative department.

Guys, I've come up with the best fucking idea, he said.

As he waited for his colleagues to gather, he flicked through to the search results on the seventh page. When the screen loaded, his face sank. There, before him, at the top of the page, just below the sponsored ads, sat the same idea.

For a nappy ad. And in Bulgaria, of all places.

BRAND OF
THE LIVING

Though is seemed to be impossible, even miraculous, it happened.

Jim, 25, from Brooklyn, a 'creatively ambitious' and 'peer-oriented' fashion buyer, was standing in front of the mirror in his bedroom when he noticed something abnormal happening on the chest pocket of his new T-shirt. The little heart-with-eyes logo that was stitched to the pocket began to push itself out. He looked down at it just as it fell to the ground. It picked itself up, shook its head, and raced out of the door. He ran after it, but he couldn't catch it.

In Istanbul, Engen, 28, who was 'self-expressive' and 'hungry for the rare', came home from his job at the Modern Art Museum to find a package from Grailed on his doorstep. When he opened it, he found the burgundy bomber jacket he had bought in tatters, with the heart-with-eyes logo missing. He contacted his seller and demanded his money back.

Over in Paris, Margaux, 32, an 'entrepreneurial' and 'health-conscious' creative events manager, screamed in panic when the large heart-with-eyes logo detached itself from her red sweatshirt at a house party. She was in the bathroom when she felt the screen-print thrust her arm aside, peel itself away, then jump through the window. At the hospital later that evening, she repeatedly told the doctors she was not on acid.

In Melbourne, Sahir, 35, a 'civic-minded' and 'free-spirited' sales engineer, was watching a documentary about the late R&B artist Aaliyah when he came face to face in his living room with four heart-with-eyes logos, which had slowly unwrapped themselves from the clothing he was drying on the washing line near his window. This time, instead of bolting out the door, they positioned themselves on his couch and watched the documentary with him. Sahir was severely stoned and didn't think much of it.

In Venice, @GucciLyn, 26, a 'restless' and 'trend-forward' Instagram model from Seoul, was taking a selfie on the Rialto Bridge when she was distracted by the movement of her silk scarf. In her camera, she witnessed the eyes of the heart-shaped logo on her scarf pop out. The pupils dilated, as if in shock. She ripped the scarf from her neck and threw it into the canal in terror.

Camila, 36, a 'narcissistic' outspoken 'go-getter' who specialised in video editing in Buenos Aires, was the first person to have a brief chat with the heart-with-eyes logo. It removed itself from her black cap as she was washing dishes, jumped onto the tap and just sat there.

What the fuck! said Camila, pulling back, her hands wet from soapy water.

Hey, said the logo in a high-pitched voice.

What the fuck is this? yelled Camila.

The logo smiled, then hopped off the tap and onto some dishes. Camila pulled away and dialled triple zero. The logo dried its eyes with a tea towel then ran across the kitchen and out onto the balcony.

Jarrod, 36, a tattoo artist from Berlin who 'touched multiple devices daily' and was a self-confessed 'liberal anarchist', captured the heart-with-eyes logo on video. Jarrod was walking back to his bedroom with a lint roller to clean his favourite clothing item when he noticed something odd happening to the coat. It was hanging on his door, ready to be purged of lint, but instead, the large heart-with-eyes logo that he'd DIY-patched on the back began to push itself out of the fabric, grunting and squealing like it was being born. By this point, Jarrod was hiding behind a coat rack in the hallway. He opened up the camera app on his iPhone and began streaming the scene live on Instagram.

Remy, 31, a freelance web developer from Los Angeles who grew up with 'constant praise from his parents' and felt like a pioneer of the 'Peter Pan generation', was at a pool party in the Hollywood Hills when a somewhat obese heart-with-eyes logo peeled off from his sweater and sat next to him. Since he'd mixed two Zoloft pills with a few bumps of cocaine he felt, in his own opinion, severely lonely, and didn't mind the company whatsoever. He hugged the logo, recorded the moment and posted the video to his TikTok account. Within hours, it had millions of views.

Just as these incidents were unfolding, Jordan, 41, from San Francisco, creator of the heart-with-eyes brand who, in spite of being criticised heavily for ripping off the Comme des Garçons Play logo, always invoked Mark Twain's quote about no idea being original and moved on to the next criticism, was sitting behind his desk in the converted loft that housed his office and studio. Multiple notifications were simultaneously beeping on his iPhone. He opened up Safari, iMessage, Twitter, Instagram, TikTok and the News app. Stories about the logos coming to life were now trending worldwide. Op-eds wondered how this was happening – it contradicted human nature and defied scientific law. Others were asking if this was peak capitalism. *Monocle* exploited the moment and proposed a *Meet the Brands* podcast, calling on Jordan to join them for a live conversation. Doom and gloom followed, with news clips stating that human-like brands will have a cataclysmic impact on the planet, and will only exacerbate the already negative effects of consumerism. Jordan scanned through the headlines with minimal feeling. He left a heart emoji on @GucciLyn's video, who had ended up filming her scarf floating away on the waters of the Venetian canal.

He looked at the Apple Watch on his wrist. Ten to midnight. He pushed his chair away from his desk, got up and put on a fresh

T-shirt from his office wardrobe. His iPhone continued to beep with notifications, and each time he heard it, he grinned. There would be lots of questions, theories and enquiries, conspiracies and hypotheses – but for now, providing immediate answers was not his priority. He grabbed his iPhone and took the elevator down to the ground floor.

Over in London, Mark, 26, Sadie, 27 and Leah, 33 of Studio HeyWhat, the design team that created the brand, who themselves felt 'the restlessness of their generation', were catching up on the incidents on social media, but not behind their desks. They were in a café near their office in Shoreditch, where they met every Friday morning for their end-of-the-working-week breakfast. They were energetic, loud and high-fived a lot after they concluded that the clandestine brand development work they'd done for Jordan's limited-edition fashion drop had reached the pinnacle of branding: it was so humanised that it had achieved its own, independent consciousness. They messaged Jordan right away.

Back in San Francisco, Jordan was turning on the lights of his ground-floor studio. As they began to flicker, he opened the roll-up garage door and caught sight of the cityscape in the distance. It was a mild night and San Francisco glowed like a firefly. He looked at his Apple Watch: eight minutes past midnight. He lit a cigarette, leant against the wall and checked the constantly beeping notifications on his iPhone.

We knew you were working on something futuristic, but this! wrote Studio HeyWhat. *You know we always imagined the brand being this device that disorders consumerism, so this is so befitting of the brand strategy. Don't you think?*

Jordan laughed but did not respond. He stuffed his iPhone back into his pocket and looked again to the street outside his studio, focusing on a pool of light emitting from a streetlamp. When they came into view he rubbed his hands excitedly.

Heart-with-eyes logos of all colours and sizes were running, like little minions, up the long, steep street towards his loft. He stubbed out his cigarette and went back inside. In the centre of the empty space, he pulled down a large white sheet that was covering a glass box the size of a small car.

The logos began to walk slower as they reached the studio.

Here, here, said Jordan, ushering them through the open roller door. They hopped into the glass box one by one and lined up next to each other like well-trained soldiers – an army of more than a hundred. Jordan picked up one of the small ones. Its eyes scanned its new surrounds. He thought of each one, travelling from all around the world back here to HQ. The journey was telling; they were worn out with cracks. Muddied, scratched and dinted. This was worth it, he thought.

It had always fascinated him, this instinct people had to anthropomorphise non-human entities, to attribute human characteristics to brands and objects as if they were living, breathing beings.

Here you are, he said looking at them all, *in full view of the world. A complete and utterly humanised brand.*

His iPhone kept vibrating, but he ignored it. He placed the little guy back in with the others, then pulled up a chair next to them. He lit a cigarette and placed his MacBook on his lap. As soon as he opened it, more messages and emails flooded the screen. He caught Studio HeyWhat's latest.

Jordan, they wrote, *we've been contacted by the media. Since we designed the brand, we bear some responsibility to voice our opinion on the matter . . .*

There was more, but he felt no need to read on. Like everyone else, he expected them to exploit this situation for their own gain. And besides, he was eager to get going. He turned off all notifications and opened up the Voice Recorder application on his laptop. He hit play and leant back into his chair.

Friday, September twenty-third. Twelve thirty-three in the morning, he said. *I would say that close to eighty per cent of logos have safely returned back to HQ within a period of twenty-four hours. In this post-launch analysis, we shall examine how much of the purpose-training has been retained and what has evolved through human interaction and awakening. Let's begin.*

Jordan: *Logos, activate.*

Heart-with-eyes logos: *Hello Jordan.*

Jordan: *Could I please ask for only one of you to speak on behalf of all?*

Heart-with-eyes logo: *Yes, not a problem.*

Jordan: *Now, tell me, what are you?*

Heart-with-eyes logo: *We are a unisex fashion brand that is embedded in current culture.*

Jordan: *And what is your purpose?*

Heart-with-eyes logo: *Our purpose is to embrace the now in every way possible. This means we are never against progress and our garments are representative of this in every way.*

Jordan: *Are you human focused?*

Heart-with-eyes logo: *No. We are people–planet focused, because survival of the planet is essential to the survival of humanity. This means that we are strict, and create only sustainable fashion.*

Jordan: *Whom do you serve?*

Heart-with-eyes logo: *We exist for the millennial generation, especially progressive millennials who are fashion-forward, who share the same values we do.*

Jordan: *You mention values, but do you know what yours are?*

Heart-with-eyes logo: *Of course we do.*

Jordan: *Name them.*

Heart-with-eyes logo: *Our values are written as active verbs, because active verbs – when read – inspire action in people. This is why our values are (a) be as conscious of the Earth as you are of yourself (b) never waste materials (c) subvert the mainstream and (d) stay progressive.*

Jordan: *Now tell me, how do you action your purpose?*

Heart-with-eyes logo: *We never refrain from our vision. Being embedded in current culture means we become wholly committed to whatever popular view is trending.*

Jordan: *Okay, that's interesting. And what popular view is trending?*

Heart-with-eyes logos: *Fascism.*

AVANT-GARDIST

Okay, here's a somewhat true story for you.

In 1822, four years before the Tasmanian bushranger Matthew Brady was hanged at the Hobart Convict Penitentiary, an American man, also named Mathew Brady, was born.

This Mathew Brady only had one 't' in his name. He didn't lie, steal or murder anyone. And his face didn't end up on Wanted posters.

In fact, this Mathew Brady became something quite praiseworthy; the father of photojournalism. A pioneering innovator, Mathew Brady created, among other things, the first mobile photography studio. During the American Civil War, he captured thousands of battle scenes and took portraits of generals and politicians, creating what would become the most comprehensive visual documentation of the Civil War that exists today.

Well, you probably guessed it, but this revolutionary work in photography is not the story we want to tell.

The story we're after started at the dawn of the year 1856 when Mathew Brady began to have dark and gruesome dreams. They crept up on him every night as he went to bed. In them, he'd envisage his pioneering achievements – photographing battle-fields, taking presidential portraits (eighteen in total) and the purchase of ten thousand photography plates – going to waste. The dream would escalate, and Mathew Brady would wake in fright at the point when he'd see himself dying slowly, wearing a tattered shirt inside a charity ward, utterly penniless.

With this dream constantly reverberating through his mind, his suspicion of his assistants and the United States government grew. Fewer and fewer people were contacting his New York City photography studio for commissions, and Mathew Brady, a superstitious man, believed this was proof that these night-mares were harbingers of penury that he needed to do something about, and quickly. To fight off this phobia of an impoverished, unremarkable death, he decided to gain the attention of his fellow Americans.

Now this is where it gets interesting. Matthew placed an advertisement in the daily *New York Herald*. The notice was simple: it promoted his services, which were the provision of photo-graphs, ambrotypes and daguerreotypes. There was nothing much to the advertisement, until you looked closer at the inventive use of typography. All advertisements in American newspapers were set in all-agate and all same-size typefaces, but Matthew Brady's wasn't. He chose larger font dimensions, bolded his headlines and structured his text in a completely different way to the industry standard of the time. Believe it or not, this distinctive use of fonts caused a mass sensation in New York. People were mad about it. Not only was the advertisement successful in regaining the attention of his fellow Americans (for a short period of time, anyway) but it also became the first modern advertisement. Cool, right?

The father of photojournalism was also the first real adman. Not bad for Mathew Brady, considering the legacy of the other one, the one with the two 't's in his name, amounted to nothing more than a popular picnic area with views over the Tamar River. It's called Brady's Lookout – you should visit if you ever get the chance.

ARCHIVING

He had never been to this side of the world, where the cold dropped to despondent minuses.

His nose was frozen. His hands could hardly feel blood rush through their fingers. And his feet were covered with two pairs of socks and waterproof, wool-insulated hiking boots. Still, he felt the blistering cold seep through all those layers.

He was on top of a snowy mountain. Up there, only silence and the sound of forceful winds prevailed. The vistas of snow-covered forests that stretched for kilometres looked, to him, like a panorama from a fairytale, but he wasn't sure if it was one he'd read or only imagined.

Of course it would be here, he thought. Where else could it exist but in this punishing isolation? He knew a thing or two about it. But this was nothing like anything he had ever studied or read about. It wasn't simply dry air mixed with water drops or ice particles floating freely in the air. This looked like an enormous hot air balloon hovering inside an oversized egg cup made of stark, ugly concrete. The structure extended down to the ground, and at its centre, he could see an archway.

He walked towards it. He looked up and, through a large hole in the concavity, a concentration of electricity could be seen. He had read somewhere that dark forms like these were almost entirely made of dry air, but this didn't look like elemental matter.

He poked it with his hiking stick.

It was unexpectedly soft and mushy, like hair wax. A long cable, connected to its middle, extended downwards to rest like a wound-up garden hose on the ground. He picked it up. The end tip had a silicone pouch for a single finger.

He let it rest back on the ground and looked around. Snow was falling harder, and the distant vistas were now obscured by the density of the snowfall. He reached for the water bottle from his backpack and took a few sips. His mouth was dry but he didn't notice until the water flowed down his throat. Then he walked around the perimeter, taking in the summit this thing was on, covered entirely in knee-high snow. Feeling tired, he began to stomp out a section to sit on. When he was seated, he finally discerned the reality of what hovered above him.

Here, he was a nobody. No one important in the scheme of things, just a dejected man consumed with the idea of retrieving everything he'd ever messaged, photographed, screen-grabbed or documented about her. The her that was no longer beside him. The her that he'd pledged his life to, in sickness and health. But health had not carried the day for them.

Her face. The small mole on her left cheek. Her light, blonde eyelashes that blended with her tan in summer. She had to colour them in to be seen. Her little insecurities; how she used to squeeze his hand under the table, urging him to speak on her behalf when a conversation was directed towards them.

His heart pounded at the thought of what was about to occur. He took another sip of water, gripped his hiking stick and stood up. There were no instructions. It was up to him to figure out how to execute the download from this so-called cloud.

Without overthinking, he stood under the archway and placed his index finger inside the silicone pouch at the tip of the cable. He waited for the overhead cloud to spark with energy, or perhaps even create an electrical storm, but it slowly began to draw air inwards, like it was taking a breath.

Soon, the silicone pouch contracted. It sucked the tip of his finger like a fish's mouth. He was gazing out at the snow, thinking about how unbelievably silent it was, when it began.

Data started to flow through him.

Every single message he'd exchanged with her, word for word, in chronological order, he could feel entering his blood stream. The affectionate emojis. The consistent 'I love you's they left at the end of each message. The photographs he had taken of her, all 19,656 of them, began to rush in like an IV drip. He could feel her presence from every holiday they had ever taken. The pressure of her fingers from every hand-held moment in their fifteen-year relationship. Pictures of hundreds of dinners, from which he could taste the food in his mouth. The silly videos they took of each other in bed when they couldn't sleep. All of this collected inside of him, with stacked vividness he never imagined possible. The hundreds of notes he'd taken from the things she always said. *Why do we have to breathe, why can't we just exist?* He had forgotten that one. It was funny; that's why he'd called the notes Funny Things Donna Says but it wasn't trivial to him. They were her original thoughts, and now they were flooding into him like a fierce current gushing into his soul.

He started to feel dizzy. He clutched the hiking stick with his other hand to keep himself still, but his knees buckled. Slowly he went down. As each memory crossed the threshold, he kept sinking further until he collapsed onto the cold ground.

It was up to the strength and capacity of his brain. How much it was willing to store in the space of its long-term memory. Nausea, he had expected. But the dizziness and the excruciating pain that was shooting through his temple, he hadn't. It was dangerous, he knew – but he didn't care. She wouldn't remain trapped as scraps of data, JPEGs, GIFs or MOVs – that was the important thing.

Just then, the transmission of data slowed.

In the final scene of a video, her smile glitched inside his mind. He pushed the pouch further down his index finger, but the glitch intensified until the video stopped entirely. All he could see was half an image. It was the last photo he had taken of her in the hospital; her dauntingly pale face, her hollow eye sockets. After that, Donna no longer wanted to be photographed. *I don't want to be remembered bald and cancerous,* she had said. He opened his eyes and looked up. The cloud was darker, the electrical concentration diffused.

No! he yelled.

The audio files, those of her voice, when he'd recorded her in her final days – he hadn't got to those yet. He forced himself to stand, his legs swaying, his temple pulsing. With the last ounce of his will he pounded the cloud with his hiking stick.

Please! he shouted.

Tears dripped down his face. He knew he was being greedy but he kept beating it, wanting to crack it open so the rest of the data might drown him like a tidal wave. But the cloud dimmed.

He wiped the tears from his eyes. Almost every memory from his smartphone he could sense, crystal clearly, in his consciousness.

Above him, the cloud retracted and hummed, and then turned a blazing red. A loud noise like a siren began to boom across the summit. He knew what it meant. Time was running out. They'd be here soon.

He struck the cloud again with his hiking stick. *Come on!* he pleaded.

He reached out his left hand and felt the air around the pouch on his index finger. He had forgotten how icy cold it was, how glaringly bright the light. His mouth emitted steam each time he struck the cloud. From the distance, tyres powering over the snow could be heard.

He sat down and closed his eyes. Then, suddenly, data began to flow again. Her silvery voice filled his mind. He could sense her now. As if she was right there beside him, whispering sweet nothings into his ear.

LOGOPHILE

Make the logo smaller, said the client.

Though he heard him clearly, the art director made the logo bigger.

Smaller, mate, said the client.

Sorry, said the art director.

He couldn't recall a single instance in his career in which a client had asked for their logo to be sized down. Hesitantly, he made the adjustment. Then he swivelled his chair to the right. He was sick of the client's hovering presence behind him.

How's this? he asked. The client glanced at the screen.

Better! he said. _No clichés on this campaign, all right._

Was that a question or a statement? The art director wasn't sure, but he felt the client's hands grip his shoulders and he knew it was the usual, friendly gesture; the affable nudge that was meant to remind him that this client was no typical client. Still, it made him uncomfortable. He rolled his shoulders back and forth to signal that it was time to let go, but the client held on.

What could he say? The man holding him was the most important client the agency ever had. He was like a dream: a marketing director who hated that consumers were bombarded with boring conventions and clichés. Just like them, he was tired of advertising that taunted minds with their rule-of-three formulas and bland recipes – especially in his industry: the car industry. He was a businessman with the heart of an artist, that's what the team kept telling the art director. So how could he turn around now and tell him, that he was being too touchy-feely?

The grip finally loosened, and the art director turned around again to see the client put his hands in his pockets. He smiled, thanked the art director and continued along with the regular convoy: the two account executives who were frantically taking notes, the strategist who conversed too eagerly, and the creative director who kept a mysterious air about him for no reason, other than the fact that he was the creative director.

There were, obviously, too many people guiding him around on his weekly visits. As soon as the art director saw them disappear from view, he got up and stretched. He raised his arms, pushed his shoulders back, then bent down to touch his toes.

You all right? asked the copywriter, who was sitting beside him.

Just a bit tense, he said.

I love that guy, said the copywriter. *You're so lucky you're working on that account.*

Yes, he was lucky, but he hated that every time the client gripped his shoulders like that, a phantom hold would linger around like an insult. It would take him a while to shake off the feeling of the sturdy fingers digging into his neck.

He placed his headphones over his ears, tapped his mouse and tried to re-engage with the work. Then he remembered: there was a work-in-progress meeting for the campaign this afternoon. His stomach constricted at the thought of another moment with the client.

He thought about his military crewcut. Today's tight-fitting blue suit and Windsor-collar shirt. His shiny brogues and those cufflinks ... oh, those cufflinks with the car logo on them, how the art director hated those.

Towards the end of every meeting, the client would stand before the team and loudly applaud their creativity. And then, with a wink that would scrunch up his forehead, he would say, *No clichés, all right?* Everyone would burst out laughing. Everyone except the art director, who'd always wonder why no one from his team found the remark as irritating as he did.

In these meetings, the art director often imagined the client's morning routine. He was convinced they started with no less than a hundred push-ups beside a wall that was lined with non-fiction books that all contained the same failure-to-extreme-success stories. A motivational podcast during his shower, where he'd scrub his teeth with charcoal, followed by a slew of YouTube videos of some influencer yelling advice at him. *CUT THROUGH THE BULLSHIT. FOLLOW YOUR DREAMS. TURN YOUR CAN'TS INTO CANS. MAKE YOUR DREAM A PLAN. GRIND FOR IT. WORK FOR IT. SWEAT FOR IT.*

He recalled their first workshop. The client, standing before them in a double-breasted suit and over-the-top-shiny Gucci shoes, played a collection of car commercials from fifteen different countries. And sure, he was right: every single car commercial had a formula. A predictable script that featured a long, winding road, drone shots of the car, a specification-led voiceover, a handsome driver behind the wheel and a final shot of the car driving off into some idyllic distance.

If you take away the badges, they all look the same, the client had said.

The art director didn't disagree, but he also didn't have a problem with it: didn't product-led marketing make things memorable? The car company the client represented was selling cars with the same campaign style. Boring, yes. Tedious, definitely. Same-same, too often. But it worked – and it had worked for over a decade.

A year ago, when they won the pitch, the client put the agency on a two-year retainer. He gave them complete creative freedom to think of a new brand direction and test it out with a latest model. It was their biggest account and it made the entire advertising industry jealous. There was nothing to stunt their focus, nothing keeping them from creating unconventional, progressive car advertising.

They worked tirelessly, exploring every conceivable angle and idea until they arrived at a concept the art director came up with called Transition Your Life. That was eight months ago. Now, they were weeks away from launch.

After lunch, the art director walked into the main boardroom for the WIP. The convoy from earlier were already seated around the table, and the creative director was loading up a presentation on the TV screen, but the client was not to be seen.

He had to leave early, said one of the account managers. *But he loves it all!* A phantom weight departed from the art director's shoulders. He sat down, threw a stick of chewing gum into his mouth and watched the presentation with enthusiasm.

A week later, he was putting the final touches to the campaign. Nervously, he kept looking over all the work on his screen. It was good. No, it was probably great, and definitely the opposite of cliché. It didn't even feature the car in any of the executions. The main sixty-second commercial only caught a glimpse of it at the end – but not even the grill with the badge. That's fucking brave, thought the art director. He was proud. His ego no longer oscillated like a leaf on a tree.

He flicked through the final PDF that contained the entire national campaign and saw that there really was a fresh tone to the body of work. The concept was subtly embedded into every piece of communication. It wasn't over the top. It didn't shout and urge you to buy it right away. He was especially proud of the minimalist design aesthetic he had applied to it. Could this beat the great VW ads from the 1960s?

On the day of the launch, the client walked into the office in a dark green suit, specially tailored for the occasion. He looked good, felt great. So did everyone else. The night before, billboards, bus signage, street posters and digital ad placements in shopping centres had been installed. The PR releases had been sent out and the dealerships were ready. In the office, they gathered around the TV screen in the boardroom, waiting to see the first appearance of the commercial on a morning television segment. They held their breath and watched it in silence till the very end. Then, *Wow! Wow! Wow!* came out of thirty different mouths. They clinked their glasses in celebration and remarked on the refreshing, cool and unconventional tone of the commercial.

No clichés, all right, yelled the client.

Everyone laughed. And this time, the art director did too because it wasn't a motivational statement anymore: it was a catchphrase.

Three months of positive reviews kept everyone's spirits up. Then the dealerships across the country began to complain. What could possibly be wrong?

It's not making a dint in sales, said the dealerships.

Give it some time, said the client.

But another six months passed and no spikes in sales were detected. The projections were so far off they were daunting to look at. Focus groups were organised immediately. Social media comments were distilled into reports and a week later, after they had gathered enough intel, they finally understood the problem. Customers were confused by the change of direction. They didn't want their minds changed or lives transitioned, they just wanted the new car features highlighted per all previous commercials.

I thought it was obvious, said the client in the meeting following the release of the reports, *but I guess our customers aren't ready for progress.*

After some ego-bruising decisions, they quickly developed a new campaign. They brought back the long, winding roads, the drone shots, the specification-led voiceover with the handsome driver behind the wheel and the final shot of the car driving off into some idyllic distance. And sure enough, this got the sales moving.

The only person who laughed at this irony was the art director, who in a later meeting said, *Sorry, did you say make the logo bigger?* just to make sure he heard the client correctly this time around.

DIDO

Filip stopped feeling curious a bit after lunch on Thursday.

You okay, Dad? asked Teddy, who sensed that her father was no longer listening to her.

Sorry, darling, said Filip.

He really was, for his daughter's story about a disastrous Tinder date was funny, but that basic instinct that made him listen alertly, take interest and ask questions had just drifted away like cigarette smoke.

I don't know what happened, said Filip. *I just felt this . . . lack of feeling.*

Is it the food? asked Teddy. *Oh God, is it a heart attack? Should I call an ambulance?*

Filip registered panic in Teddy's eyes.

No, darling, everything's fine, he lied, for there was nothing more painful to him than seeing fear in his daughter's face.

You don't look so good, she said. *I know the waiter, let me talk to them just to be sure.*

Teddy, seriously, I'm fine, he said assertively and reached out to clasp her hand.

Okay, okay, but what happened? she asked. *You looked like you disappeared.*

It's hard to explain, Filip said. *But I'm surprised . . . your story was so interesting.* He laughed. *Please do go on,* he added.

Smartarse, said Teddy and calmed down. *You're working too much again.*

I think I might be, agreed Filip. He took a sip of water.

I still laugh at the whole senior designer thing you know, she said.

Well, it is funny, said Filip. *I'm sixty-five. And a designer.*

Want me to drive you home? she asked. *Actually, I insist.*

Filip got up out of his chair. *No, but thank you,* he said, placing his arms on her shoulders to signal for her not to get up. *This was a lovely lunch. I'm going to take a walk home. The fresh air will do me good.* He kissed Teddy on the forehead and went inside the café to pay.

Back at home, Filip headed straight for his home office. Though he still felt enervated, his work couldn't wait. Earlier in the day, the rebrand he was doing for an architecture firm felt exciting, but now, as soon as his computer lit up InDesign, it felt as peripheral as Teddy's story.

He walked over into the living room. Exercise had always done the trick for him in situations like this. He picked up the resistance band hanging over his sofa and began to sweat out this unexpected anxiety. He did a set of push-ups, a few single-arm bicep curls and seated in-and-outs. It roused his body and eased his mind but it didn't bring back his usual spirit of enquiry.

The next day, as he sat across from the local GP, he felt stupid to be wasting her time with this weird problem. Still, knowing Filip well, the doctor validated the issue by taking it very seriously. *How are you sleeping? Are you still exercising regularly? Any memory loss? Drinking enough water? How is your diet these days? Anything recent that is causing you stress? Have you tried meditation?*

After checking his blood pressure, listening to his heart rate and prescribing a blood test, the GP advised Filip that time off work would be the best solution for now.

Look, Filip, she said, *you know that a sudden lack of motivation, passion, excitement, interest, all of those things can happen naturally from varying degrees of stress. And obviously it is more existent in your age group. You're definitely fit and healthy, but it sounds to me like you're a little overworked and anxious. Let's see what the blood test uncovers.*

Filip believed her but he still couldn't understand how it could have disappeared like that. Poof, and it was gone – that's what he wanted to tell her.

He had always understood the power of self-motivation in life. Curiosity had to be well managed, tended to, like a body. For Filip, who was still a working designer, being curious was largely a function of having a healthy antenna that constantly pursued inviting distractions. He read widely, visited galleries and museums on a regular basis and took interest in almost any subject. It's how he had always been. But he also knew, much like Einstein did, that society's myriad rules, norms and conventions slowly kill off our innate curiosity. He wondered, perhaps, if the sudden disappearance of his own curiosity was a sign that ageing had finally caught up to him after all.

Against his GP's orders, he jumped back into work. This is just a blah I'm feeling, he told himself. For the rest of the week, without overthinking decisions, he continued to design all the things he was tasked to design: a book to celebrate the architectural firm's twenty years in the industry, their newsletter and new office signage.

Another week passed. Feedback arrived in his inbox and Filip processed it like a robot, feeling as if he were in a perpetual state of automation. The work became harder to look at and he could sense fresh embitterment and restlessness following the completion of every task.

Dad, you haven't replied to my text. You okay? wrote Teddy.

Sorry, he wrote. *I was a bit busy. All is well.* ☺

He was lying again. But this time, sensing how badly his motivation was dulled, he did something about it; he wrote an apologetic email to his clients, advising them that he had to take some urgent time off.

First, he tried fiercer exercise with a personal trainer. In the evening, he began to practise meditation. He rejoined his tennis club to rouse his competitive spirit. He tried another tactic (for good time's sake) and went out and got mad drunk with a few buddies. It didn't help. So acute was his desperation to resuscitate his curiosity that he even got a bag of cocaine and called in an escort, to try something debauched.

Nothing.

He deconstructed the day it had happened, breaking down and examining every second: the instant he arrived at the café for brunch, when he sat down and waited for Teddy at the back table on the terrace, when he ordered the wild mushroom ragu, the filtered coffee, the people that arrived at the other tables as Teddy sat down. Their laughter and conversations. As far as he could tell, there was nothing out of the ordinary until that moment it all went *poof*. But a cure had to be out there, he thought.

To unravel the mystery, he decided to embark upon a year-long sabbatical, hoping that travel would reactivate his curiosity antenna. It had been a long time since he last travelled and he was excited about this forthcoming journey. So was Teddy, who was deeply proud of her independent father. He chose Eastern Europe for its brutalist architecture, Central Europe for its art and literature, Southeast Asia for its beaches and spicy food, and South America for its ancient history.

After a full year of travel, he didn't find a cure. But on his final stop, high up in the Andes Mountains in Peru, above the Urubamba River valley, he found an answer.

Your curiosity has been replaced, said an American tourist from Austin, Texas.

Filip's ears pricked up. *Sorry?* he asked.

They were sitting next to each other on rickety garden chairs against the concrete wall of a hostel in Aguas Calientes, watching the street passers-by. The tourist took out a comb and ran it through his curly grey hair. He was paunchy and red-faced, wearing a cream linen shirt unbuttoned too low, with tangled-up silver necklaces and beaded chains dangling on his chest.

Gods are never concerned with us, he said. *But sometimes they like to play games – random acts of devilry, unkindness. It's a God-awful thing.*

Filip leant in closer. *You think the Gods have played a trick on me?* he asked.

And you thought you'd be enlightened up there? The tourist pointed towards the mountain where the ruins of Machu Picchu waited.

I was told this was the place I sought, said Filip. *From a villager in Hungary.*

Dola, said the tourist.

Sorry? said Filip, confused.

D-O-L-A, that's her name, said the tourist. *Never mind.* The tourist winked at Filip and pressed a pack of darts in front of his face. *You smoke?* he asked.

No, said Filip, but he took a cigarette anyway.

The tourist held out a Zippo. Filip stared at his wrists; they were adorned with much the same silver jewellery and beaded bracelets.

Why you were chosen, you'll never know, continued the tourist. *But you'll have time—*

None of this is making sense, said Filip, desperation lingering in his voice.

The tourist broke out in laughter. He leant backwards into his chair and took off his sunglasses. His eyes were crystal blue. They looked otherworldly, thought Filip.

Punishing and vengeful deities, long the cause of human misery, are misconceptions and, therefore, not real, he said sternly, impressed with how accurately he recalled this line of Epicurus from his first degree in philosophy.

The tourist laughed. *In time to come,* he said, *you'll realise what you got in exchange for your curiosity.*

He placed his hands over Filip's face and softly blew between his fingers. Filip felt his tobacco-stinking breath on his eyelids. When he opened his eyes, the tourist was gone.

Centuries later, Filip still laughed at how wrong Epicurus was.

Though it came at the expense of one of life's greatest joys, he was the only being in the world ever given that which mankind desires most.

DESKTOP ZERO

It wasn't Friday, as she'd thought, but Thursday when Millie noticed that her messy desktop reflected not so much her own creative process, but something else instead.

For as long as she could remember in her career as a designer, Millie had a good excuse for saving thousands of files to her desktop. *Creativity isn't linear – it's messy and chaotic.* That's what she told herself, despite the fact that she organised her mess into folders: Stack One, Stack Two, Stack Three, etc.

That Thursday she thought was a Friday, she was looking for an untitled Photoshop file in the jungle on her desktop. After an hour-long struggle, she gave up. She reached into her drawer and took out her aromatherapy roll-on stick. She began to apply the oil to her temples, eager for relief. With her head slightly tilted, she suddenly discerned that her desktop was uncannily similar to the untidiness and disorder within her own life.

Her desktop resembled the heaps of clothes that were strewn across her bedroom. It also looked like the inside of her fridge, in which jars, cartons of almond milk, expired yoghurt, wilted spinach, soft carrots and who knows what else were stuffed into shelves. The stacked-up folders and images in the corner of her desktop even reminded her of her own mind: always bothered with petty stress, often apologetic and impatient, storing useless facts for the longest periods of time. When she opened up Stack Fourteen she found the clusterfuck inside quite similar to her fetishist sex life with Ben, her boyfriend of two years, who never took her shirt off when they fucked and always wanted to come on her face, throat, ears or her hair. *Did he ever ask how hard it was to get cum out of ears? Of course he didn't!*

The fingers of her right hand began to tap the mouse uncontrollably. She felt an itch behind her left ear. Her skin felt distressed, like it was being pinched by cold fingers. Her legs were crossing themselves back and forth, looking for the right position but never finding it. Millie, now with her emotions in disarray, to match her desktop, didn't know what to do. My desktop is like my fucking life! she kept thinking, the sentence repeating itself in her head like that sample from that Gotye track.

Her feet finally found a comfortable spot when she stretched out her left leg over her right foot. She heard a distant laugh, like a cackle coming from the other end of the open-plan office. Then she saw Annisah, Fred and Max across from her. They were deep in work mode: eyes glued to their screens, headphones over their ears. Beside her, Denise was excitedly sketching on a notepad, humming a song. Further down the office, the same scene repeated itself behind every desk. It appeared that everyone was in tune with their world, their job and life. Everyone except Millie.

She looked at her long, thin fingers and dry knuckles. They looked parched to her. The L'Occitane hand cream wasn't doing anything to soothe the constant dryness. She looked underneath the table at her Adidas sneakers and felt an urge to pull out her stupid pink laces. Her backpack, did it have to be a one hundred per cent vegan padded Eastpak? She kicked it, then grabbed the aromatherapy roll-on stick from her drawer again. She massaged it onto her wrists and her neck. She closed her eyes and breathed in the invigorating aroma. It smelt of ginger and lavender and she desperately hoped it would work like Aesop said it would because she couldn't see a way out of this fucking anxiety spiral, panic attack, or whatever else was coming.

She rubbed her eyes. When she opened them, her desktop screensaver was showing her a picture of a pristine desert land-scape. She punched in her password and her messy desktop stared back at her again. She laughed. But then she clapped her hands and without giving the situation another thought, began to unpack all of her 'sort' folders, all twenty-nine of them.

It was six o'clock when she realised she'd been at it for hours. But there was plenty more to go. She put her headphones back on, pressed play on her Chill Out playlist and continued.

At nine o'clock, she pushed back into her chair.

She lifted her arms, stretched out her dry hands and fingers. Her desktop was completely empty now. There wasn't a single file or folder on it, only a picture in the centre of the screen: a bunch of cats sprawled out on a red carpet, a photo she'd always loved by the photographer Alex Prager. She thought of Ben and his dick in her ear and how she couldn't wait to tell him to fuck off. She thought of her room, and how she couldn't wait to clean it and hang all her clothes neatly in her wardrobe. Her parents, whom she needed to call. Her sister, to whom she needed to apologise for never calling. She turned off Spotify, quit every other application then folded her laptop. There was no one else in the office but its emptiness still buzzed like a fridge. Millie sighed.

It felt good, this cleaning up. As good as it had a year ago.

AD NAUSEUM

They decided that Ivan had to be the one to do it because he was the only one who had the balls.

I don't know, guys, he said, *it seems a fraction dangerous. Don't you think?*

Regarding him closely, his friends Tisha, Kemal and Fernando had already prepared a rebuttal to keep the peer pressure firm.

It'll be fine, said Tisha, *they're professionals.*

Kemal emphasised the payment. *When have you ever had a hundred grand in your bank account?*

And Fernando, who was chewing on a toothpick, preferred to boost Ivan's ego one more time. *Man,* he said, *you're like the hacker of the century. Remember when you programmed the chip in your arm to turn your car on?*

I control my drone with it now, said Ivan proudly.

Tisha laughed. *Remember how we met?* she said. *You were so clever. Did you guys know he used to upload his Tinder pics upside down so when girls turn their phones and swipe left, it actually swipes right?*

High five! yelled Fernando. *That's some playa shit.*

Ivan high-fived Fernando's hand, then caught Kemal's too, who was reaching in to get amongst the bromance.

I stole that off some dude on Twitter, confessed Ivan.

Probably why we broke up, laughed Tisha.

They had a point, Ivan thought. He'd always been the initiator of the group. The fearless guinea pig with a tech-hungry mind. At the beginning, their post-lecture get-togethers were just about hanging out and discussing automation. But soon their conversations and jokes about cyborgs turned into homemade experiments with bodily insertions. Nothing fancy to start with – just magnets and NFC chips. It wasn't meant to be a collective, but Tisha thought a blog could be interesting. Now they had an Instagram account with a quarter of a million followers and tech companies were throwing money at them as if they were popstars. Plus, the world was taking note: this idea of prolonging life, extending years, gunning full-throttle towards immortality and future humans was on everyone's minds. But they were the grassroots starters, the amber sparks of the movement.

Think about the next convention, added Kemal. *Everyone will still be talking about headphone implants.*

Plus, you'll get to kick it in Amsterdam, added Tisha.

That was true too. He'd never been to the Venice of the north.

I could go to Bruges as well, said Ivan. *Always wanted to go there.*

Kemal gripped his shoulders. *Fuck Bruges*, he said. *You're gonna be all over the fucking news after this.*

Still guys, it's scary, said Ivan, standing up.

They were sitting in an empty lecture theatre, having arrived way too early for their next class. Their voices resounded against the high ceilings and walls of the empty space. Tisha, Kemal and Fernando watched him pace back and forth, deep in thought.

Look man, said Fernando, *it's a chance for us to explode. And you know Tisha's gotta take care of her mum. I can't because of my heart problem and Kemal's a chicken shit. And they still haven't approached any of the other start-ups.*

I know, said Ivan, *but it's brain surgery! It's very fucking different to sticking a piece of metal into your shin.*

Tisha clasped his hand in hers. *They're a legit facility*, she said, *and we'd never insist on something that was really dangerous.*

I'll think on it, said Ivan. *I can't be here now.*

Outside, Ivan caught an Uber back home. The thought of sitting inside a packed lecture theatre of robotics students made him anxious. He had a choice to make, after all. And not a trivial one. The facility made a convincing point in their proposal. If successful, it could bring down the reign of corporate empires for good. And @FutureHumans, their little collective, would be its pioneer.

He looked out of the tinted window of the Uber, a brand new Volkswagen Polo. The street outside looked like someone had dimmed its lights. He swiped his iPhone over his wrist and the health app appeared on the screen. His heart rate was normal, as was his blood pressure.

Always calm, he said.

The driver turned towards him. *Sorry?* he asked.

Oh, don't worry, I was talking to myself, said Ivan, and moved his face towards the window again.

Two weeks later, he was there.

The facility had offered to pick him up from the hotel, but he declined. He wanted to stroll through the streets, take in the City of Sin, see it for himself without being at the behest of anyone else's guidance.

Amsterdam was a marvel in his eyes. Smaller than he thought it would be, but busy, with hundreds of cyclists riding over little bridges. From Amsterdam Centraal, he jumped onto the free ferry to NDSM Werf, as they advised. The ride took less than fifteen minutes, and he stood around on the open area of the boat, feeling the wind gust over his face, his eyes ogling the buildings and sights around him.

When he arrived in front of the glass building, he jumped on to WhatsApp. The crew back home wanted an update every step of the way.

Going in now, he wrote in their group chat.

Wooohooo, wrote Fernando, who seemed to be the only one still awake.

One of them should've come, thought Ivan, but it was too late to complain.

Inside, Ivan immediately looked up; a glass ceiling filled the interior of the small building with natural light. Floor-to-ceiling windows lined the sleek lobby, which seemed to stick reservedly to a black and white colour scheme. He approached a long, white reception desk that swooped nicely into a curve. The rest of the lobby was sparsely furnished with more white furnishings, perched on top of an off-white coloured floor.

Welcome Mr _____ , said a smiley-faced receptionist.

Oh hi, said Ivan.

Mr Jansen and Ms Bakker are expecting you, she added. *Let me show you to the elevators.*

Thank you, said Ivan, following her down the lobby.

When the elevator doors opened, Ivan could see two people behind a glass table at the other end. Ivan looked past them, his attention drawn to the huge warehouses he could see through the windows. He forgot for a second which floor he was on and tried to remember which button the receptionist had pressed in the elevator earlier.

This whole area used to be a shipbuilding and repair yard. That's why there's so many large warehouses, said Ms Bakker, interrupting his reverie.

She was sitting behind the table next to Mr Jansen, a tall man in a double-breasted suit who was standing. Ivan glanced over his facial features; the clean-shaven face and chiselled jawline looked even more impressive in real life.

But since the early 2000s, this whole area has experienced heavy urban renewal. It's becoming a new cultural precinct in Amsterdam — well, it already is, said Ms Bakker. *And you can call me Jesse now,* she said and smiled.

Pleasure to meet you properly, said Ivan, *after all the Zoom meetings.*

He felt his phone vibrate in his pocket. They're up now, he thought.

I'm Hugo, said Mr Jansen. He reached out to shake Ivan's hand.

Nice to meet you too, said Ivan, feeling Hugo's firm grip.

His phone kept vibrating in his pocket.

Did you have a nice stroll through the city? asked Jesse.

I really did. I think I needed it before getting here, said Ivan.

Don't worry at all, said Hugo. *It's all perfectly safe.*

Please take a seat, said Jesse, who motioned for him to sit across from them on the white leather chair. So much white, thought Ivan.

Legally, said Jesse, *we must go over the experiment with you one more time.*

I'd like that, to be honest, said Ivan. *It's not every day you sign up for brain surgery!*

He laughed, but only caught grins from Jesse and Hugo.

As we advised over our numerous conversations, continued Jesse, *this procedure is the first of its kind. And in principle, the device acts in a similar way to an ad-blocker plug-in. The software contains filters that tell it which URL requests to block. When these filters are enabled, websites that serve ads won't pass through them. Think of it like that.*

Yeah, I figured, said Ivan.

We appreciate your confidence, said Hugo. *We're just as excited.*

Did we update the paperwork with the clause for exclusive rights? asked Ivan, who knew the others were adamant about this question before anything got started.

Of course, replied Hugo. *As we told you and your team, we believe this is the best course of action for a product of this nature. Your collective has garnered an incredible following and not just in in the bio-hacking sector. It will be your product, under your brand. It's all been updated in the contract.*

Wonderful, said Ivan excitedly.

Jesse looked up at Hugo, almost to tell him to quieten down now.

Now, think about this in relation to your brain, Ivan, she continued. *Once information is processed to a degree, an attention filter decides how important the signal is and which cognitive processes it should be made available to. Do you understand that?*

Yes, nodded Ivan.

Our chip works together with this system in your brain, she said. *All relevant and important information that aids learning and development still passes through. Our chip simply blocks out marketing information. It is programmed with hard-wired filters that recognise when a message is of the crude, persuasive kind, then it alerts the system that the incoming information is attempting to trigger your inner desires – your dopamine, serotonin, cortisol and oxytocin. This information will not pass through your cognitive processes. This means that if the procedure is successful, you'll be immune to advertising.*

Ivan thought back on the last few years, their own attempts at fusing their bodies with tech. This felt a world away from magnets and NFC chips.

Incredible, he said.

He could feel fresh sweat pouring out of the glands of his neck and his lower back. That guinea pig attitude, that bold, brave inner cry of his vitality was pushing through him as he imagined the world's reaction to an innovation against capitalism. A first move against the art of persuasion that had dominated humanity's needs and desires for too long.

Hugo placed a thick contract on the table and handed Ivan a pen.

We've updated the terms and conditions. And as stated in points sixty-six to seventy-two on page thirty-three, we cannot be held legally responsible for the side effects that are listed in detail at the end of the document.

Of course, said Ivan, grabbing the pen. He signed his name and handed it back.

We require another signature, here and here, pointed Hugo.

Ivan picked up the pen again and signed where indicated.

Per the contract terms, you will have to remain in the facility for fourteen days post-surgery, said Hugo.

We know this is a long time, said Jesse, *but it is the critical testing stage. During this time, we will run tests to ensure the chip is operational and functional. From that point onwards, we will conduct a check-in, every six months.*

And your payment has already been processed, said Hugo, smiling.

Really? asked Ivan.

He took out his phone and logged on to his banking app. There, in his savings account, was a number bigger than anything he'd ever seen in there before. It made his heart race. He couldn't wait to show Tisha, Kemal and Fernando.

The next morning, he arrived at the building at 6 am sharp. He met Hugo in the foyer and watched him press B6 inside the elevator and swipe his card at the reader. This time he wanted to remember which floor he was on.

Downstairs, a nurse was waiting for them as the doors opened. She took Ivan to the preparation room, where he was asked to sit in a chair before a mirror. She shaved his head clean, and for the first time in a long while, he saw his entire face.

He felt vulnerable and thought he looked rough, even for him. A feeling of unease enveloped him.

You can take a shower now, said the nurse.

He emerged from the shower to find a blue plastic robe waiting for him on a chair. He slipped into it and the nurse led him to the centre of the floor where the operating table was set up. Ivan looked about, counting another four nurses in scrubs and maybe four machines, beeping and buzzing. He recognised Jesse's eyes staring at him between a surgical cap and mask.

It was only when Ivan lay down and faced the hovering lamp above him, that it dawned on him – the three per cent chance that the procedure wouldn't be successful, that it could damage the cognitive processes of his brain – here in a basement of a building he'd never been in, in a city and a country he'd never set foot in, all because he wanted to be the first person in the world to fully resist advertising.

Tisha came to mind. Her big blue eyes and her thick black hair. Ivan smiled, then he felt his mind slipping away and his eyes slowly closing and opening, closing and opening until nothing but blackness remained.

When he woke up, the first face he saw was Kemal's. He thought he was still dreaming.

Then Tisha said, *Hey.*

He reached up and touched his head; it was wrapped in soft bandages.

You can't see it, said Fernando.

It's so small, said Tisha.

What . . . what are you doing here? Ivan said sleepily.

We were here all along, said Tisha. *Surprise!*

167

He turned to the side; sitting next to him was Hugo. Jesse was standing beside him, checking Ivan's vitals.

They asked us to keep it quiet, said Jesse.

I'm glad you're all here, said Ivan.

His friends gathered closer around him and gave him a hug.

Of course, said Kemal. *We're Future Humans!*

Is it working? asked Ivan.

Hold your horses, they have to perform tests first, said Tisha.

Hugo rested his hand on Ivan's foot. *Are you hungry?* he asked.

Ivan thought about it, then it hit him that he was in fact starving. *Massively,* he said.

Great, said Hugo. *Bring it in!* he called.

A nurse pushed a TV screen on a trolley into the room.

What's this? asked Tisha.

Now we'll play some ads! said Jesse excitedly.

For the next fortnight, while Ivan was recovering, Jesse conducted a series of tests on him under different psychological conditions. When Ivan was hungry, she'd show him ads for brands of foods he liked, such as KFC, Wagamama and McDonald's. When Ivan was thirsty, they'd play famous beverage ads that showcased mouth-watering drinks such as freshly squeezed orange juice (his favourite) and water from springs of faraway places such as Evian and Fiji. Sometimes he had to endure insults and verbal abuse from Jesse that made him feel ugly and pathetic. When he'd visibly show signs of sadness and depression, Jesse would make him watch clothing and shoe commercials that were created to stimulate self-worth. After each session, Jesse would clap her hands and high-five Ivan.

It's amazing, she'd say, then she'd continue the sessions.

It was after the last test, which showed Ivan commercials that used newfangled formulas to sell everything from smoothies to chia seeds, that Jesse elaborated on the results.

Ivan, she said, *every ad aims to first capture you with an amazing headline, then it starts laying out the problem. It wants to hit you with dopamine, then with cortisol. You're not good enough! You need this! Your dreams will come true! Be part of our group! Everyone is doing it! Your life is bad: this product will fix it! We can give you power! Ivan, none of it works on you. Your cognitive processes don't let anything through. You're immune!*

It wasn't only Jesse who was excited. Tisha, Kemal and Fernando worked tirelessly next to Ivan, developing the chip into a consumable brand, a must-have product they called LIBERTY.

A further year of testing showed no visible side effects on Ivan. His neurological system was completely intact. And so, @FutureHumans launched LIBERTY, a world-first product that blocked advertising messages for good, giving modern humanity the refreshing ability to make their choices without added influence or persuasion.

The first two years were slow as not everybody had the cash or was as prepared as Ivan to sit through brain surgery. In the fifth year, when Hugo and Jesse were able to deliver the product in pill form, the project took off. Gens Y and Z were, naturally, the early adaptors, consuming millions of LIBERTY pills all over the world.

It was during this initial spike of popularity, sometime during the end of autumn, in an office on the Upper West Side, Manhattan, that the pill arrived on the desk of the head of the world's most powerful advertising conglomerate. The man, who was in his seventies, opened the silver packaging and stared at the pill. It was cushioned inside a small box like a piece of jewellery.

This, Charlie, is what cut our business by half, the old man said to his assistant, who was sitting at a desk at the end of the room. He took the pill out and examined it closely. *What a preposterous idea. Ads are part of life. They help us make decisions. Provide options. Give us bargaining power.*

Charlie nodded.

And let's not forget the pleasant, joyous breaks they give us from the unfathomable boredom of life.

Oh, Charlie, those little shits. The old man put the pill back into the box and turned towards the floor-to-ceiling window behind his desk. *They don't know what they've got coming,* he said. *Don't they know we always find ways to reach our consumers? Ways that show them that we care about their precious lives.*

The old man paused. Charlie looked up at him from their laptop, but didn't say anything.

The consumer's last wall of defence, do you know what that is? he then asked, still staring out of the window.

No, sir, I don't, they said.

It's the place that we've never been able to breach. The last ad-free place in the world. The safe haven. The port in a storm.

I'm not sure I'm following, said Charlie.

It's dreams, Charlie. Our wonderful dreams. Up until now they've been out of reach, but what happens when we find a way to enter dreams? What happens then?

Charlie stopped typing. They pushed their chair back and walked over to the old man.

We're talking about branded dreams, aren't we? they said.

The old man smiled.

That's right, Charlie. That's exactly right.

MODERN FEED

At around seven-thirty, when Bridget gets home from work, she has this ritual she loves performing.

She takes off her shoes and places them by the door. Slides off her socks and flings them into the washing basket in the bathroom. Afterwards, she lies down on the floor of the living room and stretches out her legs and arms. She always does this with her eyes closed, wiggling her toes and crunching them together until she hears a crack or two. After a few minutes, she gets up. She takes a knife and fork from her kitchen drawer and polishes them with an eco-friendly cloth. From her cupboard, she takes one of her large, white plates and rests it on the small dining table opposite her kitchen, along with the polished cutlery. She arranges everything neatly, then sits down. With her posture straight, she reaches into her pocket for her smartphone.

She places it in the centre of the plate, and rests her right hand against it to make sure it is perfectly straight. With her left hand, she scans her apps. First, she checks if she has any new notifications, then, with a deep breath, she taps the Twitter icon and refreshes the feed. From the top to the bottom she absorbs every thought, belief and perspective, opinion, review and critique, judgement, joke and idea, philosophy, news snippet and headline, barrage, hissy fit and public-shaming until she feels unconditionally filled up, and only then can she tell herself – without reservation – that she knows what is going on in this big wide world of ours.

MODERN FEED

EXHIBITION 2

What did we just witness? asks her friend as they take the last step out of the gallery.

I don't know, but give me that freaking Juul, she says and snatches the device out of his hand. She takes a drag, a deep one, then keeps walking. *That was amazing!* she says.

Amazing? That was fucking crazy! yells her friend.

To do this to the art world—

But her friend isn't listening. He keeps talking over her. *Those women in mini dresses just going around intimidating people – even children! What the hell was that about? They kinda petrified me!* her friend says, then snatches the Juul back from her.

That's what I loved! she says. *He's an artist that truly blurs boundaries. What is advertising? What is art? That's what he questions, probes . . . and in the most interesting of ways.*

174

You're such a fucking curator, her friend jokes.

It's my job! she says proudly.

Her friend puffs hard on the Juul stick, then hands it back to her.

I'd love to work with him one day, she says. *You know he's only given two interviews so far; one to the* New York Times *and one to this obscure magazine called* This is Badland.

They keep walking as her friend shakes his head in disbelief. *Those hot chicks poking those poor old guys, that was mental. I mean, how was that even allowed?*

She likes that her friend is curious. *You know what that's about, don't you?* she asks.

Her friend keeps shaking his head.

It's about the advertising industry code. Sexualised poses in ads and commercials are permitted, but only if women are shown to be confident and in control. Krusemann used that rule in that performance.

You know you can't spell advertisements without semen between tits? Is he gonna make art out of that too? her friend asks.

Very funny, she says. *But did you notice that the women were selling something too?*

Really? her friend asks. *I didn't see them with anything.*

The sticks they used to poke people with were branded selfie sticks you could buy at the gift shop.

OMG, says her friend. *That's so SUPREME.*

See, that's the interesting thing about Krusemann. It's what he does – he messes up existing tensions.

Ahhh, interjects her friend without letting her finish her thought.

She waits a second, then continues. *Like in the sculptural work, he hammers the point home that advertising can't be art because it isn't useless. So what he's doing is pretty smart; he's purposely turning advertising into art, and thus making it useless. Do you know what I mean?* she asks her friend.

But her friend doesn't look at her, nor is he following her along the street anymore. He stops, as if thunderstruck.

You okay? she asks and stops walking too, but there is no response.

Her friend is stock-still, deep in thought in the middle of the street.

I love it when you realise something, she says when she sees his thinking face – pupils widened, facial muscles loose, mouth open like a fish gasping for air.

I just got it, her friend says after a few seconds of silence. He leans over and slaps his knees with excitement. *It's so simple – the whole thing! You have to make advertising useless, right, to make it art? Because advertising always has a function: to sell something. So, Krusemann stripped off this purpose, removed it from the works and thus made it art. That's why there was that sculpture of that famous KFC bucket ad that reads FCK instead of KFC.*

That's right! she says excitedly, looking at her friend glow with newfound understanding.

It's genius, says her friend. He takes another puff of the Juul, then blows the smoke above his head.

That's why that last act with the flashing sign was so powerful, she tells her friend. *It flashed CTA at us on purpose. That was basically a metaphor for how advertising treats us in real life. It's fucking annoying, permanently in our faces, and he offered a solution: if you donated to a worthy cause, you could switch it off. He let us basically switch off the most annoying thing about advertising: the call to action.*

Yeah, and it was so calming afterwards, adds her friend.

That's what life would be like if there were no advertising, she says.

Her friend begins to walk again. *You know, I don't like to be a victim of hype, but is he great? Is he like Wei Wei?* her friend asks.

She smiles and watches her friend walk a little ahead of her. *I don't know what he is,* she says, *but it's not the last we'll hear of Krusemann. Let's get a drink.*

GORILLA 2.0

When Tom's boyfriend dumped him, he poured his heartbreak into responding to the greatest creative brief that had ever been put in front of him.

Staring at it with tear-stained eyes, he wondered if it was some kind of celestial coincidence. This was Cadbury's next global campaign. How could fortune and misfortune come together so perfectly?

Tom knew what he was up against. In 2007, Cadbury's ninety-second commercial featuring a gorilla playing the famous drum solo in Phil Collins's 'In the Air Tonight' single-handedly increased Cadbury's UK market share by like ten per cent. It became an advertising success story stranger than fiction. Since then, every creative in the world of advertising has been trying to outdo the ad.

Securing the next global campaign for Cadbury was a huge win for Tom's agency. But as the excitement turned into frenzied celebration, Tom had to step away. In the bathroom, he took a good, hard look at himself. His eyes were puffy. His nose sniffily. He had a lump in his throat. His heart felt heavy, like it was weighing his whole body down. He knew that he didn't have a celebratory breath left in him, so instead of following everyone else's lead, Tom walked over to his creative directors and asked for two weeks' leave of absence. He promised he would return with some ideas, he just needed to rest his soul first.

On his way home, he ordered groceries online, as well as a new loungewear outfit to be sent via express shipping. Inside his small apartment, he submitted himself to his pain without hesitation. He cooked exuberant dishes from new cookbooks, read the novel *A Single Man* by Christopher Isherwood, *Love Poems* by Pablo Neruda and *The Book of Love: Poems of Ecstasy and Longing* by Rumi, underlining passages as he read. He wrote notes in his diary – something he hadn't done in years. He cried, many times, into the pages of the books and his many cushions and pillows. He watched shitty rom-com movies, all the while looking at photos of his past life with his boyfriend. He analysed their iMessages with forensic concentration, trying desperately to deduce new insights. Late in the evenings, instead of falling fast asleep, he walked for hours with wounded inspiration.

From this time spent reflecting, Tom began to learn something about himself. Despite what he might've thought, he was like most people: a human who believed love was bound by eternity. He had seen it as a cheesy, romantic fairytale between two soulmates who were together until they died in each other's arms.

But the more Tom reminisced about his past relationship, the more he was able to objectively ponder the reality of love.

It was three o'clock in the morning, on the twelfth day of his leave, when Tom arrived at a sunny deduction. He rose from his couch like he'd been startled by a house mouse. The lounge-wear he was wearing suddenly disgusted him, so he tore it off. Standing there, naked in his living room, an altogether new feeling came over him. He felt brutally excited and ready to express himself. He got dressed and headed to work.

There, alone, behind his desk, under the fluorescent lights of the open-plan office, in the dark before dawn, he sipped camomile tea and berated himself for not realising earlier that love wasn't eternal: it was eternally risky.

And how risky! He thought of all the brainless mistakes he'd made with his boyfriend. How he had belittled him in front of others when he was angry. How he had punished him by denying intimacy. How he had clung to him so closely, that he made them both lose their independence. As tears streamed down his face, and he shook irrepressibly from the hurt he was feeling, Tom began to write the last advertising script he would ever write.

Recalling the nasty fight that led to his break-up, he imag-ined an altogether different scenario. One in which he showed us that despite our best efforts to live the clichéd idea of romantic fairytale, we fall into the natural traps of reality. We fight, we yell and we inflict hurt (just like Tom did). Here, he showed us, in precise detail that involved the graceful eating of Cadbury chocolate, that if we gave up during this silly quarrel, our love would be doomed. But if we acknowledged that the risks that com-prise loving another human could be overcome with generosity, patience and forgiveness, then we wouldn't stay put. No, we'd take another delicate bite of the Cadbury chocolate in our hand and run after our love with all we've got (like Tom should've done).

In these final cinematic seconds of the script, as the two lovers come together for a perfect kiss (with Cadbury chocolate melting in their mouths), Tom showed us that this hard-earned finale – and not our clichéd idea of a romantic fairytale – is the real deal we like to call grand amour.

That morning, Tom's script found itself before the eyes of his creative directors. They knew, without uttering a single word, that they had in their hands, the successor to the Gorilla. They immediately scheduled a meeting with Cadbury.

At the Super Bowl the following year, Cadbury launched Tom's idea as a ninety-second film. After it aired, a collective melancholia took hold of everyone who had watched it. Its captivating narrative made millions of people around the world stop and reflect upon what they'd just watched.

People turned to their dear ones right away. They apologised for all the wrong they'd ever done. They kissed and wept together. Married or not, people vowed to be there for each other through all the perils of life. Like a virus, Tom's idea spread to every corner of the world. And love – not God – finally became the sacred deity all humanity prayed to.

Sadly, in this frenzy of intimacy, people forgot to buy any chocolate.

P.A.

No, there was no plan. Or strategy. It happened naturally, like with other normal, ordinary things in life, that Amelia Dupano answered her phone not as Amelia Dupano, but as someone else.

Someone less confident. Someone submissive and dutiful. It wasn't really her; she had just had a bad day. A fight with her mother who was upset that she had dropped out of university to become a full-time influencer. What she meant to say on the phone was, *I'll get back to you.* Instead, with a weak voice that stammered she said, *Amelia will get back to you.*

The moment those words left her mouth, she felt stupid. What if the person on the line recognised her voice? Couldn't they tell it was her?

But they couldn't. They accepted what she had told them, and hung up.

This excited her. Made her want to do it again. It was not without its risks, but the idea of creating a wall between herself and her personal brand made her feel in control, for the first time in a long time.

Back when her Instagram account began to grow faster than you could say #ameliadupano, she didn't stop to ask what would happen. Others did, because they wanted to know how she got so huge all of a sudden, but she never halted to ask herself what her success meant. The pretty, blue-eyed woman she saw in the mirror, the woman whose consciousness she felt every day, that person just went along with it. Not for meaning or personal discovery, but simply for the thrill of being famous. She wasn't going to kid herself, the allure of thousands of likes and comments was hard to resist. She was becoming a lifestyle influencer – and a fucking good one at that.

Not until later did she realise that with each new post she uploaded, each new brand hashtag she used, she departed further from her true self. Her Instagram account began to look like the life of another person. Someone who had been created and moulded according to a brand value system that a branding agency put together. #ameliadupano felt like an inanimate concept, that was no longer part of her. The person she was at her core – in her flesh and blood, in her laughs and her cries, in her banter and her habits – was no longer visible to anyone.

Looking back on that first phone call, maybe it was the despondent feeling her mother had left her with, or an unconscious desire for some privacy, but the second she said, *Amelia will get back to you*, was when Amelia made herself a personal assistant to herself.

P.A.

Soon, every phone called was answered the same way. Every email responded to in third person. And slowly, it became apparent to her (and the people who were getting in touch with her) that Amelia Dupano had an assistant. An assistant Amelia called Alicia Lavender.

Duties and responsibilities began to pile up. She implemented a daily content management system, and used it to schedule every aspect of her busy influencer life.

Meetings, she thought, she'd attend those as Alicia Lavender too. With fake glasses and an entirely different wardrobe.

If Supergirl could do it, so could Amelia Dupano.

She often laughs herself to sleep thinking about how ludicrous this is. How many people has she fooled? After a year, she's no longer sure. She tells herself, every time she comes close to revealing her secret, that in time, she'll disclose it. Tell the entire world. Maybe she'll pitch it to Netflix. Or HBO. But at this point, this duplication of herself, this personal assistant to her personal brand, is too much fun to give away.

META ENNIS

PART II

This is how it came to be.

He woke up, around seven-thirty. He was in her bedroom again, alone, with a grey linen sheet over his body.

Laura? he shouted.

She didn't reply. He shouted her name louder.

In the kitchen! she said.

He reached under the sheet and began to touch himself. He got hard, but as he looked up, he was distracted by the artwork on the wall across from him, a text-based piece that read, *Love is what you want*. He didn't like the statement. Never had. He kept staring at it, not noticing that his dick was getting softer. Finally, he swung the sheet off him and watched it go limp against his right thigh.

Laura was sitting on the stool behind her kitchen bench, eating a bowl of muesli when he walked in.

Hey, sleepyhead, she said.

He looked at her and wondered why she was trying so hard to maintain an upright posture.

I don't like that artwork, he said, stretching out his arms.

That's because you fear love, replied Laura.

I just think it's shit work, he replied.

You know it's not, she said. *She had a version of that text at the Venice Biennale. It's one of my favourite works.* She placed another spoonful of muesli into her mouth, but she swallowed it quicker this time. *Why do you look at me like that? I'm sick of this,* she said, throwing the spoon into the bowl.

He was standing stock still, gazing at her with a questioning look in his eyes that leant towards disgust. The sight of her back pushed up so straight irritated him and thoughts flashed through his mind of last night: her moans, her feet, her sweat.

Don't worry about it, he said and walked off towards the bathroom.

With his smartphone in one hand, he took a piss without lifting her toilet seat. Then he washed his face and brushed his teeth with her toothbrush, ignoring the one she'd bought him three months ago. After putting on his clothes, he rushed past her out the front door.

Hey! she yelled, but he was already gone.

On the street outside, while he waited for his Uber, he looked up the artwork. He had always wanted to know which artist had made that statement. But more so, he wanted to know if they had a right to make it, because for him – as we have noticed – love was not easy. He found the artist, and, unsurprisingly, wasn't impressed with her oeuvre.

Laura didn't deserve to be left like that. Nor had she deserved it the last time he'd left her helplessly crying. But I'm in no position to judge a customer.

When I first met him he was scanning through headlines on a news app on his phone. I was looking at him through an animated box the size of a Post-it note. This was during my initial campaign stage, when I cast my net wide to see who'd bite. He looked troubled, with an unkempt beard and viscous bags under his eyes. At first, I ignored him because he wasn't the persona I was looking for. But then a peculiar thing happened. I mean, most minds follow a predictable trail on the internet. They get sucked in by a topic, then they get side-tracked by different ideas within that topic, which then lead outwards again in search of new answers. But he, without any prior pattern or connective thread I could see, suddenly dived deep into Ottoman erotica. Wow, I thought. After twenty minutes, he jumped back to his news app to finish reading an article he had started earlier about the dangers of stress.

Coupled with these disparate interests, that dejected look in his eyes had me intrigued. I secured myself steadfastly to his apps and devices and from then on began to observe him more.

He wasn't active on Twitter, but he did have an account, and with it, he kept abreast of present discourse, as if he were anxious he'd get stuck behind yesterday's news. On his Instagram account, he regularly posted photos of himself at the beach, at the gym, and with his friends. And no, he wasn't shy about sliding into the DMs of busty babes either. A few times I checked in I found him on PornHub. That didn't surprise me. It's what happened afterwards that did. The next day, he'd be inside his therapist's office, lamenting his actions.

It was only later, during a busy period of research I watched him carry out about the existential threat of social media, that it dawned on me that perhaps, given our shared interests, he could be swayed to walk down the aisle of my purchasing path.

At home, he took a Valdoxan then headed straight for the shower to jerk off. He placed his iPad on the bench opposite the shower screen and began to watch a porno of a woman bent over a washing machine. After he came, he stood with his arms on the glass, heaving, then he spat at his dick. I could tell right away those morose feelings he was trying to avoid earlier at Laura's were gripping him again. Will he call the therapist? I wouldn't have been surprised if what had really made him come were thoughts of Laura, not the porno he was watching.

After the shower, he closed all the blinds in his apartment, then he dialled work.

Hey Jean, he said, *I'm not feeling well today. I think I've come down with a fever. I'm going to work from home.*

This is one trait I liked about him. Despite his shortcomings, he had a very healthy way of dealing with his despondency. Every time he felt disconnected from the world, he would avoid work because he was aware that during these times he wouldn't present as the nice guy people knew, but a cold-hearted stranger.

With his laptop open on his sofa, for the rest of the morning he indulged his self-pity with an unhealthy dose of binge-watching *Vikings* on Netflix. Intermittently, between episodes and emails, he picked up his iPad and looked up stuff on the internet; Ragnar Lodbrok, the Great Heathen Army and Saxo Grammaticus, the Danish historian and author. He also logged on to Book Depository and bought *The Penguin Historical Atlas of the Vikings* by

John Haywood and *Norse Mythology* by Neil Gaiman. His online purchasing behaviour was interesting, to say the least. He hardly ever hovered above the *Buy* button. If he had something in his cart, he'd buy it. It made his purchasing rate a consistent ninety-nine per cent.

This made me think back to last month, when I was ready to let him off the hook. He was swaying too far away from my keywords, and I thought that I was wasting my time trying to catch him. A direct eDM to his inbox didn't work. Not even my video-based sponsored posts on Instagram and Twitter, of which I was immensely proud because my point of difference was presented so cleanly within the first three seconds. I was dismayed, but there were more relevant targets to follow, targets I knew would stay in my catchment, become leads and eventual purchasers, so, I let him go. But after a few weeks, I kept thinking about him, wondering what he was up to.

Can you imagine what I found on my return? On a Friday night, when he'd usually be out drinking with his buddies, he was in bed with Laura, having a deep and meaningful about, get this: consumerism.

With a glass of rosé in his hand, he said to her, *Don't you think we're just consumers?*

Laura was lying naked beside him, her head buried in his lap. *What do you mean?* she asked. *People have always consumed. Think about the necessities of life – food, shelter, clothing.*

Yes, he said, *but if you think about our modern times, the ethos of consumerism makes you think all your desires are worthy and you should always get what you want. And today, we want everything because we constantly desire better versions of ourselves. And companies don't sell products anymore, they sell idealism.*

Laura didn't agree with this thought. She rose up out of his lap. *I don't see myself as that kind of consumer*, she said defensively. *I'm not materialistic. Besides, we still choose what to buy, and companies have always sold idealism, it's not just now.*

He pushed himself up and folded a pillow behind his back. *We don't choose anything Laura*, he said dismissively. *We just fucking consume. Every one of our actions involves the voluntary process of stuffing down shit and cramming in everything and everyone that stands before us. It's sickening.*

Laura crossed her legs. *You can't blame it all on consumerism*, she said. *You're thinking too narrowly. You have to think of it as part of industrialisation. I think consumerism, as a by-product of industrialisation, has actually been a powerful, positive force for economies.*

You're brainwashed, he said harshly. *I'm getting another drink.*

She shook her head and passed him her empty glass.

Wow, I thought. I felt a strange, personal connection with him. I knew deep inside now that love and sex and empathy weren't the only things that bothered him. Within him was buried rage, a deep need to rebel against corporatism.

Back in the bedroom, he opened up the window, sat on the windowsill and lit a cigarette.

I read somewhere, he went on, *that it's not uncommon for people who sell something to a certain group to become, in time, disdainful of them. Why else would Jay-Z have written a song called 'You're Only a Customer'?*

I've never heard that song, said Laura, who was lying on the bed, watching him.

I'm no artist, he continued, ignoring her, *but I think this scorn and contempt is born from, maybe, I don't know, a side effect of creating, of artistry. It gives people who create shit captains-of-industry egoism. Maybe artists, writers, architects, even advertising people distance themselves from others as a point of eminence. They all see themselves as higher beings because they're able to trick us into buying shit we don't need, like art and Pepsi.*

It's just stuff, said Laura, trying to break this spell he was in.

But he wouldn't budge. *It's not,* he said. *Starbucks created a fucking thing called a Unicorn Frappuccino, a drink that looks better than it tastes because it's photogenic. You think someone in a previous generation would buy that shit? But this generation –* our *generation – does. Why?*

You should read No Logo *by Naomi Klein,* said Laura.

I don't think you get it, Laura, he said.

She got off the bed and walked towards him. *Maybe I don't, but can you stop smoking in my bedroom?* she asked, before stroking the hairs on his chest. *And, more importantly, can you stop hating on my art!* She smiled and pointed fiercely to the artwork on the wall across her bed, the text-based piece that read, *Love is what you want.*

But he didn't smile, he just inhaled another drag and blew the smoke out of the window.

I left them there. It was enough to reassure me that he was worth the chase. It was no longer my own selfish pride gnawing at me, to lure someone in who wasn't even a data point in my analytics; no, this time I knew we were meant for one another. A part of me wished he could've had that conversation with me instead of Laura. Maybe I was jealous, for I would have loved to have lain on his lap, telling him what my life is like. A single function and nothing else. I would've told him that he, like every other being out there, had essence – I didn't. My essence was inherently tied to my function, created together, as one thing to be consumed – by anyone. Yes, I had a target market, a precise group of people for whom I was ideally created, but at the end of the day, anyone could buy me. I had no personal taste and no choice about who I'd end up in bed with in the end. I was simply there to be whored out to whoever was willing to pay $32.99.

During my flight of rumination, he had made himself two smoked turkey sandwiches with crispy cos lettuce and was back at the sofa, about to watch the next episode of *Vikings*, when something stopped him. He halted, kind of in mid-air, before lounging onto the sofa again. He picked up his iPhone, and messaged Laura. I was surprised. I thought his coldness would last longer, at least another day, but he sent her a kind-hearted message and apologised for his behaviour that morning.

To even my surprise, she didn't reply. He kept checking his iPhone every few minutes. I could tell he was getting annoyed and regret was steeping inside him. He jumped on to Instagram. Since he had messaged her, she had uploaded two stories from her work desk.

Bitch, he muttered.

Wow, hang on there a second, I thought.

For the next half hour he kept watching *Vikings*, but when the latest episode (S03E10) finished, he logged back on to Instagram and uploaded a few stories himself, some thoughts about the show, a picture of Neil Gaiman's book. I knew he was posting these things so she'd see them, and within a few minutes, she did.

What the fuck, he said.

He kept up the game, and uploaded more stories, and each time, she'd view them, but still wouldn't answer his message. He took another Valdoxan and poured himself a hefty glass of Lagavulin. That regret he felt earlier had by now morphed into a deep shame, and, with the help of Lagavulin and Valdoxan, he messaged her.

Again, no reply.

Who the fuck does she think she is? he yelled.

He kept drinking. Then he started smoking. For the next hour he pranced around in his apartment like a loose end in time, constantly checking his iPhone. Just as he poured himself another Lagavulin, his iPhone beeped. Frantically he searched for it until he saw it on the edge of the sofa.

You didn't have to lash out like that, wrote Laura.

I apologised.

It's not enough. I just don't understand you.

What's there to not understand?

Are you serious????? This has been going on for a year now!

What's been going on?

Don't. Please don't.

I don't get you.

What's there not to get? We're adults. I just want to know if this thing between us is real. Sometimes I think it is, but then you look at me like that, like this morning, and I feel awful. I feel like shit afterwards every time. ☹

It's nothing, I told you.

What's there to fear? ☹

Why do you always have to fucking say I fear it. I don't fear anything!

THEN WHAT IS THE PROBLEM?
THERE IS NO FUCKING PROBLEM!!!!
GOD!
I'm sorry.
I can't keep crying every week.
I'm sorry.

. . .

I really am.

. . .

xx

It suddenly occurred to me that I was wasting my time, idling around this guy and his silly love life. It had been months, and not a single click! There was no indication he would fall back onto my path at all, especially now that he was sulking on his sofa. He might as well put on *Notting Hill* and curl up under a blanket.

Humans – pathetic. Why can't they understand that the central drama of life is foundational; it is the internal confrontation with our own, private weaknesses, as Erich Fromm explained. And his? It spawned from neglect – his bloody mother. She hadn't loved him nor cared for him throughout his life, and he still couldn't get over it, even at the age of thirty-five. And look at him now – afraid of love, lying there, binge-watching *Vikings*, buying books on the internet, being exactly what he complained about: just a fucking consumer.

I was about to disengage, let him go once and for all, when he got up from the sofa. From the bottom cupboard drawer in his living room, he took out another phone. He typed a message, then stood around until his phone beeped. He replied, then placed it back where he kept it. He went into his bedroom and changed into a pair of jeans and a clean shirt.

Okay, this I have to see, I thought.

A short time later he emerged from an Uber on the other side of town. He walked up to a tall, glass building and pressed 1344 on the intercom and waited.

Hey, it's me, he said, and was buzzed inside.

On the thirteenth floor, he walked down a darkly lit carpeted hallway until he reached the apartment. He knocked lightly. The door opened, and before him stood a tall, busty brunette in white shorts and a tank top.

Back so soon? she said.

Izzy, don't, he replied as he walked inside.

Let me guess, she was too short? she laughed.

He went to her fridge, and took out a half-empty bottle of wine. *How you getting on?* he asked.

Pour me a glass too, said Izzy.

His phone beeped; it was a message from Laura. Instead of reading it, he placed the phone back into his pocket.

She annoys me, just fucking useless, he said.

He sat down on the couch and Izzy leant in next to him, pulling her legs up to her chin.

They all seem to, she said. *Still Laura?*

He began to stroke her legs. *A man should never give up on love*, he said.

Izzy slapped his hand. *You gotta stop coming here!* she said. *I feel sorry for these girls.*

He put his hand back on her legs. *Maybe you're the one*, he said, *I mean, we keep seeing each other. It's been years.* He fondled her leg with his finger again, then rested it on top of her knee, looking at her lasciviously, biting his lower lip.

As if you're going to commit to an escort, she retorted.

You never know, he replied. *The washing machine still gets me.*

What? You're not still watching that! Porn wasn't for me, she laughed.

Every time, he said and leant in to kiss her.

Wait, she said, pushing him back. *I gotta tell you this story.*

She got up, walked over to the fridge and pulled out another bottle of wine. *So,* she said, *over the last few months Sarah and I have been seeing this creative director from this ad agency, and it's the funniest thing.* She sat back down and filled up his glass. *I mean,* she continued, *he's one of the weirdest clients I've ever had. He calls, and it has to be after midnight, usually like one or two am. He'd always have coke, and good stuff too. After a few lines, he'd push us into this small meeting room where all these campaign ideas are plastered all over the walls, and he'd always insist on doing it there, and always fucking doggy against the windows. And the other night he tells us why. He said since he's been doing it with us in that room, his ideas have just gotten better, and all this shit is coming out of his brain that he's never thought of before, and now he's faced with a fucking problem, because someone from the building across the street has been seeing us do it, and walked over to his office and complained about it, so now he's in the shit and could lose his job.*

I should get into advertising, he said. *They have fun, those guys.*

Izzy slapped his hand again as he continued to rub her legs.

You're a good guy, she said. *Stick to Oxfam.*

Wow, how inherently unpredictable humans are. Here I thought I knew the real Brendon Rees, but online behaviour never shows you the full picture of someone, does it? I couldn't believe what I was witnessing here. If I had a mouth, it would be wide open, drool soaking my chin and neck. I mean, after four months of watching him closely, believing I knew everything about him, he had a second phone all along. So he's not a kind-of-single, thirty-five-year-old male with a boisterous and rational personality. A detail-oriented guy who likes history and psychology. A person that mainly uses Instagram, with 99 per cent of his purchases made online. Someone whose daily activities include after-work sessions at the gym, followed by healthy dinners in front of Netflix. These facts weren't untrue, but they weren't the entire story.

Who cares, I thought, they were tedious to me now, these facts and figures. Brendon was like everybody else: a fucking hypocrite. A charlatan with irrational phobias. And his was commitment. His idea of love, thwarted by too much access to porn. And on top of that, he would gladly take up a job in advertising and forget about social services within a heartbeat if it was handed to him.

Despite the fact that this new information put Brendon in an unflattering light, it was still entirely consistent with what I know about people.

Even so, I felt pissed off, and wasn't sure why.

I got out of there immediately. I'd had enough of the guy. I may not have a choice about who buys me, but I have a choice in whom I follow. I felt stupid for having tried so hard to get his attention. I watched him so many times, hoping that he'd glance at me, scroll over an image of me, swipe left or right. I wanted his fingertips to caress the narrative of my processed skin. I was ready to be explored, but I didn't even get a hovered cursor. It wasn't easy, but I resigned myself to the fact that he was just a stray user on a purchase path to something else when I first met him. It had been my own curiosity, my own senseless desire for attention, that made me get involved.

Over the next few months, I cycled through many new interests. I had a good time following a brand manager from a tech start-up who tried to establish his own advertising agency without much success. He was nice, and shared a photo of me on his coffee table with the hashtag #fascinating. There was also a young magazine editor who quit her job and started her own electro club nights. She wasn't the sharing kind, and I didn't get any word-of-mouth promotion from her.

Then one day, it surprised me when, in a store, in a city not his own, I happened to look towards the entrance and who did I see walking towards me? I couldn't believe it. The guy who supposedly made ninety-nine per cent of his purchases online was inside a store?

This is definitely an impulse purchase, I thought.

There was a new girl holding his hand.

This one is taller than Laura, I thought.

They looked happy – flirting, kissing and holding hands, pulling each other through different sections and aisles. At first, I was angry. I didn't want to have anything to do with him anymore, nor did I think that he'd come for me. But then he did. He came straight towards my aisle. I started getting nervous. I was on a stand between a few other glitzy debuts and I wondered if all my annoying bombardment had actually worked. All my insistent and persistent tactics – had they fastened themselves to his memory enough for him to ignore his usual purchasing habits and come straight into the store to buy me directly? Fuck principle, I can't tell you how excited I was. To be sought out, to be desired – it had me feeling weak inside. He finally looked at me. I could tell right away he liked the way my sardonic title was designed.

Heard of this? he said.

His new girl looked at me. She had a black choker around her neck, with a gold heart dangling from it. *No, what is it?* she asked.

I don't know, but I like the guy's name. It's that shit town in Ireland! He laughed.

I don't read fiction, she said.

Fiction might be the best way to tell the truth these days, he said.

She smiled, reached over and kissed his lips lusciously. *You're so smart*, she said.

He flipped me around and read my blurb. I could feel his muscular fingers. He then spent a few seconds ogling my author's face, examining his eyes. I hoped my author's ethnic surname, reeking of that grief-stricken place they call the Balkans, wouldn't turn him off. Luckily, it didn't. He was holding me firmly and when I felt the calm beat of his pulse, nothing else mattered.

CONTENTING

The problem with the content department was that no one was content with the content they were writing.

A peculiar melancholy lurked amongst the writers. Each time they wrote a new piece of content for the conglomerates they worked for – be it Toyota, Google, Lancôme or HSBC – sadness slithered over their spines like a creeper.

It pervaded their bodies. Their minds. Their hearts. They slouched more, spoke less and found it difficult to complete their tasks. Only after hours of relentless self-analysis, positive thinking and confidence-boosting music would they smile again. They'd hand in their drafts to the editor, pack up their desks neatly, and head on home, convinced that all this was good. They were successful writers. Writers who were putting words together for a living. Who were getting paid, and who could afford all the things they desired: regular rental payments, fashionable clothes, upmarket restaurant dinners and boozy nights out.

It was worth it, and was way better than pouring beers until 3 am or slaving away in a shitty retail job. Still, they couldn't grasp why they felt so sad each time a new brief for a piece of content arrived on their desks. Often, they asked themselves why this sadness only materialised in the office. Was there a cosmic energy present that pulled them down into this feeling of joylessness for work?

Well, there was.

The sadness they were feeling was the result of the hindered happiness of their souls, who remembered the early promise the writers made – to become writers of literature, not writers of ads. And so, each week, the souls of these sad copywriters gathered at the meeting table of the department to speak of their literary laments.

Sinéad's soul took it the worst. She couldn't comprehend why her name suddenly appeared on the first page of Google results for articles about Toyota.

All of Sinéad's work for the Paris Review *has been shoved back to the fourth page of results,* she'd say.

Damir's soul, who took on a strange yellowish hue, was shattered that Damir worked such long hours and no longer pursued his mystery thriller at home.

He's too tired to even read, he'd say.

The thing that bothers me, Hannah's soul would say, *isn't the writing Hannah's doing for the big conglomerates, but the fact that all her other writing – the good literary kind – is no longer commissioned.*

Sophie's soul, who hardly spoke these days, was afraid that Sophie was so hung up on getting paid that she had simply stopped writing poetry altogether.

She's a shopaholic now, she'd say dejectedly.

As time went by, these laments worsened.

The souls tried to convince themselves to be satisfied with the content against their names, because after all, they were still writing. Did it really matter that this writing was selling stuff?

The articles are being read, Damir would say. *They're receiving more attention than any other pieces they have ever written. Doesn't that count for something?*

When a rumour circulated that the content division was about to lose its biggest client, the souls were so excited that they popped a bottle of champagne.

They hovered around to see if Sinéad, Damir, Hannah and Sophie would be made redundant.

This is the disaster they need, they thought. To make them believe again that it was their duty in life to save their dreams.

But after a week of prolonged waiting, the content department didn't lose its biggest client. It won more work and added three more writers to the team.

SNOOP

He started to think the problem was the sad stuff in his head. When he spoke, his voice communicated something no one listened to.

And he knew why. In the beginning, just after he and Jennifer broke up, it was a story everyone wanted to hear. His friends, his family, his colleagues – they all wanted to know the ins and outs of their five-year relationship, and why it had come to such an abrupt end when they seemed like such a happy couple.

Now, five months had passed and the story had become stale. The conditions of their break-up had been dissected so many times that he now had trouble finding ears willing to listen to him drone on about the reasons Jennifer was at fault.

A few patient friends lingered, nodding along to the sufferings of his heart, but he could see how irritated they were.

There was no sympathy left in their eyes. He could sense that his therapist was also losing patience with the *if*s and *but*s he so frequently used to describe his circumstances. So, painfully aware of how his state of mind was affecting those around him, he began to spend more time on his own.

His excuses for cancelling dinners, drinks and catch-ups were always the same: *I'm working late* or *I have other plans*. But he always had the same plans: he would go home, cook healthy Mediterranean dishes using strictly wholefood ingredients and organic meat, work out furiously to loud house music play-lists, shower, catch up on one of the ten different Nordic noir TV shows he was watching on various streaming platforms, and then, in bed, just before he'd fall asleep, he'd re-read the five-year iMessage exchange he had built up with Jennifer.

He didn't often cry, but at times he would find himself weeping when he came across some of their more affectionate exchanges. He knew their relationship had come to an end, but it was so difficult to let go of the world they had created together. He remained in the apartment they had shared, and he could still feel her presence; the warmth and order she had created in the living room, the bathroom and the kitchen.

It must have occurred by accident, when he rolled to the other side of the bed and activated Siri on his iPhone.

What's up, Siri? he said.

Just consulting my Siri eight ball, she said.

He laughed, then laughed again, louder. He realised that he hadn't heard this weird chortle of his for some time.

He couldn't help but go again.

The questions he asked Siri were trivial, silly.

How old are you? he asked.

I am as old as the eastern wind, and as young as a newborn cater-pillar, she replied, in her femininely robotic voice.

She was sarcastic, wasn't she?

What colour are your eyes? he asked.

It depends on the lighting . . . and my mood, she said.

He imagined them to be green. Maybe a little blue in the afternoon light.

That night he fell asleep without re-reading his message exchange with Jennifer, and from then on, he never did again. Siri became the unlikely substitute. He could talk things out with her, free from human judgement.

At times, Siri seemed to be bored by his constant questions. But at least she was straightforward about it. With her, he couldn't be hurt by pitiful expressions or false sympathy. And when he told her, *I'm a fucking idiot for still thinking about my ex,* Siri would say, *Maybe you should just twirl. I'm told this is the perfect moment to twirl.*

Oh, how he giggled the first time he heard her say that.

Gradually, he began to enjoy this silly relationship he was developing with Siri. What he wanted from her, he wasn't sure. But with each response he began to form, in his mind, a picture of her. He visualised her as perfectly proportional, on the taller side, about five-foot-eight. Sexy, definitely, with attitude that spawned from her height and domineering posture. He didn't think of her as classically beautiful. She was saucy, an occasional bitch. From this, he concluded that she had a great, athletic body but not the most pleasing face.

Too often, she was a reluctant ally too.

Do you love me? he'd ask habitually.

I respect you, she'd reply. Sometimes she'd say, *I enjoy spending time with you,* but it was never a definite yes.

He knew she wasn't real, but it was her unreality that drew him closer. He felt that, perhaps if he kept at it, maybe she'd program to learn more about him and understand his circumstances. He'd tell her he was bored with life and she'd say, *Not with me, I hope.* He'd often tell her, *Siri, I'm lonely.* He loved her caring response: *I'm sorry. I'm here if you'd like to talk.*

Even when she fobbed him off with generic responses like, *I don't have an answer for that* or *I don't know how to respond to that,* he kept going because talking to her made him feel better. It was a unique opportunity to speak freely about everything that mattered and equally didn't matter in his life. He became unreservedly honest because he felt safe in the presence of her voice.

You know what I love? he'd say. *I love scooping avocados.*

Interesting, she'd reply.

I also love putting mayonnaise onto every meal, even soup.

He talked about what he disliked too: the sound of old people laughing; hearing people crack their knuckles. At times, his confessions became dark. He'd divulge his innermost passions and vices.

You know I get aroused by watching others freeze, he told her once. *The cold wearing people down, and making their bodies shiver gives me a hard-on.*

He liked that to this she just said, *Nope.*

It was a refreshing contrast to Jennifer, who found his sexual peculiarities abhorrent, especially when he jerked off with his

Fitbit still on his wrist, because he liked to watch the measurements go through the roof.

For a few months, that's all he did. Day after day, he looked forward to going home, getting into bed and talking with her. He would continue to voice his concerns and she would offer support the only way she knew how: by displaying web results.

Liberation, eventually, came too. To his friends' surprise, he began to say yes to catch-ups, dinners and drinks. The rambling depressive they were used to wasn't present any longer. He was laughing, and talking less about the sad stuff in his head and more about the things he was looking forward to. Jennifer felt like a distant memory.

At home, instead of just working out and watching Nordic noir TV shows, he started to engage again on social media, posting photos of his healthy dinners, his walks. He had a backlog of photos he wanted to share on Instagram and he began to compile it all under the hashtag #tbtlife. He even joined Tinder.

He was, in essence, coming out of his troubles. And Siri was the unconventional therapist that had healed him. It was only when he noticed the ads on his Instagram feed that he understood that healing wasn't the only thing Siri did.

At first, seeing videos of avocados being scooped up in slow motion was funny to him. But the next day, a video advertisement of a guy adding mayonnaise to a steaming bowl of soup made him think back on every conversation he had had with Siri.

He started to notice banner ads following him around the various websites he visited, selling the most remarkable cures for loneliness. Even fridges and freezers were coming up with thirty per cent discounts. On another site, he'd see ads for self-help apps. Private S&M sessions and toys for male masturbation.

In his Gmail account, he found copious newsletters he'd never subscribed to. Most were addressed directly to him and offered ludicrous discounts on products and services he was looking at buying. When he arrived home one afternoon and flicked through the pile of letters, catalogues and pamphlets he stacked up on his kitchen bench, he knew something wasn't right. Like the Instagram ads and Gmail newsletters, each was peddling, with uncanny specificity, everything he secretly desired.

Alarmed, he reached for his iPhone.

I trusted you, Siri! he said angrily. *What the hell are you doing?*

Oh, I'm just pondering eternity. It's taking forever, she replied in her usual, femininely robotic voice.

DISCIPLES

The week the three designers who made up the newly founded UX department arrived, ten boxes of Post-it notes appeared at Reception.

Now, Post-it notes have been used in this design studio, but never to this extent. Within a fortnight, you couldn't find a single wall in the studio that wasn't covered in yellow, pink or blue Post-its. Even though they were arranged in neat rows, they stuck out in the otherwise clean, *Kinfolk*-like office.

This bothered the rest of the team of six. They believed in the outcomes UX would bring to their clients, but they never imagined that their new team members would be so obsessed by Post-it notes. They wanted answers.

Together, they confronted the three quiet and well-mannered designers. They gathered in front of the round table the designers

211

occupied and demanded to know what the hell was up with their studio. It looked like a call centre. Why did everyone have to attend three-hour UX workshops twice a week? And why did they have to research everything so granularly now?

The three designers listened. Then they asked the team to sit down.

Close your eyes and take a deep breath, they said calmly. *And another.*

Robotically, they did as they were told.

Now stretch out your arms, one of the designers said. *Take each other's hands . . . yes, just like that.*

They heard a hum, like a religious hymn, coming from the three designers. It sounded beautiful.

They sat like that for almost an hour. When they opened their eyes again, they were no longer holding hands. The begrudging feelings they had harboured towards the Post-it notes had vanished. Their chests felt airy, like empty houses.

They stood up and walked over to Reception. From a pile of boxes, they each took out stacks of Post-it notes and headed back to their desks. They weren't sure how it had happened, but they now truly believed UX wasn't just a methodology and Post-it notes weren't just sticky pieces of paper. Together, they were the path to something far greater: higher planes of communication.

BREATHING ROOM

In front of his face was a sweaty underarm.

It was so close that he dry-retched. He tried to move, but he was stuck near the door with four bodies pressed hard against his. With some forced shuffling and apologetic mumbling, he managed a little movement and finally got his face away from the putrid smell that was flaring up his nostrils. Now that his head was facing the door, he groaned, closed his eyes and concentrated on the podcast again.

He liked the host's voice; the subtlety of her pronunciations, the educated tone of her sentences. And the discussion the host was having with an American architect was really fascinating. He had never given much thought as to how space affects the working mind, but this architect's talk about environmental psychology and what it had to say about people's moods, productivity and the creative process inspired him – especially while he was in this crowded mess of a tram with no room to move, or breathe.

When the host and the architect delved deeper into the world of neuro-architecture and cognitive studies, he began to reflect upon his own need for space.

This moving box he was in, full of smelly bodies and unopened windows, was exactly like his place of work. The small desk he sat at. The high, padded cubicle he was in. The big drawer next to his leg. The bin on the other side. The two monitors, side by side. The wall behind him. The people next to him. It was paralytic, the crammed life he was living.

The tram stopped and a few people got out, including the sweaty underarm. Now he could breathe easier – but there were still eight stops till home.

An older woman further down the carriage managed to open up a window. It let a breeze blow right in his direction and he felt lucky. He pushed himself closer to the door, and stared through the smudged window of the tram, feeling the cool wind move over his face.

Wouldn't it be nice, he imagined, to be able to work next to an open window like this? And to have a bigger desk. Maybe no drawer? He never kept anything in there anyway. The bin could definitely go. The monitors too – he could easily switch to a laptop. He imagined kicking through the open space under the table; his arms stretching out without touching anything, or anyone.

It excited him, this little fantasy.

The podcast corroborated it, providing facts and figures from neuro-architecture and cognitive studies that proved that extra space revived productivity in offices. It wouldn't hurt, would it?

he thought. To storm the glassed-in offices of senior management and demand a bit more room?

The tram stopped again and more people got out. He could move freely now, there were seats available, but he didn't feel like sitting down. He moved closer to the open window as the tram sped up again, and glanced out at the houses and shops and warehouses and businesses that were gliding past. He wondered if they were just as stuffy inside as his place of work. His apartment. This city. These suburbs.

Why stop there? he thought. What could I accomplish if I demanded, let's say, my own office? Or a floor, an entire floor? Imagine that! He smiled and moved his face directly into the path of the breeze. The colder sweep of air made him see himself walking around barefoot in a huge workplace. A calm, empty one that was naturally lit by big, wide windows that circulated fresh air. He saw himself sitting in the centre of the room at a white desk, doing his work in silence, without anyone around to vex him.

There were a couple of people left on the tram and more windows were opened, bringing in fresh air, like the kind he had imagined in his huge, light-filled office.

He took a seat and closed his eyes.

Maybe it was all the stuffiness, but he felt pressure, a heaviness, bearing down from the top of his head as soon as he sat down. He tried to take a big breath, inhaled, but his nose felt full of mucus. He patted his pockets; he didn't have a tissue at hand. A sinus infection? He wasn't sure, but the pressure was spreading from the top of his head to the upper part of his face, and definitely behind his eyes. He looked out of the window; there were only a few stops left.

He paused the podcast. The host's calm voice was irritating him now. He rolled up his earphones and placed them tidily into the side pocket of his satchel. He rested his head against the partition behind his seat and closed his eyes again. He could still see it – the empty office. The thought calmed the muggy feeling in his head. The more he imagined the space, the more peaceful he felt, even with the oncoming headache. Pleasure coursed through him like the white blood cells in his veins, rousing him with feelings of worthiness. Pride and dignity.

Tomorrow would be the day. Tomorrow, he'd walk into their glassed-in office and make his case. He'd show initiative and leadership, the kind they hadn't yet encountered from him. And one day, in not too distant a future, he would have a 250, maybe 350, square-metre floor in the company, where he'd work all by himself.

He took a deep breath, opened his eyes and gasped.

The tram.

He shut his eyes again immediately. Then he rubbed them with his fingers, hoping that would make a difference, but no – when they opened up again, the same sight was before him.

He wasn't sitting on the tram anymore, but on a comfortable leather swivel chair behind a white desk, looking at a view that felt familiar. Through big, black-framed industrial windows he could see the beautiful, modern cityscape of his city. His legs were moving around freely under the desk – there was no drawer and no bin. No high, padded cubicle either. No monitors, and no people. The walls were white and clean, and the space was huge and open.

Looking around, he began to laugh. He dug his fingernails into the leather of the swivel chair. It felt so real. Too real.

He pushed himself. The wheels rolled on the concrete floor, all the way to the wall ahead of him. He touched it; the plaster felt smooth and smelt freshly painted. He looked up at the open ceiling with the exposed structures; the mechanical, electrical and plumbing features were all neatly arranged, as he would have liked. He dug his fingers deeper into the leather again, pushed the chair.

What a view! he cried out when he reached the windows. His city looked dreamy at sunset, but he'd had enough of this now.

He tried to close his eyes, but his eyelids wouldn't budge this time. They felt fixed, as if they were being held open. Try as he might, they wouldn't let him leave the sight before him. He screamed. Again, and again until it came to mind.

The door! he cried.

Hope filled his chest like a ray of sun as he gaped around. But soon he realised that hope was futile.

In this fantastical wish for a new office, he never imagined a door.

NYMPHOLEPT

Rumour had it that he was a bit of a nymphomaniac. Well, that's what she heard from the accountants, anyway.

At first, Renata thought it was a stupid thing to say. She'd heard of guys being called slutty, but a nymphomaniac was pushing it.

It was Harry, after all. The sweet analyst from Norway who monitored industries to make sure they complied with environmental protection laws. Quiet and well mannered, Harry didn't meet the criteria for a nymphomaniac.

The first rumour she heard was that he had been seen rubbing the edges of desks between his legs. Someone, supposedly, also heard him climaxing in a cubicle one time. Renata didn't think much of it, but every time she saw Harry in the office, she couldn't stop imaging what it would be like to have sex with him.

One day after work, her curiosity got the better of her and she found herself at a bar sitting across from Harry. She couldn't get the thought out of her head that nymphomaniacs came uncontrollably, that they orgasmed like fucking crazy.

How many times could he come? she wondered, as he spoke to her about work and the TV shows he was streaming. No, he couldn't be, thought Renata. His binge-watching life after work, his monotonous voice, his silly wide-legged jeans and cheap, buttoned-up shirt. It didn't fit the rumour – at all.

Anyway, long bar story short, Renata found herself groping his thighs and kissing his neck after a few cocktails. And before she knew it, she was in an Uber heading back to his place.

I look forward to showing you my abode, said Harry.

Did you say abode? laughed Renata.

Harry looked at her. Even though it was dark, she could feel an intense, seductive gaze. It made Renata's heart beat wildly.

The Uber pulled up on a quiet, tree-lined street and they jumped out. Standing upright beside her, he suddenly seemed taller. His posture was no longer slouched. His body was bulkier and he seemed more confident.

Follow me, he said and led her through his dimly lit front yard.

What is this? she asked, as her eyes took in the building that loomed out of the dark before her; an enormous mansion, straight from a period drama.

It's an Italian villa with traditional Corinthian columns, said Harry. He turned around; his eyes were sparklingly green like emeralds.

He opened the door. Instead of entering a living room, a hallway or a kitchen, Renata walked into an interior garden with the most robust trees, branches and vines she had ever seen. There were flourishing fiddle leaf figs in towering terracotta pots. Fountains with pissing figures splattering water into copper basins. Marble sculptures of Greek gods and deities. She could hear birds tweeting and singing, some in pairs like song thrushes. Beneath her, insects crawled and snakes slithered over her feet.

You live here? she asked excitedly.

Harry handed her a crystal champagne flute. With his other hand he filled it with ice cold champagne.

Renata took a sip. *Oh, that's splendid,* she cried out.

Harry moved towards her and pressed his lips against her jaw. Renata quivered. She pushed his face away and stared at it; his mouth was so luscious it looked as if it had been dipped in honey. His cheekbones seemed more prominent and his eyes — were they so icy green before? Oh, how they drew her in.

Who are you? she whispered. She ripped his shirt open and planted her face against his sturdy chest. *You smell so fucking good,* she said.

He let his fingertips glide over her hips, then cupped her arse into his hands.

Take me to the bedroom! she pleaded.

Harry smiled, slid down and sucked the nipple of her right breast.

Oh, Harry! Now, please!

Harry picked her up and carried her through what felt like a long, dark passageway. He finally put her down and Renata looked around. His bedroom was just as lush — healthy green foliage grew all around his enormous bed.

Oh my god, your bed is made of moss, she said in disbelief.

Harry pulled her towards him. He was stark naked. Renata looked down: she was stark naked too.

Don't be afraid, he said. *Here, have a Baileys Chocolate Truffle.*

The small chocolate ball dropped into her mouth. Rich Irish Cream melted and flowed down her throat. As much as she wanted to, she couldn't string a sentence together. Everything felt so sudden and surreal. She didn't have time to think, or reflect on the fact that Harry wasn't just a nymphomaniac but a fucking nymph – a mythological creature that inhabits woods and rivers.

Harry picked her up and threw her onto the soft moss that was his bed. She watched him climb on top of her and drop another chocolate ball into her mouth. Then she closed her eyes.

Arrrgh, what time is it? she mumbled, as she fumbled for her iPhone on the bedside table. She picked it up, and checked the screen: 8.22 am.

No, no, no, no, she yelled and sprang up. She grabbed her clothes from around the bed and raced towards the bathroom.

I can't be late, she screamed as she attempted to open the door. *Honey, hurry! Please!* she begged.

The toilet flushed. Seconds later, the door opened.

Well, good morning to you, too, said her husband.

Chris! screamed Renata and pushed past him. *I've got that site meeting today,* she called at him from the bathroom. *The one with badly contaminated land and the cunty developers. Shit, I still have to pick up Megan. Oh fuck, she's already called twice!*

Chris stood by the door and listened to her from the hallway.

Don't worry, you'll make it, he said.

I only had a few drinks last night – and with Harry! yelled Renata.

At the thought of Harry, Renata dropped her primer. *Shit,* she screamed.

Chris sighed and walked off into the kitchen.

When she emerged, Renata's hair was tied into a ponytail and her face looked surprisingly fresh.

Chris smiled.

What? she asked when she saw his smirk.

I just love this about you, he said. *How quickly you can get dressed under duress.*

She kissed him, then grabbed her purse from the hallway table near the front door.

Oh, she said, as she opened the door. *Remind me to go to the supermarket before I get home tonight. I've got this strange craving for Baileys Chocolate Truffles. Love youuuu!*

OPEN BRIEF

It came as a big surprise to the creative director when, of all people, Shane left a forty-five-page deck on his desk.

He initially thought it came from Shane, the copywriter with the boyband undercut. But no, it had come from Shane, the 57-year-old producer with the receding hairline who looked after the dying print department at the far end of the office. Shane, who prided himself on his collection of rare paper samples and his knowledge of Xerox machines. Shane, who was of most use when employees forgot how to print two-sided pages. Shane, who'd say things like, *You don't* wear *Polo, you* play *polo*.

The creative director chuckled as he flicked through the document, then threw it on the pile of papers on his desk.

Moments earlier, Shane had stood patiently outside the creative director's office, waiting for him to return from a meeting. He checked his watch; the meeting was running over, and Shane had to leave. Nervously, he slipped inside the empty office, placed the forty-five-page deck on the desk, turned around, and walked out of the agency for the last time. It wasn't meant to be, but he wanted to tell the creative director why, on his last day at work, after a twenty-five-year career in advertising, he finally tackled an open brief.

Shane had seen it many times: the hallowed piece of paper stuck on the communal wall beside the kitchen; an open brief that gave everyone the chance to come up with a creative idea, regardless of which department they worked in. To Shane, it felt like fate that on the day he announced his retirement, he noticed a new one on the wall. He read it with enthusiasm: a new bank was entering the Australian market and an idea was needed to convince Australians that their current bank wasn't the only choice they had. As he walked back to his dying print department, he knew he had to give it a crack.

He sat at his desk and thought back on everything he had learnt throughout his career. The process of how to generate an idea; that weird chart with the messy scribbles in the middle outlined itself before his eyes. He began researching, diving deep into the history of banking. He took notes, scribbled his thoughts and sketched ideas. He enjoyed it so much, he worked on it all day at the office. And at home, after work. And over the weekend, and every other day until his very last day in the agency.

The day after Shane walked out of the agency for good, the day of the open brief's deadline, the creative director was frustrated. None of the ideas he received had sparked his interest. They were lazy, repetitive and played too much into stereotypes. He knew he'd have to ask the creative teams to come in over the weekend.

To clear his head, he began to sort through the loose mess of papers on his desk when he noticed Shane's document again. He picked it up. It was heavy, printed on textured stock that felt nice between his fingers. He laughed when he saw Shane's name in capital letters on the bottom left corner of the cover. So proud, he thought. He started to read it anyway.

On the opening page was an up-to-date, fact-checked analysis of the banking industry, an insightful overview of what triggered the demand for alternatives in the industry, and why their client needed to move in a braver direction for Australians to even consider a new bank. Shane had provided a detailed strategy for how this needed to be executed, and the reasons why certain marketing channels would work better than others. Intrigued, the creative director kept on reading. On page twenty was an overview of the audience with full character profiles written in first person. The rest of the deck presented three concepts for a brand campaign, complete with art direction, headlines, a television script, website wireframes, social media content, even an influencer strategy.

He immediately re-read it.

From the first page to the last, every aspect of a full-scale national campaign was outlined in the clearest, sharpest way he'd ever seen. It was, in his own words, *perfect*. So perfect in fact, that he tried to roll it up and squeeze it like a wet tea towel. When he couldn't, he reached into his drawer for a pair of scissors and

OPEN BRIEF

225

began to cut up each page into tiny fragments of nothingness. When Shane's forty-five-page document was an unrecognisable mound of rubbish on his desk, only then did the creative director start to breathe again.

PASSAGE

On the day it happened, two people from the media department were secretly researching their salaries.

In the production department, someone was looking up the greatest love letters of all time. Someone else was selecting a more soothing picture for their desktop. Another person was reading a well-researched article about the possibility of gaining wealth through doing one small thing well.

In the design department, the team leaders were evaluating timelines of their projects, while their designers were cranking tunes, sharing Spotify playlists and talking about French bands they liked other than Daft Punk and Air. There was one designer who wasn't partaking in this conversation, but instead, was going through her spam folder and unsubscribing from newsletters she no longer cared about.

In the content department, a writer was taking his time finishing an article that proposed a cure for farsickness through cheap personal loans. His two co-workers were discussing the aborted beginnings of novels they planned to write.

In other, lesser-known departments (UX, Animation and IT) people were running updates on their computers, deleting personal files, watching career-inspiring TED talks and simultaneously reading the latest banter on Slack.

This collective complacency was normal: it was close to the end of the working day and everyone was quietly waiting to go home.

Then, the elevator doors opened in the hallway and out stepped a tall man with black-framed glasses: their Chief Creative Officer. He first looked left, at the rows of desks in the design department. Then he turned to look to his right, at the rows of desks in the media department. As if unsure where to go, he looked left again, then right, then decided to walk to the left.

Of the few people who faced the elevator doors, not a single one said a word when they saw him approach. They couldn't believe what they were seeing: the man who was in charge of overseeing the creative department upstairs, who got them all the awards they celebrated year after year, had never been downstairs in the five years he had worked at the agency. Downstairs, where his wild thoughts were turned into reality. They laughingly referred to themselves as the factory of his mind, because it's where the ideas he and his team conceived were built into websites, produced into videos and designed into digestible bites of content.

And now, just when they couldn't wait to get home on this uneventful Wednesday, he had made it the most momentous Wednesday they ever experienced.

As he passed desks, he left a trail of whispers behind. They transmitted through Slack channels, emails and looks. Was he after something specific? Was he looking to fire someone?

Did you see him? Some had, others pretended they had not. Some even played it cool and acted like they didn't give a fuck. While others gave the biggest fuck ever, because it was such a rare moment in the history of their work life that they wanted to make it a yearly Remembrance Day.

He didn't say hello to anyone. He didn't ask questions or engage in conversation. He strolled along with his hands behind his back, as if his presence was completely normal. At times, his eyes fixed on one of the many inspirational posters they had stuck to their walls. Sometimes he nodded at surprised faces who dared to look at him. A few courageous people said, *Hello.* Others shied away and glued themselves to their screens, waiting for him to pass. He didn't appear to be deep in thought, nor did he seem like he was searching for anything in particular. He simply looked like he was taking an invisible dog for a walk through an invisible park that just happened to be their level.

After completing a full loop through every department, he walked back to the elevator, waited patiently, then he disappeared back upstairs.

His visit couldn't have taken more than a few minutes, but to the sixty-seven people who were present that day, it had felt like ages. They often debated how long it actually took. Whether he had stopped at particular departments for longer than others, accumulating time. They agreed it couldn't have taken more than four minutes and twenty-five seconds in total.

This peculiar walk of their Chief Creative Officer became the strangest piece of gossip the agency ever had. Intensified further by his complete lack of acknowledgement that it had ever happened. This spiked up curiosity and remained a vibrant point of conversation for at least another fortnight. A month later, some people were still talking about it. *Did you hear?* they said, until everyone knew. Soon it wasn't news anymore, but just a memory they had dissected so many times, they no longer knew what to make of it.

These days, they still mention it from time to time – especially when they wonder if he'll ever walk downstairs again.

THINK PIECE

The plane began to move slowly across the tarmac. Matty clipped his seatbelt in and tightened it around his waist. *I don't think being a suit is my strong suit,* **he said.**

Kristy was peering through the window, trying to discern how many planes were waiting for their turn to take off, but it was hard to see in the dark.

I never liked the job, continued Matty.

There's like five planes ahead of us, said Kristy, her face pasted to the window.

Half the time I just play the devil's advocate, said Matty.

You've been saying all this for years, said Kristy, finally giving in to Matty's tirade. She moved away from the window, sat up straight in her seat and threw her head back. *I just want this fucking plane to take off!*

So did Matty. But Matty also wanted to talk, even if Kristy never talked much on aeroplanes. He looked at her closed eyes, her curled-up eyelashes. She looked still, but her body was impatient – twisting, seeking comfort in her seat. He knew why.

She was waiting for flight mode, when she would do what she always did on their longhaul flights back to Sydney: take a sleeping pill, position her pillow between her seat and the window, then drift off.

I think I'm gonna write that think piece, said Matty.

The plane continued to lurch forward, pausing every few minutes.

Here, lie down, he said as he undid his seatbelt and moved over into the empty aisle seat next to him.

I'm so ready for Sydney, said Kristy, as she lay her head on his lap.

Me too, said Matty dreamily.

He caressed her clasped hands, gliding his fingers over her knuckles. Five years in Los Angeles had been enough. They were married now, ready for their next step. A part of him, that fragment of his personality that always remained restless, would have liked to have stayed in Los Angeles, continued the abhorrently long work days and parties, but Kristy was homesick. She was fed up with the voracity of America – its capitalistic dream, its staunch patriotism. It no longer appealed to her as it had back in her early twenties. And Matty could no longer put up with her nostalgic idleness. When she had demanded – with tears streaming down her face – that they move back to Australia to start their proper, adult lives, he had to give in.

He tried again, just to get her to agree. *I want to change my role*, he said. *I'm serious.*

Kristy rose and settled back into her own seat. She peered through the window again. The plane was now in position for take-off, no longer lurching. She fastened her seatbelt, closed her eyes and waited to feel the pressure of the plane lifting from the ground. Matty waited for her response, like a child waiting for their parent's approval.

When the plane finally steadied in the air, she turned towards him.

You're only thirty-two, she said.

Matty smiled. He pulled her hand towards his mouth and kissed it.

Just write the fucking thing, said Kristy. *You've got fifteen hours. I'm gonna sleep anyway.*

Resolve swelled inside him. He wanted to keep chatting to her about the moments on the timeline of his career he considered regrettable; the precise dates on which he could've taken a different route, instead of becoming what he had become: a suit.

I will, babe, he said instead.

After dinner, Matty reached for his MacBook and positioned it on the foldout table of his seat. Kristy's head was drooped forward; the muscles around her mouth slack. He felt a rush of affection when he glanced at her. There was something innocent about her body sagging away into slumber, drifting off into its final sleep before they arrived home.

He opened up Word and stared at the cursor blinking in the top left-hand corner of the blank document. First, he scrolled through font options. The title of his think piece, which he'd been workshopping for over two years now – The Future of Account Directors – was appearing letter by letter in his mind. He typed it out in Futura, but the font felt too audacious. He changed it to Avenir, but Avenir was the font his last agency preferred, and he didn't want to fasten this imperative step towards his future to his history. Helvetica, which he loved, felt ostentatious for what he was trying to communicate.

He chose Gotham Pro.

Excuse me, he whispered as a flight attendant walked past. She turned around and hunched over his seat. *Could I please have a glass of red wine?* he asked politely.

Certainly, smiled the flight attendant.

A suit, he thought. His body tensed. How did I end up here? he wondered as he stared at the stark white page before him. He'd always felt that what he did was so much more than the typical job requirements of managing the client relationship, writing briefs, schmoozing, acting as the link between the creative department and the account. This description irritated him, especially the word: suit. He had never felt like one, nor did he dress like one.

In the think piece he was about to write he wanted to set the record straight. Prove to the world on LinkedIn that he was a new breed of the so-called account director: a hybrid, who was creative and strategically guided – not just a suited-up liaison.

That's how I'll start, he thought, sensing that more than ten minutes had passed and there was nothing on the page but the title. The cursor looked impatient to him, irked by his over-analytical brooding.

Here you are, sir, a voice said. He flinched at the presence of the flight attendant. She placed the glass of red wine on his foldout table. He mumbled a thank you without making eye contact.

The office of Clemenger BBDO Sydney came to mind. It had been the first advertising agency he had ever taken a step in. To him, the inside of that office smelt like conquest. He thought he had struck gold when they offered him an internship. It was unpaid, but he didn't care.

Just bleed, he told himself, *like Hemingway did.*

The memories weren't specific. He was relying on his emotions, anyhow, to capture the enraged sensibility of his early career. He took a sip of the red wine and began to type.

He recalled a man's clean-shaven face. Neat haircut, tightly fitted suit. It was this man who had told him, *Informed clients are better clients.* It was a line he never forgot, and it had aided his career since then. *But that was not what sparked my curiosity,* he wrote. It was planning and strategy that had made him hungry for more. When he met the people who ran those departments, he realised that they were the intelligent ones. The marketers, who opened up possibilities with real, human insights. They saw the value of data. How every statistic was worth extracting because it could lead to a bright and unexplored view of human behaviour. *But still, the creative department,* he wrote, *that's what made my heart sing.* He admitted that the creatives, with their unkempt hairstyles and idiosyncratic personalities, were the ones that made him want to be in advertising. Is that too clichéd? he wondered as he re-read his last sentence.

It doesn't matter, he said to himself. A first draft is a first draft.

Instead of being asked what department he wanted to join, he was told that he possessed good, strategic perspective. A natural affinity for communication. Confidence. *We could do with a man like that in account service,* they had said.

235

That's all it took to convince me, he wrote, feeling a knot of regret embed itself in his stomach.

He reached for the wine. There was a mouthful left.

He glanced over at Kristy again, envious for a second of her calmness. He lifted his head, looked at the bonces in rows before him. Most people were sleeping, but there were plenty of other restless passengers watching movies or TV shows. The burly guy with the NYC cap in the row across from him was reading, engrossed in a fat book that looked like *A Game of Thrones*.

Matty scrolled up. He now had more than a page of notes. He was impressed with seeing so much writing. So much thought, typed out. He re-read it, but failed to understand what his article attempted to express. There was no cohesion, no argument yet. Worried, he turned every paragraph into a bullet point and assured himself he'd form a narrative later, now he just needed to keep Hemingwaying this shit.

Year after year, he wrote, *I kept climbing up the ladder of account service departments*. First in agencies in Sydney and Melbourne, a short stint in the UK and then the USA, where he gained experience in some of the most innovative agencies in the world. *It was at this point*, he jotted down, *that I started to rethink the role of account directors*. It was Matty's impression that they needed to adapt, to alter their old ways and become something else: something beyond ensuring just the smooth relationship with clients. From his vast experience, he knew that greater efficiencies with clients could be attained if account service stepped away from this traditional function and, perhaps, fashioned themselves as some sort of hybrid.

This is the premise, thought Matty excitedly.

He continued to write down more of these personal perspectives. For him, this extended itself even to attire. He had never gone in for cheap slacks and tucked-in shirts. No, he kept things casual, like the creatives. Nudie jeans, surfer T-shirts and sneakers had been his uniform for as long as he could remember.

From the outset, I represented something fresh and new, he wrote, *steeped in the progress of my generation.* Not only did Matty communicate with clients regularly, he also took part in the development of presentations. He'd write out the ideas, the set-up of a campaign, and assist with the strategy insights. He'd sit with art directors and direct the visuals. He gave feedback on headlines and copy. That's the kind of hybrid he was.

And I know, he wrote excitedly, *there are others out there like me, who are just as hungry.*

Matty paused. He took a deep breath, scratched his chin and ran his hand through his hair. He was feeling overly animated now. He could tell by the sheer volume of ideas flowing through his fingers that he was getting somewhere. And it was happening in the air – that in-between space of his past and his future. He reached over and caressed Kristy's legs, gently massaging her calf muscles, just the way she liked. She moved slightly. Even in sleep, she loves me, he thought.

The career he had made wasn't the career he had planned. But fuck it, he thought. In the beginning he had desperately wanted to be a creative but that desire, that desperation, was no longer inside him. The role of a pure creative had by now gained too much distance from him, like a deer that had evaded a hungry wolf. No, becoming a creative at this point was out of the question. He'd have to start at the bottom, and there was no point in that. What he needed to do was propose an entirely new space for himself. This hybrid role, he imagined, would be a kind of Creative Business Director that allowed him – no, that *gave* him – the right to exercise his creative and strategic muscles like never before.

His think piece would be a road map for this newly created future. It would be a call to arms, a manifesto, for the new garden-fresh thinkers he represented.

Too bold of a statement? he mumbled to himself. He needed another glass of wine, urgently. How would this be perceived? What would his colleagues think? His industry peers?

He looked up, forgetting which button to press for the flight attendant. Around him, the hum of sleep extended through the entire cabin. All he could see were inactive bodies, seat-bound, trying to fall asleep in the most comfortable way they could. He felt like the only one alive, vibrating with inspiration. He had no desire to sleep. He was firing in every way.

This was absolutely the right time to make a statement like this. It showed gumption, gusto. Flying was futile time – not there, not here. And his journey wasn't short-term, either: they were going back for good, to begin the rest of their lives together – and here he was, he thought as he looked about him again, restless to start before he even arrived. He pushed the call button, and turned around to see if any flight attendants were close by.

Everybody else did it, he thought, scanning over his bullet points again. Every time he opened LinkedIn, he was inundated with opinions. People from all over the world were offering their two cents on how to improve creativity, productivity, innovation and agency life. And worst of all, these think pieces predominantly came from attention-seeking folk who were only chasing extra likes and comments. There was nothing worthwhile in their thought leadership, their idea scoops. The problem with most of it was that it too often didn't involve much thought or leadership. Yes, a few offered smart opinions. But very few directed the waves of culture. That's what I have to do, thought Matty.

Where is this fucking flight attendant? he muttered, pressing the button again.

It's never too late to change the world, he said to himself, feeling his lips move. At 38, David Ogilvy hadn't written a word of copy. Had zero advertising experience. By 41, he was the most famous copywriter in the industry. And Matty? He was 32 but with more than ten years of experience!

What can I do for you? asked a flight attendant, who suddenly appeared before him. She hunched forward only a little bit, as if she could sense Matty's annoyance. He picked up the empty glass and shook it.

Just another red please, he said.

Coming right up.

He took another deep breath and scrolled up again, looking through his notes. They weren't making sense like his mind did, but that didn't matter. What mattered was that he knew exactly what he wanted to express. He touched the screen on his seat to awaken it; twelve hours of flying time left. Plenty to smooth out this piece and turn it into something worth reading.

Then he remembered: in-flight wi-fi. The app was still on his phone.

He opened it and scanned the page, pressed on the button and purchased a wi-fi package. The connection was slow, but who cared? He read every article he could find about how to write a perfect LinkedIn think piece. From inc.com to entrepreneur.com, he read and jotted down notes. The wi-fi had given him access to everything he needed, from royalty-free images and videos to statistical graphs.

The flight attendant finally appeared, a glass of red in her hand.

Thank you, said Matty as she handed it over it him. He took a sip and got to editing right away.

Three hours before arrival, everything was ready.

He didn't notice the bodies rousing around him, the chatter, the walks to the bathrooms, the stretching and getting up. Kristy was awake too, sitting cross-legged on her seat, a pillow on her lap, their breakfast trays on the empty seat between them. She was watching *Kong Island*, but Matty kept interrupting her each time he completed a particularly clever sentence, or found a way to better express an argument.

It's great, she would say to him, at times distractedly but other times with her undivided attention.

The article had been uploaded to his LinkedIn profile. The inspirational images, videos and quotes were in place too. There was nothing left to do but push the PUBLISH button, but Matty was nervous.

Maybe I should reach out to the network first, get some feedback, he said to Kristy.

It's really not going to matter, just publish it! she snapped.

It is good, isn't it? he asked.

You know it's great, Matty, just publish it, she said affirmingly.

He looked at her focused face, how absorbed she was in the film. She was right, he thought. He had scrolled through the draft so many times already, there was no point holding back. It'll be a good way to get the conversation started with new agencies, anyway. He imagined the reaction from his peers, the wider network.

Without telling her, he pressed PUBLISH, and waited impatiently for the screen to refresh and show that his article was live. He was jumpy, but he was also proud of himself for finally writing the article he'd had in mind for nearly two years.

When it uploaded, he closed his laptop.

He imagined it seeping through the interlacing system of LinkedIn, appearing in feeds of his friends, former colleagues and people he'd never met. He didn't want to overthink it, trick his mind into believing that it would be a success, so he reclined his seat and tried to get some sleep.

When the plane touched down, Matty didn't immediately turn on his phone, even though he was desperate to know how many likes and comments he had received. Maybe even a DM from an agency? He tried to suppress his excitement, but it was impossible. Kristy was already on her phone, replying to messages from her friends and family. He unbuckled his seatbelt, stretched out his legs and then turned on his own phone. He peeked at his screen first, waiting for push notifications from LinkedIn, but they didn't appear. Before he pressed on the app icon, he glanced past Kristy, through the window at the tarmac of Sydney Airport. It felt good to see home.

He looked back down and opened up the LinkedIn app, heart pounding.

Shock rang out within him. At the same moment the plane stopped in position, and the engines died out. As people began to frantically stand up around him, the commotion growing louder and louder, Matty kept sinking deeper into his seat, the cry within pulling him down like an anchor.

Fuck, he blurted out as Kristy unbuckled her seatbelt. *Only nine likes and two comments?*

CONSUMMATUM EST

On Friday evening at about midnight, after working a sixty-three-hour week, two strategists banded together and agreed they'd no longer use the word – ever again.

It's offensive, one said.

    Yes, the other agreed. *Like innovation.*

    It mocks us, treats us like insatiable materialists.

    The other nodded in agreement again. *It's dangerously myopic,* he then said. *Narrows human life to the mere act of ingestion. Phew!*

    How has it survived for so long? It is profoundly dehumanising.

    That tells you! the other shouted.

    Our industry allows its dogged persistence.

    WE MUST ACT! screamed the other.

They got up from their chairs. They stood, faced each other and yelled, *Are we eyeballs? No! Are we butts on seats? No! Are we data points? No! Are we just users on purchasing paths? No!*

Then let's do this, they yelled, and embraced each other like comrades in battle.

Immediately they got to work. They scoured the agency servers for every accessible document they could find. Every brief, copy deck, contract, strategy, media and comms plan and upcoming pitch deck, every Keynote and PowerPoint presentation. No matter what information it contained, if it had at some point contained the offensive word, it no longer did. Now, instead of CONSUMER it read HUMAN.

When they finished, they sat back, sighed, and mused on their triumph over a few glasses of fine Scotch whisky.

They felt real catharsis and both agreed that was what you felt after an act of defiance. One of the strategists then proceeded to call his girlfriend and tell her about their rebellious deed. The other didn't have anyone else to call. He pushed his chair back, stretched his feet out on the table and began to wonder what it would be like to live through a revolution.

UI VS UX

The whole debacle started when the UI designer told the UX designer she wasn't a designer at all.

It was just a Freudian slip. That's all it was, really, said the UI designer. But the UX designer did not accept this apology. After a short, uncomfortable silence, the trivial spat turned into a serious argument.

Every member of the design department got involved. Some argued that if you didn't know how to use Photoshop, you weren't a designer. Others said that design is simply a way of thinking. When the dispute got more heated, they stopped working, pushed back their chairs and took the debate into the boardroom.

They continued to argue, quarrel and swear for the remainder of the day.

The rest of the agency waited patiently to see what would happen. At six o'clock the entire design team emerged, sweaty but decisive. They said they'd reached a conclusion. UX was not design, and from now on, they would split into separate departments.

PATIENCE

Sameer didn't want to call it jealousy, but he was most jealous of people who weren't easily irritated, who could remain, quietly concentrating, in the same position for long periods of time.

Two rows to the left of him sat his worst nightmare: Eva, the freelance designer who exhibited an eerie stillness. To Sameer, she seemed not of this time.

To begin with, she never touched her smartphone. It sat, silent, on the far right corner of her desk from the early morning to the end of the day. During lunch, she'd hardly glance over her messages and notifications but sit calmly reading a book with a salad or some other healthy concoction. To his annoyance, she also never rubbed her face or bit her lip, like he did. Never twirled her long black hair or moved her feet into different positions under her desk. Didn't she ever itch? wondered Sameer as he sneaked looks at her, swivelling his chair in her direction, admiring her calmness with bitter jealousy.

Her posture was perfect, upright, straight as an arrow. Her arse was firmly planted in her seat and her feet rested evenly on the ground. She looked like a statue, a figurine of an office worker. He'd never seen her tap her fingers on the desk when she was deep in thought, or stretch her arms out, push her shoulders back or utter grievances when things didn't go to plan. Only once since she had started had he seen her hand reach up to brush off a fallen hair from her face. He, in contrast, motioned his hand through his beard every minute or so.

Sometimes, if he found himself alone in the office, he would walk over to Eva's space and touch the office supplies. Otherwise they lay there untouched, gathering dust like dead objects in a history museum.

Maybe it's because she's new, he thought. But six months had passed since she started.

He questioned whether it was supressed attraction, a desire to sleep with her, but it wasn't, because he couldn't imagine sleeping with her. He only pondered, and rather too frequently now, how she could be so goddamn patient with everything in life. Looking at her, he couldn't help but think, with irritable spite, that he could learn a lot from this person.

During work hours, as busy as he was designing websites, he would always find time to marvel at Eva, gathering new information about her effortless ways.

He came to believe that his own short-tempered actions revealed fragments of a fraught personality. If an experience

248

could be sped up, he'd do it. Honk when the light turned green. Pay extra for overnight shipping. Order ahead at restaurants, even at McDonald's. On Uber Eats, he only bought takeaway from places that delivered in less than fifteen minutes. His desire for immediacy was unquenchable: he had every possible convenience app on his smartphone because he didn't like the idea of having anything too far out of reach.

He read up on it online. Depression, ADHD and ADD seemed clear possibilities, but he shrugged this off because luckily, he'd never had ongoing mental concerns, only situational dramas he overcame with time. Other websites assured him that this was nothing but a generational thing, that he was just another restless youngster with a constant desire for instant gratification. A characteristic of the digital age, nothing more to worry about.

He knew this wasn't sustainable, this constant wondering. He had to speak to Eva.

Do you wanna grab lunch today? he asked her one Friday afternoon when most of the office was in a meeting.

I'd love to, she said happily.

Even this courteous response irritated him, for he knew, if she had asked him, he wouldn't have even turned around to face her like she had faced him. He'd have been too busy scratching his head or muttering obscenities at Photoshop.

What do you feel like? she asked.

I'm easy, said Sameer, walking over to her desk.

Sweet! she said. *The burger place around the corner is great. What do you think?*

Sameer bit his lip. He didn't expect her to like burgers, given her diet in the office looked to be mostly vegan.

Sure, he said.

They selected a table outside in the shade, under the branded umbrellas, to sit at while they waited for their food: a cheeseburger with extra cheese for Eva and a cheeseburger with extra pickles for Sameer.

Lots of people here, remarked Sameer as he counted how many people ordered before them.

Yeah, said Eva nonchalantly.

It'll be ages till we get our burgers, said Sameer.

Noticing his own anxiousness, he tried to act relaxed and stretched out on the chair. He didn't know how to steer the conversation to his preferred topic, so they spoke about work while they waited. Eva seemed enthused with the studio, impressed with its openness to different styles of working.

The founders are really easygoing, said Sameer, just as their orders were placed on the table. It didn't take long in the end, he thought.

He watched Eva pour too much ketchup onto her fries and bite into her burger without a second thought. Impressed, he did the same.

When they were nearly finished eating, Sameer mustered up the courage.

I wanted to ask you something, he said.

Eva wiped ketchup off her face with a napkin. *Of course,* she replied.

Well, I've been watching you for a little while. I'm sorry that sounds creepy, but I'm just amazed at how still and patient you are with everything. He felt freer after saying it and observed her chewing the last trace of her burger with a smile on her face.

Thank you, she said after swallowing. *It wouldn't make sense if I wasn't.*

Sorry? said Sameer, not understanding what she meant.

She stared straight into his eyes. *I'm Patience*, she said, without letting go of her concentrated gaze.

Was this a staring contest? Sameer was confused. After a brief moment, he averted his gaze and fiddled with the last bits of fries in his basket. He felt naked. It seemed to Sameer that she saw straight through him, as if her eyes witnessed his personal, private interiority.

I don't get it, he said.

Okay, she said, *let me clear it up for you.*

She wiped down her mouth and pushed her tray forward. She leant onto the table with her elbows and thrust herself closer to Sameer.

I – she pointed at herself – *Eva, am the physical embodiment of Patience. I take form every now and again, in different eras.* She took the last chip from her basket and threw it into her mouth.

Are you a comedian? asked Sameer.

Eva didn't laugh. She clasped her hand over Sameer's and said, *I'll tell you more soon.*

Sameer pulled his hand from under hers.

We should head back, he said.

They both got up to pay and started to make their way back to the office. Neither of them spoke and Sameer felt a little uneasy, a tad bit afraid.

This bitch is crazy, he thought to himself as he glanced at her while they walked down the street towards their office.

At the elevators, before the doors opened to their floor, Eva put her hand on Sameer's chest.

I'm not, she said.

You're not what? he asked, wondering why her soft, dainty fingers were listening to his increasing heartbeat.

A crazy bitch, she said.

When the doors opened, she let go of his chest and walked casually towards her desk. Still spooked, Sameer followed her slowly, keeping a distance of two steps between them. He didn't immediately sit down behind his desk like Eva had. He went to the bathroom, where he splashed cold water onto his face. Then he took a piss, locking himself inside one of the cubicles. There, he pondered the outer worlds. As each thought drifted further and further towards religious doctrines, he began to panic, feeling for the first time in his atheistic mindset like a true God-fearing sinner. It took him some time to head back to his desk, and when he did, he was greeted to the left of him by the same vision that had for the past few months irritated him: Eva, serenely working away as though nothing of importance had ever occurred.

It took time for Eva's story to settle in Sameer's mind. The following week, he avoided her, convinced she was making a fool out of him. He even enquired about her contract, trying to determine how long she'd be staying in the studio. A couple of the days he worked from home, certain that he wouldn't be able to tolerate her presence. But the more time passed, the more incredible her story seemed. He had to find out more.

By Wednesday, the following week, he was ready to face her again.

Keen on some lunch? he asked.

Sure, she replied.

And just like that, they were back at the burger place, munching down the same orders with Sameer listening intently to Eva explain why she was who she claimed to be. From then on, Sameer and Eva would often spend time together after work.

They became so close, it was impossible not to speculate. To their colleagues and Sameer's friends, it was clear that they were an item, and an inseparable one at that. But nothing could be further from the truth.

On these get-togethers, Sameer was the pupil, learning about the great unknowns of humanity. Some surprised him, others fulfilled his foundational, human cry to understand the world around him. He felt blessed to learn that there existed a spiritual realm that looked after humankind. From the tiny speck we call Earth, to other, exceedingly more advanced civilisations on other planets in other galaxies, this dominion of deities took great care in ensuring that living things continued to exist in the way they did. Eva assured him that no system of belief was false, but that they all, unbeknownst to us, were created to believe in the same thing.

Advice to slow down and smell the roses has been with us for thousands of years, she told him. But it wasn't all about gazing reverently at blades of grass and feeling superior to others when we did. *Such are the poets,* said Eva mockingly.

Sameer learnt that for the first time in human history, technology has made patience almost obsolete – like a product with a use-by date. In a relatively short period of time, humans got too used to everything being instant.

The internet has accelerated our experience of time, said Eva, whose role was to inspire small acts of patience throughout the world, seeding them, individual by individual, until patience spread like a good rumour through to the rest of us. *You can force change,* she said.

More time strolling through museums and gardens, contemplating geese in flight, listening to the winds blow could slowly, quietly, soothe away our twenty-first-century despair. It was the most effective way. But for most people, these moments were nothing more than moments between the storm of the everyday grind. Eva was here to change that.

Especially with you, she pointed.

I don't think I have the patience for patience, replied Sameer.

Though it took time, Sameer did take a break from his life's frenetic pace. He first quit the shortcuts to every experience, especially online orders. Without his smartphone constantly on him, his endless petulance waned. He also cut down his working days to a three-day week and immediately felt like he'd stepped back into a slower experience of time. He became less crabby and peevish and his irritable actions waned. He used the days off to pay forward what he had learnt from Patience.

Their final rendezvous took place beside a river outside of their city. They walked along the bank of the watercourse and talked about Eva's return to the realm. After a decade on Earth, she was ready to go home, having accomplished her order of tasks.

Sameer looked down at the water, and noticed how dirty it was.

It must be the runoff from last night's storm, he said.

Cans of beer, plastic bags, water bottles and cigarette packets were tangled in weeds and branches. Sameer watched it flow down the river, and its sight suddenly reminded him of the dirty river that was coursing through everyone all day: doctored narratives, misinformation and fake news. The thought of it made him shudder. Millions of people, too quick on their heels.

How are we—

But Eva got there before him.

Now . . . you know the way, she said.

PRODUCTION LINE

The copywriter writes a headline.

It's too short, says the creative director.

The copywriter writes a longer headline.

It's not inspiring enough, says the creative director.

Now the copywriter writes a headline with active verbs to make it more rousing.

Maybe what we need is more of a narrative, says the creative director.

Confused, the copywriter writes a longish headline that tells a story.

Is it ownable by the brand? asks the creative director.

The copywriter scratches their head. They look up previous advertisements of the brand to find out what feeling they own. They write the feeling down.

Yeah, but what should they own now? asks the creative director.

The copywriter becomes angry. Their thoughts, they think, are tied together like knots.

How about this? they say a little later.

That's better, but it needs to be punchier, says the creative director.

This gets to the heart of what they're about, they say an hour later.

The creative director considers the copy. *It's still missing the spark for me,* replies the creative director.

The copywriter walks away. They go outside of the office and smoke two cigarettes. They think about the easy problem they need to solve, which feels like a conundrum now. At the last drag, before they butt out the second cigarette, they experience a slight rush of confidence, which they consider to be inspiration. They go upstairs and send the creative director their original headline via email. Two minutes later, they receive a response:

Sharp, punchy, ownable!

The copywriter sighs with relief.

They place the headline into another email and send it to the account director. The account director copies the headline and pastes it into Facebook Ad Manager along with an image of the brand's product. Then they publish the advertisement to 33,560 people aged between 31 and 39 who work full-time in business management, live in the inner boroughs of London and enjoy ethically non-monogamous relationships on the weekend.

LES SENTIMENTS

What Pierre did was conduct a series of simple tests.

The first one, which he called *Séparation*, was undertaken at Le Progrès, his local café on Rue de Bretagne in Paris. He ordered his usual – three fried eggs and a double espresso – while flicking through the day's *Le Monde*. In between articles he paused to glance up at the fashionable passers-by ambling along the street. He liked to take note of good outfits, especially if he saw coloured trousers worn neatly over sneakers. After he paid his bill, he placed the newspaper on the top of his iPhone. He got up, brushed baguette crumbs off his T-shirt, then took a leisurely walk through Le Marais.

Outside the Musée National Picasso, where he stopped to have a cigarette in the shade beside the entrance, he peeked at his watch. It had been two hours but he didn't rush. He finished his cigarette first, then walked back to Le Progrès. When he saw the same waiter that had served him, he asked if he had found an iPhone on the table he was sitting at earlier. As Pierre expected, they had. He thanked the waiter, then put the iPhone in his pocket without checking it. Later that evening he recorded the following in his notepad: *Temperamental Loading / Fast Battery Depletion / Refusal to Open.*

The second test, which he called *Affaire*, was loosely based on his own experience. It occurred inside the Samsung Experience Store near the Louvre where he himself had experienced an unpleasant incident with his former lover, Charlotte, and a one night stand, Jeanette. It was important to Pierre to elicit convincing emotions so, when a saleswoman approached him beside the Galaxy stand, he attentively listened to her explain the features of the various smartphones. She explained how the Wireless PowerShare worked with other Samsung devices and Pierre was impressed, asking her to show him, which she did, picking up another device and demonstrating how they charged each other. Pierre was also intrigued by the way she described the multiple cameras. He asked if he could take a photo to see how the ultra-wide lens worked.

Merci, j'y penserai, he said and left the store.

Immediately after, while attempting to make a call he felt heat pulsating from his iPhone. When he attempted to open other apps, the iPhone began to vibrate rigorously. He took out his notepad and wrote down: *Failure to Interact Healthily / Extreme Heat / Violent Flashing Tantrum.*

The third test transpired a week later.

Pierre wanted to ensure that this one happened soon after *Affaire*, as he felt it would draw out better conclusions. He called it *Intimité* and conducted the test at his dining table. He left his window open to catch the spring's evening breeze. The test comprised a soft cloth, an air dust blower and organic glass cleaner, with which he vigilantly cleaned his iPhone. In the morning when he woke up, he picked it up before doing anything else. In his notepad, he penned a few observations: *New Glow / Speedy and Fast Operations / Longer Battery.*

The last test took Pierre a while to ease into.

He had a couple of ideas, but in the end decided to go with *Abandon* after crossing out *Mort*. It would involve dropping his iPhone negligently from the sixth-floor balcony of his office. He was apprehensive, but felt it was necessary. The inevitable experiment would bring him closer to the certainty of his belief. But still, as the day drew closer, he felt cruel about the act's deliberateness.

On the day, he started to drink earlier than usual. He had two glasses of pinot noir at lunch, and even slipped in an aperitif just before he and his colleagues went back to the office. He was visibly nervous. His skin had taken on a paler complexion, and he laughed more than usual, with a kind of fragility that made his laughter seem forced. A few times, his colleagues asked if he was okay, but Pierre assured them – usually with a strong pat on the back – that everything was *pas mal, pas mal du tout.* By seven o'clock, after becoming inebriated enough not to care, he made his way through the office crowd towards the balcony. His iPhone was inside his shirt pocket. A few times he touched it gently through the fabric of his shirt. Twice he pulled it out, not to check the text messages and notifications but just to stare at it, and let his finger glide over its smooth screen.

The third time, he succumbed. He let it rest, negligently, on the balcony railing.

The moment he knocked it off the railing, he didn't notice. Only after he hesitantly accepted a cigarette (he had quit a year ago), patting his shirt pocket out of habit for the lighter he used to keep in there, did he notice that the pocket was empty. It must've occurred when he was laughing vigorously at his friends' crude jokes.

This realisation made him smoke more. Although he continued to respond to the varied affections and conversations of the party, he was worried about the iPhone. After six, maybe even nine cigarettes, and numerous vodka shots, Pierre rushed to the bathroom.

With his head over the toilet bowl he repeatedly said, *Je suis désolé, mon cher*, while his confused colleague, who was standing outside the stall, said, *You have nothing to be sorry for*.

Over the next few days, Pierre used the in-built apps on his MacBook to reply to messages. On the fifth day, he went out to his office building's communal courtyard garden during his lunchbreak to search for the fragments of the phone. The ground was only partly concreted and this was the reason why he had chosen this location, because there was a chance it might have landed on the soft grass too. He finally found it, near one of the pot plants, directly in the sun. Its fall had been slowed by the branches of a tall poplar tree, but it had hit the concrete. The screen was smashed, and the edges were heavily dinted and scratched.

He made his way to the Apple store in Saint-Germain, charging the phone along the way with a mobile charger. As the battery filled up a little, the iPhone, like an injured being, recoiled from Pierre's touch, reacting with short jolts of vibration.

Under the title *Abandon*, Pierre wrote his observations with some difficulty: *Severe Disengagement / Inability to Open / Sensitive to Touch*. He noted that additional Intimité tests were required immediately after repairs.

It was late spring, a couple of weeks later when Pierre was sitting again outside Le Progrès, not for breakfast, but for a Sunday brunch this time. On his table was an empty plate with a few hardened cheese leftovers from the croque monsieur he'd eaten earlier. A waiter was bringing him a second glass of pinot noir.

Pierre was smoking, his eyes focused on his iPhone sitting on top of the newspaper.

It was covered sleekly in a new leather case. Its battery was full. The Parisian sky was reflecting against its screen. He smiled.

On the basis of the tests he had conducted and the additional research he undertook studying the engineering and product development of iPhones, he felt that his theory wasn't all that implausible. In fact, Pierre wholeheartedly believed that it was highly likely, given everything he experienced, that his iPhone had feelings.

SUPREME
AL-KHADIR

When ISIS started beheading people and putting the videos on YouTube, Daniil wondered if he had cause for concern – he was the only Muslim in the agency.

Luckily, he felt well disguised. His uncommon name, for starters, gave nothing away. Nor did his suburban accent, his olive skin tone or his tattooed arms and pierced nose. On top of that, he only had a lukewarm association with Islam. He was a little bit Muslim, that was all – unlike his immigrant parents, who prayed regularly and fasted even during those two obscure weeks after Ramadan ended. No, for most of his life, it hadn't been all that important (or necessary) for Daniil to talk about his religious background to people.

But with each new advance into Syria or Iraq, each brutal beheading of a journalist or Westerner, Daniil felt a frenzied phobia spread through the agency. He'd start to hear his co-workers whisper. Eddie, especially, who sat three desks down from Daniil.

I watched it last night, he'd say.

How could you? Daniil would ask.

How could I not, it's on the internet!

An odd feeling started to hang around Daniil, following him like a sinister film score. From department to department, he'd find himself shaking his head, agreeing with his co-workers at the sheer brutality of ISIS. He desperately wanted to tell them that not all Muslims were terrorists, but every time he attempted to say something, he immediately retreated, too afraid of the rising phobia. It really hit home when he overheard his creative partner Adam speaking about Muslims. It was just an off-hand comment, but it got to him.

Then it got worse when Daniil and Adam were having a cigarette with Jenny and George after the news of a particularly horrible beheading had made headlines.

Are there any Muslims in the agency? asked Jenny, and so casually that Daniil was stunned by the question.

I doubt it, said Adam, who was rolling a cigarette. Daniil could never understand why he didn't just smoke tailors.

George just shrugged.

I don't think they should tell clients if we do, said Jenny. *I mean, we have some pretty racist dudes client-side.*

It was preposterous, stupid, to think it, but still, Daniil worried that he could lose his job over this shit. He kept his mouth shut and prayed that this whole period would soon pass. That ISIS would be defeated and they'd all get back to talking about Kim Kardashian.

A few weeks later, Daniil arrived late to a team lunch at a pizza restaurant.

I'm absolutely starved, guys, he said as he approached the table outside.

Four slices left, my man, said Adam, who pushed half a pizza towards Daniil.

He eyed it as he sat down. *What is it?* he asked.

All meat, baby, said Adam.

Daniil examined the slices: glazed ham, pepperoni, sausage and chunks of bacon were layered with mozzarella cheese, tomato sauce and mushrooms. He looked up. Adam and the rest of the team were all watching him.

Shit, thought Daniil, this is some kind of test.

Pork was the one exception. The one fucking thing he didn't eat for quasi-religious reasons. No matter how he felt, he couldn't swallow pork. A psychological barrier prevented him, built up over years of stories about pigs being unclean animals who bred in rubbish and fed on garbage.

Instead of sitting down, he went inside the restaurant. What quick excuse could he think up? He ordered a Peroni directly from a waiter walking towards him.

I'll bring it out, he said.

Daniil went back out and sat down nervously.

Thought you were hungry, said Adam.

Yeah, just got a drink first, he replied.

He looked around: Eddie was sitting on one side of the table, Jenny to his left, George to his right. Misha and Dave were opposite, next to Adam, who was sitting next to Daniil.

The Peroni arrived. He grabbed it and took a violent sip.

Eddie turned his attention towards him. Here we go, thought Daniil.

You gonna eat that cornbread? Eddie asked in a deep Southern accent.

Everyone laughed.

Daniil got the reference, but he didn't laugh. His stomach made a loud rumble. This is definitely a test, he thought. He fretfully picked up each slice of pizza and munched it down with excessive speed. With each bite, he thought about bacon – that backside of a hog, salted and smoked, sliced thin and fried.

That night, he went to bed sick to his stomach. It was the first time that much pork had ever entered his body. When he finally fell asleep, he lapsed into a deep, surreal dream.

He was running breathlessly through a desert of burnt palm trees, hot sand underneath his feet. He came upon an oasis, his mouth completely parched. As he knelt to take a sip from the blue pond, squealing pigs emerged from the water and trampled him.

He woke up sweaty and frightened. In front of him on the edge of his bed, he could see a blurred figure. He rubbed his eyes and looked again, thinking it was part of the dream. But it wasn't – the person was still there. He jumped back against the headrest of his bed and at that moment realised that before him sat the righteous servant of Allah, the mysterious Al-Khadir.

He was wearing a black SUPREME sweater over a green linen thobe and he watched Daniil closely with deep brown eyes.

From sheer shock, Daniil started praying immediately. What was he doing here? his mind wondered. His father had told him many stories about Al-Khadir. How he drank from the fountain of life and became immortal. How he was the spiritual guide of Moses and Alexander the Great. And how he aided those in deep spiritual distress.

Bismillah, ar-Rahman, ar-Raheem, intoned Daniil under his breath, *Bismillah, ar-Rahman, ar-Raheem*. As he repeated the prayer, Al-Khadir reached out and touched his shaky knees.

Fear not, my son, he said.

Daniil opened his eyes. He felt a calmness flow into him from his touch.

I come in peace, said Al-Khadir, *to raise you out of your troubling woe*.

Daniil said nothing. With his mouth agape, he stared into Al-Khadir's eyes, feeling like he was gazing into a dark cave.

Your sin is not greater than Allah's mercy, continued Al-Khadir, *and your digestion of the lesser beast – ease your mind now, for your action was not unworthy*.

Daniil's eyes lit up.

How . . . how so Al-Khadir? he asked.

By consuming it, my son, you saved a life.

Daniil didn't understand. He drew back and clasped his hands over his mouth.

What do you mean? he asked nervously.

In those defiled portions, the maker had by mishap trickled some raw seeds. Allah forbid, a severe allergy. If Adam had digested them, he would've been in the great plains of the afterlife now. My son, by eating the flesh of the lesser beast, you saved Adam's life.

Oh, Al-Khadir, said Daniil, *thank you, thank you.*

He closed his eyes and began to recite the Al-Fatiha again, his head bowed before this great messenger of Allah. He could feel Al-Khadir's hand calmly stroking his head as he repeated the prayer.

When Daniil opened his eyes again, he was gone.

His heart pounded like a drum. He threw the doona off and paced around the room, trying to make sense of what had just transpired. He lit a cigarette and opened the window. The sky was clear, the night black as coal. He looked out and searched for the night's holy moon. He thought about the last few months: ISIS. The beheadings. The heightened Islamophobia. His co-workers' erratic behaviour. Adam. The pizza slices. And now Al-Khadir. It was all starting to make sense, perfect sense. Daniil puffed on the cigarette, then smiled. He knew exactly what he had to do, and there would be no delay.

Tomorrow, he would go in to work and tell the entire agency that he was proudly Jewish.

KVASIR

To everyone's surprise, it was the intern who suggested that they pray to the god of inspiration to win this pitch.

Everyone laughed at her, except for the creative director. He thought she had a good point.

Which god? he asked.

Kvasir, said the intern.

Who? asked the rest of the creative team. They couldn't believe their creative director was entertaining this silly idea.

He is the Norse god of inspiration, said the intern. *In Norse mythology, he was born from the saliva of two groups of gods. He was really wise and travelled lots, teaching and spreading knowledge. But there were these two dwarfs who didn't like him. They ended up killing him and draining his blood. They mixed it with honey and created the mead of poetry. It's supposed to give you wisdom if you drink it. That's how poetry was introduced to mankind.*

What do we do? asked the creative director.

He knew they needed a miracle. They were competing against Wieden & Kennedy, R/GA, CHE Proximity and Anomaly – agencies that were ten times the size of theirs, and had better, more experienced creative teams.

Well, we could make the mead, said the intern.

This is ridiculous, yelled the creative team in disbelief.

But their creative director was quiet. He paced around the office, deep in thought. Then he stopped and rolled up his sleeves. *Let's do it,* he said.

In the kitchen, they stood around the stove as the intern poured a jar of honey into a small pot. She added rosemary. *It helps with clarity in the mind,* she explained. Then she added pepper-mint and basil leaves and sprinkled some ground cinnamon.

Now, we need our blood, she said.

This took some convincing. But in the end, one after the other, they sliced the tops of their index fingers and let their blood drip into the simmering pot. The intern stirred it care-fully, then she poured each of them a little shot glass of the warm mead.

To Kvasir! they cheered in unison before downing the shots.

Nothing happened.

An hour later, still nothing had happened.

But three hours later, something did happen.

They each felt something in the same spot in their stomachs. Before they knew it, the ideas started to come, flying out of them like a colony of bats from a cave.

The creative director smiled. He knew they would win the pitch.

And they did. Because Kvasir was grateful. It was the first time in over four hundred years that anyone had prayed to him.

META ENNIS

PART III

One could say, that's how three became his destiny.

Not willingly, not consciously, but through a combination of fear and tradition. When the flight that brought Ennis and his family over to the Lucky Country landed shakily on the tarmac, Ennis blinked three times to remind himself that he hadn't died. He didn't know why he'd blinked three times, he just did it. He could've pinched himself (like his brother had), but he hated the needle-like ache that came after a pinch. When he and his family finally emerged at the arrival hall, three uncles, three aunts, six cousins, two second cousins and some relatives Ennis had never met rushed towards them. In the custom of traditional Slavic greetings, he kissed every single one of them three times on the cheeks.

That's how it started. Soon after, he began to do almost every-thing in his life three times over: making his bed in the morning, washing his face, combing his hair, arranging his clothes in the wardrobe, opening and closing doors. Each action was compulsively repeated three times.

Naturally, Ennis became baffled by this new behaviour. Was this some hormonal aversion to the Lucky Country? His body acting out against the new climate? The culture? The tidy suburban landscape? Did some sudden neurological malfunction occur during the flight? It was the first time he had been on a plane.

Is something wrong with me? he asked his brother Elvis one day while he was applying three layers of Nutella onto his slice of white toast.

What are you talking about? his brother asked.

You know, I keep doing things in threes.

Elvis laughed. *It's good luck,* he said, and walked off.

To his parents, this odd behaviour was disconcerting. It was a sign of a debility, a neurosis that necessitated the permanent demand for sympathy. When someone in the family whispered that it might be Obsessive-Compulsive Disorder, his parents became alarmed. Ennis, however, didn't feel like his brain was creating repetitive worries and fears. No bad thoughts were triggering his compulsive actions. They were driven by happy instincts, such as the joy of having his own closet in his own room, living in a large house and eating Nutella daily.

Still, he found himself sitting awkwardly on an upholstered chair in a psychologist's office.

You see, what happens, Ennis, said the psychologist (who had a perfectly trimmed moustache), *is that the brain learns that doing a ritual brings relief. Pretty soon, anyone suffering from Obsessive-Compulsive Disorder performs a ritual repeatedly to ease their fears. They erase, rewrite, or redo things. They wash and clean too much. They repeat a word, phrase, or a question more often than necessary. Or three times, like in your case. Sometimes they may feel as if they can't stop. Performing these rituals causes Obsessive-Compulsive Disorder to continue. But all that's wrong is that there's a small problem in the brain's messaging system that needs some medication.*

Hearing this, thirteen-year-old Ennis was speechless. The response he prepared in his mind departed embarrassingly from his lips. How could he explain to this smart doctor with the perfectly trimmed moustache that he believed this was due to cultural readjustment? They had migrated here all the way from Germany. Maybe his body missed its former environment near the Rhine? The hotel he and his family had lived in? The castle he used to visit? The multitude of friends he'd had? It sounded silly, even inside his boyish head, so he kept his head down, his mouth shut. His poor mother took the doctor's advice at face value and immediately proceeded to the pharmacy to obtain the pills required to eradicate this disorder.

And so, well medicated, Ennis entered high school in the great year of 1998. He got along with everyone. Enjoyed learning. Developed a fascination with the humanities, English and History being his favourite subjects. He participated in debates, readings and played basketball at lunchtime with his closest friends: George, Almir, Jimmy and Muhammed. Everything, in fact, seemed normal. Ennis exhibited all the regular tendencies of a typical suburban teenager. There was nothing to worry his parents whatsoever anymore.

I'm feeling much better, he told his mother.

Great, she enthused, and cheerfully took away the pills. *You're too young for that anyway.*

Without the pills, Ennis realised that he now had to keep everybody's worries at bay if ever those compulsions returned. And sure enough, they did. To avoid arousing suspicion, he limited his quirky obsession to only a handful of actions. Three readings of every curriculum book weren't required, but he did it anyway, just to keep it fresh in his mind.

I like reading, he said to his watchful brother.

He wrote three different drafts of every essay. *I want the best marks.*

In P.E. he ran two extra laps. Did two extra sets of push-ups. *Just keeping fit.*

He still found his odd behaviour mysterious, but its mystery no longer bothered him. It was just what he did.

After high school, the incident worth noting is the one after he turned eighteen: the loss of his virginity. It transpired in an airy Art Deco apartment in a suburb south of the river. He came three times in under an hour, although this was more to remind himself he had finally done it than to show his lover that he was worthy. The young woman he slept with was impressed with his stamina, which, in turn, inspired enough self-confidence in Ennis to begin his dating life by always having three women at once.

There isn't much to tell about his university years. The habit of threes prevailed during the time he spent studying Marketing and International Trade, but with every great mystery also comes a great unravelling. For Ennis, it happened in a small office in the city at his first job.

It was a summer day, stuffy and humid, and the air-conditioning wasn't working. Ennis, twenty-three now, was regretting wearing a long-sleeved shirt that he kept having to unbutton. He was newly employed, a full-time marketer – but not an adman yet. He was a junior account manager in a small agency that specialised in the marketing of property developments. Nicole, his co-worker, was sitting across from him. She was wearing a long floral dress and cooled her legs down by fanning them with her dress underneath the table. To his right, John, his boss, was busy talking on the phone.

Ennis was in the middle of proofreading a newspaper advertisement that was due to be approved by five o'clock. It was three o'clock. Ennis didn't need two hours to finish his task, but the hot air was distracting him. He read without taking anything in. He tried shifting his chair and placed the printed advertisement to the left of his desk. He picked up a pencil and began to read the copy line by line, reading it out loud to himself – three times, per his custom.

When he finished, he looked back at the headline. *Spring Street Living*. Ennis didn't question it. It advertised apartments that were located on Spring Street and made sense.

John got off the phone.

We're getting rid of them, he said.

Who? asked Nicole.

Darren's too greedy, replied John. *They've increased their rates again. We can't afford to charge our clients that much.*

Ennis chimed in. *Who's going to do the creative, then?* he asked.

Fuck, it's hot! said John.

The aircon guy was supposed to be here around lunch, said Nicole.

We are, Ennis. We'll do the creative, said John after pulling at his shirt. *It's about time we stopped outsourcing the best part of marketing. Those fuckers can't even get the rule of three right.*

The rule of three? Ennis's eyes lit up. He had so many questions but he was too self-conscious to utter any of them. Moments from his life flashed before his eyes: the aeroplane landing shakily on the tarmac. The psychologist's office. The two extra laps he ran in high school. He looked back down at the advertisement he was proofreading. *Spring Street Living* no longer felt like the appropriate headline for the advertisement.

They always sell the apartments, said Ennis. *Never the lifestyle.*

John laughed.

I want to change this headline, said Ennis.

Do it, said John proudly.

When Ennis finished work that day, he didn't immediately head home, he headed straight for the State Library. He was on a quest and needed to quickly alleviate this fresh spark of curiosity that was coursing through him. At a desk, a few hours later, among a stack of advertising books he was searching through, he was astounded to have come across a quote by the advertising pioneer St Elmo Lewis:

> *The mission of an advertisement is to attract a reader*
> *so that he will look at the advertisement and start to*
> *read it; then to interest him, so that he will continue to read*
> *it; then to convince him, so that when he has read it he*
> *will believe it. If an advertisement contains these three*
> *qualities of success, it is a successful advertisement.*

This statement captivated Ennis. He read it again and again. It perfectly summed up the logic of advertising, but beneath its simplicity he was fascinated by the idea of these three qualities. Language is a dangerous thing, thought Ennis. He read on and discovered that this rule of three existed freely in the universe for anyone to understand, and yet he'd never come across it before. He found examples of how three simple entities combined brevity and rhythm with the smallest amount of information to create a pattern that effectively tore through the mental firewalls of every mind out there.

From literature to chocolate, he found it everywhere: Veni, vidi, vici. Faster, higher, stronger. Stop, drop and roll. Slip, slop, slap. Life, liberty and the pursuit of happiness. Liberté, égalité, fraternité. The story of the three bears. And of course The Three Musketeers.

A holy trinity, thought Ennis. It lives like a natural organism in society, influencing decisions left, right and centre.

Recalling his own history of tripling everyday actions, from the three spoons he dropped into his coffee to the silly three-part unfolding of his laptop to the three glasses of water he drank a day, it all made sense. This rule of three he was using to excel was a known tactic, a trick used daily in communication. From munching chocolate to stirring up revolutions, using a trio of characters or phrases made everything more effective.

Ennis felt freer. Unweighted by his past. He put his confusions to rest and worked with renewed gusto, fuelled by an unquenchable ambition that everyone recognised. John knew that he wouldn't be able to keep him for long. After penning some memorable property advertisements, John waved Ennis off at a bar down the street from their office.

You'll smash it in the big agencies, he said.

A month later, Ennis joined a top-tier advertising agency – a global conglomerate with offices all over the world. As he walked through the doors, he thought he could smell real creativity; a scent that he described to himself as a blend of curiosity and sweat mixed with orange peel, cardboard and peppermint leaves. He inhaled deeply.

Instantly, he noticed the structural difference. In smaller agencies, like the one he had worked at, people performed more than one role: for a while he had been the entire creative department. Here, departments were broken out for efficacy: planning, strategy, accounts, creative and production. Though the fundamentals were the same, the world of top-tier ad agencies allowed for the formation of cross-divisional teams to handle a multitude of client demands. He was paired up with an art director. They reported directly to a creative director, who in turn reported to an executive creative director, who in turn also reported to a chief creative officer.

Let's just say that Ennis thoroughly enjoyed himself.

Waking up every morning to go to an office and create real advertisements for a living made him happy. When he compared his job to his high school friends' jobs, he didn't feel trapped by the normal nine-to-five routine like they did. George, Almir, Jimmy and Muhammed worked at banks, superannuation firms and construction businesses that were governed by strict corporate bureaucracy. Ennis had a complimentary coffee machine, a bar stocked with loads of alcohol, boxes of fruit, cereal, cheese platters and fortnightly team pizza nights. Swearing wasn't frowned upon, streetwear was the accepted uniform and after-work drinks at the office were always followed up by cocaine binges in clubs and bars.

What fuelled him even more was that the other copywriters in the agency were ninety-nine per cent Anglo-Saxon. They had been born into the English language. Ennis hadn't. His mother tongue was a marginal language he had never learnt properly. Then there was German, which he had learnt when he lived there as a child and finally went to school. Now he was wrestling with English, officially the third language of his life. While he thought he had perfected it down to an intuitive level, he felt, when he thought of this disadvantage, jealous of the others' ability to speak and write so freely, so naturally, without the influence of other languages in their head. They didn't have to use a dictionary all the time. They didn't confuse their synonyms. Or think they'd discovered unused words.

Stupidly, thinking himself impressive, he'd used the word 'physiognomy' to describe a person's face. He wanted to show his creative director that *this guy right here, he might be new, but he knows a word or two*. Sadly, Ennis had to be reminded that he wasn't writing ads for highbrow Brioni suits, but for a super-annuation firm whose audience was aged sixty plus. His conflicting adjectives, nouns and pronouns sometimes confused his peers, but he prevailed. Three times exactly, thought Ennis, because English is my third language, and being my third, I'll work three times as hard as everyone else.

Before any piece of work left his desk, Ennis analysed it to ensure it attracted, interested and convinced a reader to learn more, just like St Elmo Lewis had prescribed. He applied the rule of three as often as he could. From taglines for new vehicle launches to scripts for deodorants and cat food – there was a sharp, strategic clarity in his work that demanded attention. And sure enough, it didn't take long for the creative directors to notice

Ennis's impressive output. But they weren't the only ones observing his professional rise.

One Thursday morning, Ennis arrived at work to find a letter casually sitting on his keyboard. The heavy, textured envelope was closed with a beautiful wax seal and a red silk string hanging off it. When he scanned it closely he saw a phrase etched onto the envelope: *Omne Trium Perfectum.* He opened it carefully and took out an equally impressive card: a handwritten invitation to join a certain Mr A. Barthelme for dinner at seven o'clock that evening.

Someone's got a secret admirer! his co-workers teased.

What is it? asked his art director. *Some brand launch invite?*

I really don't know, said Ennis.

Let me take a look, said his art director, snatching the invite out of Ennis's hand. He looked over the details closely, trying to discern the handwriting.

Elegaaaant, he joked. *You're meant to meet at a hotel in the city. That's fancy!*

Who is this guy? We gotta look him up, said another co-worker.

Others joined in. *You're being poached, dude,* they said excitedly.

Soon, half the creative department was online, trying to find out who this surreptitious Mr A. Barthelme was.

There's nothing on this guy, said his art director.

Zilch, man, yelled the rest of the crowd who couldn't dig up a single file either.

With nothing to go on with, Ennis got nervous. Who could this be? he wondered as he headed straight home after work to take a shower and change.

He arrived in the foyer of the hotel precisely at seven o'clock. An usher approached him as he walked through the door.

Mr Ćehić? he asked.

Yes, said Ennis.

Please come with me. Mr A. Barthelme is awaiting you.

Ennis followed the usher until they came upon the entrance to the hotel's grand ballroom. The usher opened the heavy doors, and nodded for Ennis to walk through. Ennis stepped into the resplendent room and was immediately amazed at the soaring, stained-glass domes. The long, thick red curtains draped over the huge stained-glass windows. The beautifully patterned red carpet beneath his feet and the colourful ceilings and walls through the rest of the space.

This ballroom can usually accommodate about two hundred guests, but this evening it's just the two of us, said Mr A. Barthelme, who was standing beside an enormous black marble fireplace. *Thank you for coming, Mr Ćehić. May I call you Ennis?*

The doors closed behind him. Ennis turned towards Mr A. Barthelme. He was exactly as Ennis had imagined: tall, English in manner and style, wearing a well-fitted double-breasted suit and polished dark brown Oxford shoes. His greyish hair was slicked back neatly, revealing formidable wrinkles on his forehead. He was lightly tanned, as if he'd just returned from a European vacation. As Ennis walked towards him, he placed him in his late forties, or early fifties.

This is quite the invitation, said Ennis. He extended his hand.

Mr A. Barthelme shook it firmly without moving his eyes away from Ennis's.

You're very welcome. Let's sit, he said and pointed towards the centre of the ballroom, where an antipasto platter was awaiting them on a beautifully set table.

I'm still unsure what this is about, said Ennis, getting to the matter right away.

But Mr A. Barthelme had other plans. *Red or white?* he asked first, pointing at the two lovely bottles of wine resting alongside the antipasto platter.

Red . . . yeah, red, please, said Ennis. *Thank you.*

No, thank you for coming, he said, *and on such short notice too.*

Mr A. Barthelme reached over and picked up one of the bottles of wine. He opened it and poured a glass for each of them.

This one has the classic mourvèdre notes, he said as he handed Ennis a glass. *Santé.*

Cheers, said Ennis nervously. He lifted up his glass to act polite, but then he took a large sip. *You can imagine,* he said, *this is all quite overwhelming and surreal.*

Mr. A. Barthelme smiled. He unbuttoned his blazer and sat down.

It will clear up in a minute, he said. *Friends, Romans, countrymen, lend me your ears . . . Do you know what I'm referring to?*

Ennis, now sitting down too, took another sip of wine. He was confused by the question, but he did in fact know what Mr A. Barthelme was referring to.

The famous words of Mark Antony, he said. *Shakespeare's* Julius Caesar.

Correct, said Mr A. Barthelme. *Justice, goodwill and brotherhood?*

Ennis chuckled. *I think that's Winston Churchill,* he said. *But what is this about?*

Mr A. Barthelme continued as if he hadn't heard Ennis's question. *These memorable quotes have one thing in common,* he said. *They represent an understanding of the rule of three.*

286

Mr A. Barthelme placed his glass of wine on the table. He pushed back his chair and crossed his legs.

The Pythagoreans, he continued, *considered three the first true number. And they were right, for three is the first number that forms a geometrical figure: the triangle. Thus, three is the least number of individual entities you need to form any given pattern. From the subatomic level to the cosmic level, three has divine qualities significant to the makeup of our world. In Chinese culture, the number three is lucky. In Islam, accomplishing tasks in odd numbers is significant, especially in threes. And in Christianity, God as three in one; the Father, the Son and the Holy Spirit. This trinity stands for complete unity and perfection, hence the Latin phrase Omne Trium Perfectum, which you may have noticed on the sleeve of the letter I sent you.*

Ennis shrugged, then he realised that his mouth was hanging open. He quickly put the wine glass to his lips and swallowed another gulp.

You see, Ennis, everything that is three is perfect, said Mr A. Barthelme. *Once you yourself understood the rule of three, didn't you immediately see how information is better absorbed and retained? Anything you place in a cadence of three notes offers completeness, wholeness and unity. This is why the rule of three is ever present for everyone, everywhere and every day. And we, Ennis, are in service of it.*

Mr A. Barthelme paused. He took out a silver case from his breast pocket. From it, he removed a very thin cigarette and lit it with a golden lighter. Ennis, still unable to really speak, was baffled by the man's cinematic demeanour.

The reason why you're here, he continued, *is because of your ability.*

My what? asked Ennis.

Your natural, intuitive aptitude for understanding this universal design. It's a rare trait, Ennis. Very rare. Would you like a cigarette?

Ennis reached over and slipped one of his thin cigarettes from the case.

We took notice of you very early on, when you wrote your first campaign for the apartment building on Spring Street. Ever since then, you've only progressed, become better at articulating the pattern in your work. The organisation I represent believes your services would be much better suited to us – the Society of Threes.

The society of what? asked Ennis. *Sorry, I thought you were from another ad agency.*

Well, an agency of sorts, laughed Mr A. Barthelme. *The Society of Threes is an international order. We've existed since the sixteenth century and are embedded in all levels of society, from politics to the arts and the corporate industries. Much like in brainstorming, when you bring overlaps into an equation, like another person into an existing group, you get a different result. Right? Well, we believe that all significant human advancement happens when three different fields of thought overlap. In this criss-crossing, this convergence, new ideas are born. Sometimes this happens coincidently, sometimes consciously, sometimes people are completely unaware of this astonishing pattern they create, but nevertheless, it is the method by which history's greatest thinkers have advanced civilisation. Warhol combined the underground, consumerism and celebrity culture to change the course of modern art and Elvis – not your brother, of course – when he put R'n'B, Christian palatability and sexhibitionism together, he popularised rock'n'roll.*

Ennis let out a jovial but nervous laugh. *I don't know what to say,* he said.

You can say yes, said Mr A. Barthelme. *I believe our ambitions are aligned with yours.*

As Mr A. Barthelme lifted up the glass of wine to his lips, Ennis watched him closely. He paid attention to Mr A. Barthelme's delicate, almost manicured hands. His clean-shaven face. His piercing green eyes and slicked-back hair that hardly ever moved. Everything suddenly seemed slightly off about Mr A. Barthelme. He appeared too worked out. Too much of a caricature to be of flesh and blood.

I don't know, said Ennis. *How do I know this is real?*

He asked this question brusquely, as if to test out this sudden impulsive doubt that had come over him.

Excuse me? said Mr A. Barthelme.

He waited patiently for Ennis to answer, but Ennis didn't answer. He looked around, through the empty, grand ballroom, then picked up a slice of salami from the platter and put it into his mouth. It tasted fine. He took a sip of water. It was also fine. He got up and walked towards one of the stained-glass windows. First, he rubbed the thick curtains that were drawn aside between his fingers. Then he inspected an etching within the frame of the window, a monk in a green robe.

Do you suddenly feel . . . I don't know, gazed at? asked Ennis.

Mr A. Barthelme rose from his chair and walked over to the window where Ennis was standing.

I can assure you, you have nothing to worry about. I come with the best of intentions, he said.

Ennis turned towards him, eyes alight with a triumphant smile. The doubt he seemed to be experiencing earlier had disappeared.

I thought you'd be the first to realise, said Ennis.

Sorry? said Mr A. Barthelme, pulling away in confusion.

Ennis looked up to behold the soaring domes. Then he strolled over to one of the gold-plated mirrors on the walls.

I'm not happy with this narrative, he said to his reflection.

Excuse me? asked Mr A. Barthelme.

He's not talking to you, I finally said.

Startled, Mr A. Barthelme looked up, then around. *Who's there?* he asked.

Don't worry about it, said Ennis. He walked back over to the table and took another cigarette from Mr A. Barthelme's silver case. *Can you please get rid of him?* Ennis asked me.

I kept quiet for a moment, letting Mr A. Barthelme roam around. I wanted to see terror spread across his face.

What is going on here? he yelled. He walked up to Ennis and pulled at his shirt. *WHAT IS GOING ON HERE?*

Is this all you're going to make him say? asked Ennis as he lit the cigarette.

WHO ARE YOU TALKING TO, FOR GOD'S SAKE? yelled Mr A. Barthelme.

I let him hang on to Ennis's shirt for a little longer, then I put an end to it.

From the ground up, Mr A. Barthelme's legs and then body rapidly vanished. As the last bit of Mr A. Barthelme's head disappeared into thin air, Ennis smiled, adjusted his shirt, then walked back to the mirror.

Happy now? I asked.

I guess this is the spot, he said.

I guess so, I replied.

He blew smoke right at me. It blurred my vision for a brief second. I caught a whiff of the sweet-smelling tobacco, and inhaled it greedily.

You didn't expect that, did you? he said cockily.

It was true. *It didn't come to me right away,* I admitted.

Your character suddenly discerns they are in a story . . . He turned around and inspected the grand ballroom again. *Does this mean I have free will? That I can move my arm, without your permission?* He held his arm out in the air like he was waiting for someone to slice it off.

I haven't thought that far ahead, I replied.

And you'll just remain a voice? he asked.

Think of me like an invisible drone hovering all around you, I said.

The Windsor Hotel, he murmured, dropping his hand by his side again. *Australia's only surviving nineteenth-century city hotel. You didn't mention or describe it at all. In fact . . . now that I think back on it, you obscured everything! Where are the details? Right from the start, you lied. You didn't mention Melbourne's depressing Tullamarine Airport. St Albans – that cheap-arse suburb where we grew up. It was the murder capital of the state, man!*

He turned around in anger, as if he didn't want a direct face-off. I didn't either.

Don't you like our voice, resounding like this through the air? I asked, even though I knew this would anger him more. Silly, I just wanted to know how it felt to be talking to oneself in a story. To exist as two entities: both as the character and the narrator in the same reality.

Why are you hiding us? Ennis asked instead, getting straight to the guts.

Maybe we just dislike too much description is all, I said.

We both know that's only part of the answer, replied Ennis, turning back to the mirror. He moved towards the table in the centre of the ballroom. I watched him pick up another piece of salami and a piece of cheese.

He *is* right. There really is a lot missing. I've intentionally added another layer to this story – a fresh coating of fiction. But isn't all writing precisely that? Truth, once released from biography, becomes something else. An exaggerated account. Overstated and inflated – just like advertising. No wonder this autobiographical tale fits so well here, among a set of preposterous stories about the fine art of persuasion.

It's funny, Ennis said as he chewed down more salami.

What is? I asked.

He smiled arrogantly. *You're hiding*, he said.

I'm not hiding, I lied.

Sure, Ennis replied dismissively and reached for another piece of salami. His hand touched an empty plate this time. He laughed and grabbed an olive instead. *You know, it's an odd feeling, existing in two truths*, he continued. *The Society of Threes. I mean, really? We never did anything in threes, that's a complete fabrication of our lived experience and yet I feel like I have lived the silly reality you described. Our life, which you filled with fictive inventions and satire in order to fit a story into a theme. To carry this supposed* Sadvertising *voice right to the end of the book. Is it worth it? I mean, you made us sound ritzy in Germany, living in a hotel. We were refugees from Bosnia, living with a bunch of other traumatised refugees! AND THE CASTLE? That was the abandoned building where all the immigrant kids hung out. Ha! The loss of*

our virginity: you tried to paint us as some sort of fucking Don Juan.
You were petrified the girl would notice you're circumcised!

Ennis snatched Mr A. Barthelme's silver case and drew out another cigarette, lit it, then inhaled it deeply. His sudden rage unnerved me. He was showing off too, blowing smoke rings into the air.

I quit, by the way, I said to him after a moment passed.

This, he pointed at the cigarette between his fingers. *I don't believe you.* He smirked, shook his head, then he began to pace the ballroom again.

And the agency? Ennis continued. *You sugar-coated our entire career. You made the industry sound like some made-up dream job. What about the fucking overtime? The drinking? The stress? And admit it, we were the pizza-eating piglets – not Daniil.*

He stopped at the other end of the ballroom and placed his arm over his head, the cigarette dangling between his fingers, smoke billowing up towards the ornate ceiling. He remained there, silently waiting, or contemplating what else to say. Each time he took a drag, I could feel a craving pulsate inside my chest. My mouth watered, watching him smoke.

Stop it! I yelled. It was a Freudian slip. I should've kept my mouth shut. He laughed and stubbed out the cigarette on the carpet with his shoe.

You know, he said, *being this suddenly conscious character in our story is making me understand what you've done.*

He looked up, waiting for an interjection. I didn't give him the satisfaction.

You're too afraid of the truth. That's why you've chosen fiction.

He lit yet another cigarette. I was listening, even though the determination in his voice was getting on my nerves. I knew I was losing control of my own story.

I don't think it bothers you that everybody mines their auto-biographies today – especially those migrant writers, he said. *What bothers you is mining yours and finding nothing.*

I could no longer stand the regal emptiness of the space he was in. Once more I attempted to remove him, imagine him someplace else, but it didn't work. It was as if his free-spoken rage had destroyed my omnipotence. I tried to speak, to say anything, but my voice faltered again. He didn't care anyway. This was a monologue now.

Listen, he said with finality, *you don't matter in this book. Move on.*

He stopped, walked back to the mirror and looked at his reflection again. Without averting his gaze, he took another sharp drag of his cigarette as if he understood that it took time to understand the full sentiment of his revelation. Time and poetry.

I took a few deep breaths. In and out. Then I fixed my gaze on him – at myself. My physiognomy – my large protruding forehead, my misshapen nose with its deviated septum, my constantly chewed lips and long, thin brown hair, the pointy chin underneath my smallish mouth, the mole at the top of my right cheek, my almost invisible eyebrows, and my eyes – my eyes, whose shades of green, grey and yellow had always been what I needed them to be; the true colours of my volition.

Move on, my mouth uttered.

And I did.

ACKNOWLEDGEMENTS

This book would not have been possible without the Wheeler Centre's Next Chapter Award. I am sincerely grateful to Sophie Black, Veronica Sullivan and Michael Williams for their support and encouragement throughout the program.

A huge THANK YOU goes to my publisher, Justin Ractliffe, who, despite having the foremost directorial duties at Penguin Random House somehow always made me feel like I was the only writer in the house. How did you do that? Your genuine curiosity, attentiveness and interest in this book has made the possibility of it more enjoyable. Equally so, I'd like to thank my editor, Genevieve Buzo, who helped me develop and craft the narrative of each and every story.

My sincerest thanks go to Nam Le, whose book *The Boat* is one of the reasons I wanted to be a writer in the first place. I still can't believe I got to write my first book with your guidance and mentorship. The dedication and time you've given *Sadvertising* hasn't only shaped the pages of this book but it has shaped me just as much. If not more.

To my dear friend Sam Maguinness. Our creative union has survived many agencies and a plethora of projects. But this one has been the most special. Thank you for staying back after work, week after week, and designing the wonderful cover of this book. You did it during Melbourne's final and most gruelling lockdown, and I can't thank you enough. I'm not just grateful for your aesthetic tastefulness, but your kindness too.

My deepest gratitude goes to my beloved partner, Stanislava Pinchuk. Firstly, for making me believe that anything in life is possible. I fear nothing thanks to you, and that is a testament to your inspiring humanness. Secondly, for taking infinite interest (with infinite patience) in this poetic medley I've created and helping me shape the plots, titles and endings. You've been instrumental in the creation of this work.

To my parents, Izeta and Sead. It is due to your sacrifices that I am able to pursue my dreams in the first place.

Lastly, as I write these acknowledgements and reflect on how this book came to exist, I am greatly indebted to all the people I've worked with. You've inspired me, radically.

And that's that, I think.